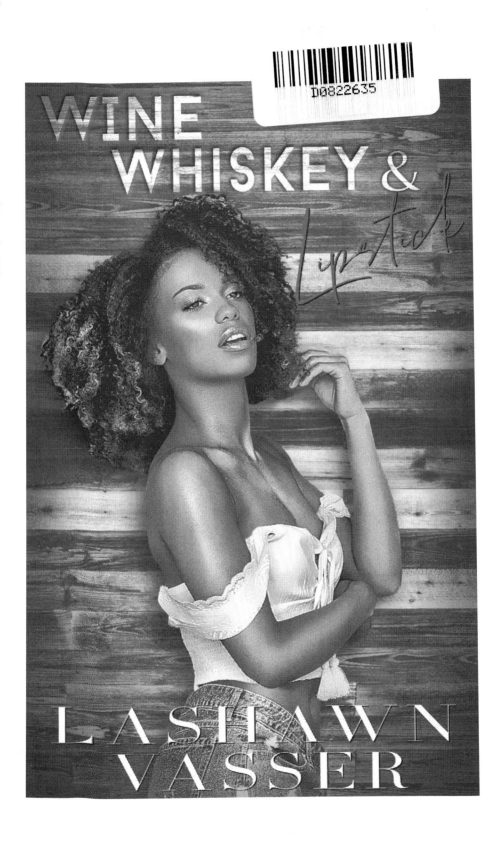

WINE
WHISKEY &
Lipstick

LASHAWN
VASSER

Table of Contents

WINE, WHISKEY, & LIPSTICK

By

LaShawn Vasser

SIGN-UP TO LASHAWN VASSER'S NEWSLETTER (http://www.lashawnvasser.com) FOR THE LATEST NEWS & RELEASE INFORMATION.

EXPLICIT ADULT CONTENT
WARNING

This novel is considered romantic fiction with erotic elements or erotica. This book is for mature audiences only. This book contains profane adult language, mild violence, and strong sexual content.

Dedications & Acknowledgments

This book is dedicated to my love. I can exhale because you breathe life into me every minute of every hour of every day. Thanks for being on this journey with me.

Melissa Harrison you always do the impossible! Thank you for always being up to the task.

Tiffany you push me to be better even when I don't want to. Thanks for the sunshine!

Chapter 1

Benjamin Cash couldn't keep still. He tapped his cell against his right knee while bouncing his leg up and down. *Something isn't right.* A nagging sense of foreboding had Ben's mind racing, and the feeling of dread wouldn't go away.

For the third time, Ben checked the time on his cell. His plane had been in a holding pattern for almost half an hour, waiting to land and pushing his return time back even further. He needed to get home *ASAP*. He'd called his wife several times before boarding, but she never picked up. *She should have picked up. Where are you, Lana?*

Almost immediately, Ben had second thoughts about leaving in the first place. Unfortunately, he needed to take this trip because it was too important to his business. *I shouldn't have been gone this long.* He had been apprehensive about leaving for so many reasons but mostly because it took him away for more than a week. *This was a bad time to travel.* Ben took little solace in having spoken with Lana several times while he was out of town. Those calls hadn't been reassuring because she seemed distant—more so than usual. If Ben were honest, he and Lana hadn't been clicking for a while. Over the last couple of months, she had threatened to end things, but this time, Ben thought maybe she would make good on her promise. His thoughts were interrupted by the voice that came over the intercom.

"Ladies and gentlemen, welcome to O'Hare Airport. The local time is now five-fifteen p.m., and the temperature is currently a balmy thirty-eight degrees.

"As we make our descent, and for your safety and comfort, please remain seated with your seat belt fastened until the captain turns off the fasten seat belt sign. This will indicate that it is safe to move about. Once the fasten seat belt sign is turned off, you may also use your cellular device."

It took several antagonizingly long minutes before Ben's plane was finally on the ground. As it taxied toward the gate, he looked at his phone once more. *Damn, still no reception.* Frustrated, he sighed heavily and rubbed the back of his neck, waiting impatiently for the plane to come to a complete stop. It took an eternity, but that green fasten seat belt sign finally turned off.

Immediately, Ben checked his phone. This time he thanked God services had been restored and tapped the redial button. Ben's call immediately went to voice mail. "Hi, you've reached Lana. I can't come to the phone right now. But at the sound of the beep, you know what to do." Ben waited for that all too familiar tone. He held the cell between his ear and shoulder as he stood to retrieve his carry-on bag from the overhead bin. "Hey. It's me. Just wanted to let you know that I've landed. Call me when you get this message. Miss you and ladybug." Reluctantly, Ben disconnected.

Dammit.

"I remember those days." Ben turned to see an older gentleman watching him with compassion. "It's one of the reasons that I always fly first class." The man smiled. "I don't like to waste any time getting home to my wife either."

Ben returned the man's smile with one of his own. "It's been a long week." He then threw his bag over his shoulder, stepped back, and allowed the man to walk ahead of him as they got off the plane. Fortunately, Ben didn't have any checked luggage and didn't need to stop by the baggage claim. He could go straight to get a Lyft or an Uber.

Hailing a car almost immediately, Ben tossed his bag inside the trunk. He slid into the backseat and, once the driver pulled away from the curb, decided to call home *again*. This time he dialed the landline. It also went straight to voice mail. He released an exaggerated breath as he glanced out the window. It was only five-thirty in the evening but looked more like nine. This time of year was always dark but seemed to foreshadow the feeling he had in the pit of his stomach. Ben could arrive home in about thirty minutes if traffic were good, but that felt like thirty minutes too long.

"Let me try Aimee," Ben said aloud. His live-in nanny should be around as he knew she wouldn't have Rylee out after dark. *Someone should be home.* Ben punched in Aimee's number. It rang several times before also going to voice mail. *Why the fuck isn't anybody answering their goddamned phones?!* Ben hoped he was overreacting, but he had a strong sense that he wasn't.

After an excruciating ride, his car finally pulled up into the circular drive of Ben's high-rise condo. He retrieved his bag and tipped the driver. Quickly, he walked into the building and waved to the on-site security on his way to the elevator.

"Good evening, Mr. Cash."

"Hey, Ronald." Ben stopped in mid-stride and backed peddled. "By chance, have you seen Lana in the past couple of days?"

Ronald stood up from behind his desk as he took a quick minute to think about it. He frowned. "Actually, I haven't. Now that you mention it, I haven't seen Aimee or Rylee either since Thursday night. However, I did take a vacation day on Friday and switched shifts with Tony yesterday. So, it's possible I just missed them."

"Everything seemed fine, though?"

Ronald nodded. "Yeah. Everything seemed fine."

"Good to hear." That bit of information should have given

Ben a bit of relief, but he knew that lately, Lana had been frustrated. More frustrated than usual. "I'm sure everything is fine. I've just come home from visiting my family and taking care of some business. I miss them like crazy. I haven't been able to reach them today and can't wait to hug my girls."

"Then quit talking to me and go see about them." Ronald laughed.

Ben put his hand up waved him away. "You're absolutely right." Unfortunately, Ronald's words didn't relieve his unease. With a sense of urgency, Ben rounded the corner and pressed the button on the elevator. The doors slid open, and he stepped inside. Ben pushed the button to the thirty-seventh floor.

He glanced up and watched the numbers of the building's floors changing inside a little digital box. As the elevator ascended, Ben's heart beat a little faster with each passing floor. As soon as the doors opened, he bounded out and walked swiftly to his door. *What if they are . . .* Ben admonished himself. *Don't panic. Lana and Rylee are probably home, watching a movie.*

Ben put his keycard inside the slot on the door and pushed it open. It was evident from the moment he stepped inside that Ben's greatest fear had occurred.

Chapter 2

Dillyn Anderson was more than satisfied with her efforts as she glanced around the living room. She placed a hand on her slim hips and admired her hard work. "Perfect," she whispered. Everything was in place. Dinner had been delivered and set up in the formal dining room. Dillyn strategically placed candles throughout the downstairs giving her home an ethereal glow while soft music played in the background.

She heard a noise. Going completely still, Dillyn listened intently until she recognized the sound she had been waiting for—the garage door—it was opening. *He was home.*

Dillyn smoothed her hands down her now svelte figure, and a satisfied grin appeared on her face. It seemed impossible, but Dillyn was finally back to her normal weight. The fertility cocktail she'd been taking had wreaked havoc on her body. It had taken Dillyn all of six months to get herself back together after deciding not to continue with the process. It was the hardest decision she'd ever made, but after making it, Dillyn was relieved. Afterward, Dillyn worked her literal ass off to get back into shape just for this moment—for Steven.

He was so visual. Appearances meant everything. Dillyn knew that her stomach wasn't completely flat, but it had lost most of its bloated appearance. Those squats she'd subjected herself to in recent months had kept the hands of time from completely dropping her ass to the ground. It was plump, rounded, and firm, just like it had been on the first day they met. Dillyn's sheer black teddy was going to drive Steven insane. It didn't leave anything to the imagination and made her breasts sit up like a Playboy Bunny. Dillyn's body wasn't perfect, but it was close enough to celebrate their tenth wedding anniversary.

He was inside. The door from the garage to the kitchen opened and closed. Dillyn hurried over to the dining room and picked up one of Steven's ties from off the table. She put it loosely around her neck and sat down in her chair. *Why the hell not?* Dillyn lifted her leg and rested it on the table, displaying a good bit of inner thigh and a brand new pair of black stiletto red bottoms.

"Dillyn?" Steven called.

"In here." Dillyn positioned herself in the sexiest pose she could manage.

Seconds later, Steven appeared in the doorway, carrying a bouquet of roses. His smile grew slowly from ear to ear. "What a way to come home."

Steven was still the sexiest man Dillyn had ever seen. He stood just over six feet and almost filled the entire doorway. His body. Those wide shoulders. Absolutely everything about him was almost pure perfection. It wasn't his sex appeal that drove Dillyn crazy, but it was the way he looked at her. The magic he wielded with those gray eyes was surely a crime. Anytime he really focused on her, Dillyn would become putty in his hands. Tonight, she wouldn't be distracted. Not when this plan had been six months in the making.

Dillyn knew she had outdone herself when Steven bit into his lower lip in anticipation of their night ahead.

"Welcome home." Her voice was husky.

"It is indeed." Steven walked over and bent low. He planted a kiss hard on her lips with a silent promise of more to come. Slowly, he pulled back. "These are for you."

Dillyn locked eyes with his for the briefest moment before forcing herself to pull away. She glanced down at the flowers. A

9

slight frown appeared on her forehead. *Is that a sticker price for $9.99?*

Dillyn sighed softly. "Thank you." No. She would not get upset that her flowers seemed like an afterthought. *Follow the plan. You'll get your reward later,* Dillyn reminded herself as she accepted the flowers and laid them on the table. She began to caress the tie around her neck. "Why don't you have a seat and let me pour you a glass of champagne?"

His voice was a husky timbre warm as honey. "I think I'd rather have you instead."

Dillyn pretended to pout. "C'mon, be patient. A lot went into pulling this night together."

After a moment of hesitation, Steven nodded in agreement and took a seat opposite her. Slowly, Dillyn lowered her leg and placed it on the floor, and his eyes followed her every move. Knowing she had his full attention, Dillyn added a little extra sway to her hips and wiggle to her strut as she walked over toward him. She was being extra and knew he was eating it up. Dillyn picked up his champagne glass and filled it with the chilled bubbly that she had placed on the table.

As she handed him a glass, her eyes connected with his. The corners of her lips edged up into a sultry smile. *It won't be long before the real fireworks begin.*

Steven couldn't stop staring as he accepted the glass. His eyes had darkened to a charcoal gray. Dillyn knew that look. He was so turned on. Even if his eyes hadn't revealed it, the large bulge in his pants was a dead giveaway. *Good. That's how I want him. Hard and needy.*

Attempting to be patient, Steven seemed to go along with Dillyn's plan . . . for now. He brought the champagne glass to his lips and took a sip.

Dillyn watched as she continued to caress the silk tie that was hanging around her neck. Steven was nothing if not predictable. She didn't know how much longer he would last. Suddenly, she was hit by a spray of liquid from Steven's mouth, drenching her. "Dill . . . what the hell is this?"

"You don't like the champagne?" she asked, seemingly confused as she picked up a napkin, dabbing herself dry.

Steven wiped his mouth with the arm of his jacket. "I don't even know if you can even call it that. It's terrible."

Dillyn knew Steven liked the finer things in life. He demanded it. Still, she pretended to be surprised. She lifted a perfectly sculpted brow. "Really? I thought it was just right for the occasion. A cheap ass drink for a whack ass man."

"What?!" The confusion on his face almost made her laugh. It was clear Steven had no idea what was about to hit him.

Dillyn took off the tie she knew he didn't recognize and threw it at him. *Narcissist.* "Sam sent you the tie. I'm pretty sure that's her shade of lipstick smeared on it, along with that." She pointed to the manila envelope sitting on the table beside the champagne bottle.

"Sam? Why would *your* friend send me anything?"

He deserved an Oscar. Lying bastard. Dillyn's tone was calm when she was anything but. "Open the envelope. The answers you seek might be in there."

Steven was hesitant but tentatively picked it up. He pulled out some papers. Dillyn could see the rise and fall of Steven's chest. There was no explaining that shit. "Six months ago, my so-called friend, *accidentally*—or hell—maybe on purpose, sent naked photos to my phone. Clearly, they were meant for you. I blew them up and printed them out just to make sure you didn't miss anything."

He glanced up. Steven's words started to tumble out like vomit. "Dillyn, you are overreacting. I can explain. Sit down, and let's talk."

Dillyn clenched her hands at her sides. She had too much anger stored up to sit. "Am I? Please explain how a wife, who received nude photos of another woman meant for her husband, could possibly be overreacting?"

Steven raked a hand through his perfectly styled dark hair. "This is not what it looks like."

"I knew you would say that. I knew you would continue to lie. If we must play this game, then you might as well take out the rest of the contents in the envelope."

"This is crazy, Dill. I'm not about to do this with you." Steven stalled. He wasn't an idiot. He knew that Dillyn was nothing if not thorough.

"Good because neither am I."

"Sam doesn't mean anything to me."

"Oh? Now the woman you've been sleeping with over the past year doesn't mean anything to you?" Dillyn blinked back tears. "You tried to break me, Steven. You tried to make me feel inadequate by suddenly complaining about the things you claimed to love, like my hair. After all these years, I wondered why you would want me to straighten it? Or start making rude and insensitive comments about my body every time I gained a pound or two."

"That's not tru—"

She cut him off. "We were trying to bring life into this world! Why would you let me start taking fertility drugs if you'd already checked out of the marriage?" Dillyn was doing her best to stay calm but held on by a thread. She spoke through gritted teeth. "The day I saw those photos was the day I stopped taking them. We didn't need to bring a child into this mess."

"You act like this is all on me!" Steven started, trying to turn the tables. "The breakdown of our marriage isn't just my fault. If you would have—"

Furious, Dillyn raised her hand to slap him but managed to stop herself in mid-motion. "You're really going to stand there with a straight face and blame *me* for *you* being a whore?!" Dillyn glanced heavenward and took a few deep breaths. "Yes. I knew that our marriage was in trouble way before you started sleeping with Sam, but it took those pictures to snap me back to reality."

"That's not true."

"C'mon, Steven, stop. Just stop!" Dillyn backed away for fear of actually assaulting him. She had never put hands on another human being in her life but was afraid today might be that day. Her eyes narrowed. "You are married to a digital forensic investigator! You know I have proof. I have pictures not just of Sam, but you *and* Sam! I have text messages, phone records, and credit card receipts!"

Steven quieted, no longer trying to explain.

"I must have been out of my mind thinking a baby would save our marriage. After all the surgeries and years of trying to conceive, you made me feel less than a woman for not being able to give you a child." Dillyn slapped a hand hard against her chest. Her heart was pounding. Her voice broke. "How could you?"

Steven turned away. He wouldn't look at her. "I never wanted kids with you."

Tears stung her eyes. Dillyn wasn't sure she could beat them back but fought hard to keep them at bay. If it weren't for her anger, she might have let them fall. *I've still got some pride.*

"You're still doing it. Trying to mess with my head. I won't let you revise history. It was me. I didn't want kids, and for

13

years, you tried to talk me into having them. Why? It just doesn't make any sense. I wish I had known about your concerns over having biracial children before I went through all of that hell. Yeah, I read those conversations on your phone too. The ones where you were worried about how any child we might have could affect your budding political career." Devastated, Dillyn whispered, "You knew that I was Black before you married me. You have eyes. I'm a brown woman with full lips and a wide nose. I wear my natural hair in coils. I've never shied away from my Blackness."

It was Steven's turn to feign righteous indignation. He slammed his hand on the table. "We were in college when we got together, Dillyn!"

She remembered. It was always them against the world—*and his family*. Steven was her champion in a place where she most definitely felt out of place. "Was our relationship really just about sticking it to your parents who never really liked me?" Dillyn shook her head as if answering her own question. "I don't know. Maybe it was the novelty of being in an interracial relationship. Regardless, even if you being a disrespectful, manipulative, man-whore was about your family, political aspirations, or something else, why not just divorce me instead of putting me through all of this?"

Steven would neither confirm nor deny Dillyn's suspicions. Instead, he stood, forcefully knocking his chair over in the process. "If you want a divorce, fine. Let's do it. But just know, what you came into this relationship with is what you'll leave with."

"Speaking from a man who grew up with money and power. I don't want a penny from the trust your grandfather left you. But after all you've put me through, and after being caught

14

cheating red-handed, are you really going to fight me over money we accumulated together?" *Who is this man?*

Steven was smug and dismissive. "I'm not worried about my trust. You can't touch that anyway."

Dillyn shot back. "Neither can you! Your father has been fighting you over it since before we were married."

"My father and family are not your concern." Steven released a sarcastic little laugh. "Let's be clear, you might have brought in a few hundred thousand, but I've made millions. The keyword in that statement is *I* made millions. No way in hell you're getting 50 percent of my hard work."

Hard work? What Steven really meant was his family's connections. He might have been on the outs with them but not so far that they would publicly disown him. Appearances were everything to the Havenhursts. Dillyn was prepared for Steven behaving like an asshole. She knew he might not have wanted her, but money and power . . . *that* meant something. He was not going to give up anything without a fight.

"My law partners and associates on the bench sit high and low. No court in New York will admit any of the shit in this envelope. I know you illegally obtained it."

Slowly, Dillyn walked back to her chair and sat down. "Are you so sure?" She crossed her arms. "Exactly what money are you referring to, Steven? You might want to check those bank statements in that envelope."

Steven was hesitant. He went back into the envelope and dumped out all of the contents. Steven quickly read through the statements. Dillyn had found all his accounts, including the ones he didn't know she knew about. Slowly, he looked up. His voice was menacing. "Where's my money?"

"Your money?" Dillyn deserved an Oscar for keeping

15

such a straight face. "Again, I ask, what money, Steven?" Dillyn was damn good at her job. She had erased every shred of digital footprints for more than seven million in cash deposits. She had also liquidated several offshore accounts and sold all of the properties they owned together–except for their primary residence. The proceeds from those sales were firmly in Dillyn's control, totaling an additional twenty-nine million.

Steven spoke through clenched teeth. "Where is my money, Dillyn?!"

She disregarded his rising anger. Her voice was calm. Calmer than she actually felt. "I'll make a deal with you. You sign the divorce papers, and I'll give you two million."

He scoffed at her offer. "Where. Is. My. Money. Dillyn?!"

She ignored his reddened face and the steam coming from out of his ears. "Okay, I'll sweeten the pot. I also won't reveal any of the shady shit you've done at your law firm, exposing them to billions in liabilities. Quite frankly, even I was shocked. In fact, the New York Attorney General might be interested in the information I have, considering you're planning on running against him in the next election. Funny, the things you can discover from a phone or a computer. Even when you think it's been deleted."

Steven's face drained of all color.

Dillyn lifted her chin toward the pen, which had been in the envelope. "Sign the papers." She snapped her finger as if she'd forgotten something. "Don't even think of a murder-for-hire scheme. It won't work because if a strand of my hair were to come up missing, I've built in contingencies, and all of your dirty laundry will come out. All. Of. It!"

Steven pressed his lips into a thin, firm line. As if resigned to the fact that Dillyn had executed a well-thought-out plan, he

16

picked up the pen, found the signature pages, and signed them.

Dillyn was falling apart, but she'd be damned if she would allow him to see it.

After Steven finished signing the documents, he dropped the pen on the table. "When will the money be in my account?"

That's all he had to say? Dillyn was more heartbroken than she led on. "What happened to you?" she whispered, voice trembling.

He looked into her eyes. "I want to be the next New York AG. I'll need my family to make that happen. I had a choice to make. You or them. It's as simple as that."

"Why not just divorce me?" Dillyn asked again since he'd never really answered the first time.

"If I'm honest? I planned to. I just hadn't figured out how to do it cleanly and quietly. I guess you could say you beat me to it."

Dillyn's chest wanted to cave into her back. The pain she felt was unlike anything she'd ever thought she would feel again. *How could he be so matter-of-fact? So cold and callous?* They had taken vows to spend forever together. Steven was supposed to be her happily ever after. Instead, he'd successfully managed to do what others failed to do—break her into a million little pieces.

Dillyn gathered the papers up from off the table. Her voice sounded like she felt . . . *drained.* "I'll have my attorney file these in the morning. Once they're filed, you can expect the money to be in your account within seven to ten business days."

"Seven to ten business days?! What am I supposed to do for money in the meantime?"

Dillyn shrugged. "I don't know. Ask Sam."

Steven clenched his fist and let her jibe go. There was nothing he could do about it just yet. "And this property? I didn't see any liquidation of assets."

Dillyn grabbed her black trench coat from off the back of one of the dining room chairs. "You and Sam can have it. According to the security footage, she seemed to be pretty comfortable in my bed." With her head held high and her back ramrod straight, Dillyn walked out of the room.

*****

Earlier, Steven had watched all of the emotions play out on Dillyn's face. She'd won round one, but he knew this wasn't over. Not by a long shot. Dillyn was playing at being ruthless. She wasn't that person. However, he was the real deal. *Did she think she could embarrass me? Take my money and threaten me without consequences?* Dillyn was still a liability. One, he had to figure out how to neutralize. She changed the game with this little stunt. Steven had worked too hard to set the pieces in motion to become New York's AG to have this hanging over his head. When the tables turn, because they would, Dillyn Anderson-Havenhurst would wish she'd just walked away.

Now, he was beside himself. Steven was wearing the floor out, pacing back and forth while holding his cell phone in a death grip.

Steven was dreading the phone call he had to make. *How could I have allowed an affair to bring down everything I've worked so hard for?* This was a clusterfuck. However, there was one silver lining—Dillyn seemed to have only uncovered his relationship with Sam and a few shady deals. She had no idea about the actual information in her possession.

Angrily, he ran his hand through his five-hundred-dollar haircut. *Dammit!* Steven's voice bounced off the walls as he growled out his frustrations.

Steven was so close to his end goal that he could almost

touch it. Dillyn was the key. She jumped the gun prematurely. He still needed her. More specifically, Steven needed her contacts. She wasn't the only one who could keep a secret. He knew all about her work for CyberCom.

Think . . . dammit . . . THINK! He could not make this phone call without a viable plan. Otherwise, it could cost him his life.

Tentatively, Steven dialed a number he'd rarely called and placed the phone up to his ear. After the first ring, his heart slammed into his chest.

No answer.

Steven listened to his call ring for the second time.

Again, no one picked up.

By the end of the third ring, his call finally connected. A deep and heavy accented voice responded. "Why are you calling me at this number?"

"We need to meet." Perspiration lined Steven's brow. He used his forearm to wipe it away. Briefly, his eyes closed before finally getting to the point. "I've been compromised." Steven rushed his words. "But I can fix this."

There was dead silence on the other end of the line. It lasted mere seconds but seemed like an eternity. "You better hope so. Be at our usual place in thirty minutes." The line immediately went dead.

Steven had thirty minutes to figure something out. In Dillyn's efforts to be cute, she had put both of their lives in danger.

Chapter 3

Dillyn was numb. She had spent so much time arranging a full-scale plot against Steven down to the tiniest detail, and now that it was over, her revenge hadn't tasted nearly as sweet. If Dillyn were honest, it left her feeling mostly empty and sad. She had been with Steven for thirteen years even though they were only married for ten, and they were supposed to be a team. Dillyn had trusted him with everything–*almost*. It was just starting to settle into her brain that life with him was over. It felt like someone died, and all the well-wishers went home, leaving her to deal with the aftermath alone.

Dillyn wasn't exactly by herself. She was blessed to have Cat and Palmer by her side. They were dear friends and had been her rock since the moment she found out about Steven. The women had helped her through the days of tears, depression, and despair. Without them, Dillyn might have had a well-deserved breakdown months ago. She thanked God they were always there to support one another. Tonight was an emergency. That meant a sleepover at one of their places with every tasty carb known to man available for consumption, several stupid comedies on Netflix, and lots and lots of wine. Since Dillyn no longer had a home and Cat was living out of a suitcase, that left Palmer's condo as their meetup spot.

Dillyn lay across the foot of Palmer's massive bed in her two-piece cotton pajamas, not listening to a word of their chatter. Their raucous laughter roused her from her thoughts and propelled her back to the present.

"Did Steven even notice you were playing Inayah's "Best Thing" in the background when he walked in?" Palmer asked.

"Probably not. Knowing Steven, he was too busy looking at your tits and ass." Cat took a sip of her wine. "I still think you should have used Mary J Blige's 'Not Gone Cry' as your farewell song. Maybe even Jazmine Sullivan's 'Bust Your Windows.' "

"It would have been too obvious," Palmer said in disagreement. Still, Palmer and Cat made eye contact and began simultaneously belting out off-key the lyrics to Mary J Blige's song.

That brought a small smile to Dillyn's lips. "Do you know he had the nerve to bring me some last-minute, I forgot our anniversary, grocery store flowers? Bastard. I mean, he couldn't even fake like he cared. The damn thing still had the nine-dollar and ninety-nine-cent sticker price on it." Dillyn's eyes misted, but she refused to let any tears fall. "I bet Sam never got grocery store flowers."

The room quieted.

Cat reached out and rubbed Dillyn's shoulder, offering just a bit of comfort. "Sam is a two-dollar trick. You're a precious jewel. I hope you know that."

Palmer agreed. "Tuh! That's too much money for that skank. Try a dime-store floozy. There is nothing lower than a woman who smiles in your face while sleeping with your man."

"I just don't know how I missed all of the signs." Dillyn sat up. "I mean, I know Steven, and I haven't been on the same page for a while, but I would never have guessed this. Sam has been a guest in our home."

Neither Cat nor Palmer was surprised.

Palmer filled Dillyn's empty glass. "It's such a triflin' cliché. Hookin' up with his admin. A job *you* helped her get."

"You know, he actually believes that having Sam on his arm will help his non-existent political career? I bet his mother will love her." Dillyn threw her head back as she closed her eyes in disbelief. "I've known this man for almost half my life. I would never have guessed he thought my race had become an issue. Like, when? I mean, c'mon. I have a lot to offer."

Palmer and Cat nodded in agreement as Dillyn ticked off her positives on her fingers. "I'm accomplished."

"True." Cat agreed.

"I have my master's in cybersecurity, a Ph.D. in international affairs, and I have my own thriving business."

"You're a rich bitch too. Let's not sugar coat that!" Palmer said. "And let's also not forget that you are hot!"

Dillyn seemed to waffle her head from side to side at their compliments. She didn't take them well.

Palmer cradled the side of Dillyn's face within the palm of her hand. "Let me rephrase. You are beautiful inside and out."

Dillyn didn't completely agree. "I'm a thirty-two-year-old divorcée. However, I will admit that I do have more money today than I had yesterday. Still . . ." A small part of her wondered if she had been able to have a baby with Steven if things would have been different. The Steven that Dillyn had known would have fallen in love with their child. Race wouldn't have mattered. "This is not the ending I saw for myself."

Cat wasn't here for it. She couldn't stand Steven. "That bastard played mind games with you. He had you thinking you had to look a certain way for his career to thrive–all the dieting and exercising. It was crazy. I can't imagine how hard this is, but we've got you. We're also here to tell you that you're perfect just the way you are."

Hoping to lighten the mood, Palmer added, "Now you can eat carbs guilt-free! For the next six months, you shouldn't even think about working out."

Dillyn was the thinnest of her girlfriends. She was curvy

but still thin. Cat and Palmer were both sexy sirens. Tall, curvy, and confident.

Dillyn had never been self-assured until she met Steven. He helped her find the confidence that was now shredded into teeny tiny pieces. But Dillyn was a survivor. She'd been a survivor her entire life. She would figure out a way to build herself back up into a better version.

For now, she just had to keep herself together and take it one day at a time. Dillyn sighed. "As crazy as you two are, I love you both. Thanks for tonight."

"We love you too, girl." Cat placed a hand on top of Dillyn's and Palmer's, effectively forming a circle between them. "If I'm honest, it's nice that we're together like this. I hate the reason for it, but I really miss hanging out when I'm in Paris."

"If yo ass could be still long enough, maybe we could do more of this." Palmer smirked. "Like we don't need wine tasters in the States," she joked. They all knew Cat had a restless soul and didn't hold it against her.

Cat faked at being taken aback. "A wine taster? I'm a master sommelier, thank you very much!" Playfully, she smacked Palmer on the arm. "Seriously, Dillyn isn't the only one that's been rethinking a few things."

Dillyn snorted. "Rethinking? That's what we're calling my situation?"

Cat ignored her. "Yes! Rethinking. I'll be thirty-two in less than a month, and I don't have anything to show for it. I mean, Palmer, you have your real estate business, Dillyn, you have *Dot Matrix,* and I live out of suitcases and hotels." Cat sighed. "There's got to be more to life than this. What that is, I have no idea, but I think I'm ready for more."

Both Palmer and Dillyn were shocked at Cat's words, but

they understood the feeling. Palmer leaned against the headboard of her bed and took a sip of wine before responding. "More? What does more even look like?"

It wasn't a real question for her friends. Dillyn knew where Palmer was going. They'd talked recently about Palmer feeling the pull of her biological clock ticking.

Cat answered the question dangling in front of her. "It would be nice actually to own something. To have my own slice of heaven. There's not much I can do in the States as a sommelier."

"That's not true," Dillyn said.

"Yeah, it's true. Unlike you two, I'm not rich. I have to travel internationally to make the big money. I'm tired of traveling."

"Who's rich? I'm not rich. I might be upper-middle class, but rich? Girl, bye." Palmer pointed toward Dillyn. "That's her."

Dillyn hated talking about money with her friends. "I do okay." She quickly changed the subject. "What would you do if you had money?"

Cat fell back onto Palmer's pillows. She looked up at the ceiling, saying wistfully, "I'd like to have my own vineyard. Create my own wine brand."

"You'd have to move out of the city, and you, my dear friend, are a city girl." Dillyn reminded her.

"I'd do it for a fresh start," Cat replied.

"A fresh start does sound nice."

"You too?" Dillyn asked, shocked. "You love your life."

"I did . . . in my twenties. Do you know how cut-throat real estate is? I have ulcers from this job. I would gladly give it up for something new and exciting. Unfortunately, somebody has got to pay for this high-priced condo we're enjoying since you

24

heffas are homeless. That someone is me."

"Condo with a magnificent view, though," Dillyn responded cheekily, then turned serious. "Too bad we can't find a vineyard and buy it. We could call it The Chicks Winery."

Cat giggled. "You, my friend, are corny. It's adorable. But if we were living in dreamland and could buy a vineyard, we would not leave you in charge of naming it."

Palmer sat up and glanced thoughtfully between her friends. She hesitated at first before speaking quietly. "I could find us a vineyard."

Dillyn and Cat stared at Palmer, waiting for her to erupt into laughter. She didn't.

Dillyn wasn't shocked why Cat wouldn't believe Palmer was serious. She knew her friend would tell them why buying a vineyard couldn't work. "What part of my broke ass can't afford to buy one did you miss? I can't even afford to be a partner."

Dillyn didn't hesitate. "What if I fronted the money?"

Again, the room grew quiet. They all wondered if the other was serious.

"Do you all remember that Bed & Breakfast we stayed at a couple of years ago for our girl's trip?"

"The Steele Orchard?" Cat asked.

"Yep." Palmer nodded. "It's for sale. The owner reached out to me several months ago because I playfully told him to contact me if he ever wanted to put it on the market."

It was then Cat realized they weren't joking, especially when she saw the look on Dillyn's face. Her friend was reeling and would agree to almost anything. Now wasn't the best time for her to be making big decisions. "I couldn't agree to a significant purchase like that."

Dillyn pointed at her. "You have the expertise in wines,

Palmer has the expertise in real estate, and I have the money." Dillyn lifted her shoulders, a small smile playing on her lips. "Maybe we *could* do this. It would be the fresh start we've been talking about."

"Would you seriously consider doing that?" Palmer asked. "Even a cheap vineyard ain't going to be cheap. It might run in the millions."

Cat chimed in. "Developing wine and turning it into a profitable business can take years, and that will cost a lot of money too."

Dillyn didn't care. "I am now twenty-seven million dollars richer than I was yesterday. The more I think about it, the more I love the idea."

"Developing our own brand of wine will really eat into that," Cat said.

Palmer's smile grew wide. "I have to admit twenty-seven million is a lot of money but may not enough for a vineyard either. However, if the property is still for sale, I own a couple of properties I could liquidate for more capital. Plus, with my negotiation skills, it just might be possible. The rest we can figure out."

It was clear that Dillyn and Palmer were on board with this crazy scheme. They just had to convince Cat. Palmer negotiated multi-million dollar deals every day. *I can certainly close one of my besties. Can't I?* "*We* could do this, but it doesn't work without you. As Dillyn said, it could be a fresh start for all of us."

Cat was adamant. "I'm not a charity case."

"We know that," Dillyn said softly but firmly. "But you know wine. I can barely tell the difference between a seedless green grape and a red one. That's as far as my expertise goes."

"It would be a big risk, Dillyn. That's a lot of money and

pressure on me if it fails. I would hate to let you down."

"Cat, I don't give a shit about this money. Steven did. It's the only reason why I took it. I still have my business which I can run from anywhere. And in all honesty, I'd love to move to a new place with new faces. Not having to run into Steven's friends and them gawking at me when all of them knew about his affair would be a godsend."

Cat was still hesitant as both Palmer and Dillyn stared at her while they waited for an answer. "We've been drinking. I'm sure this is the wine talking."

"Maybe. Doesn't mean it's not a good idea." Dillyn turned her glass up and finished off another glass of wine.

Palmer nodded. "It's actually a fanfreakintastic idea and one I would never agree to if I were sober. Better take advantage of me now."

Cat glanced between her friends. She was hesitant but wanted to come home for more than a weekend at a time. The more she thought about it, the more Cat realized it was what she wanted. "I'll only agree to this crazy scheme if we speak with a lawyer. They would have to structure any agreement between us where I would pay you back a third of your investment and give you my shares totaling that amount in the event we decided to dissolve any partnership."

Dillyn agreed. "We can do that."

"You would? Seriously?" Cat asked.

Dillyn was more than sure. "Yes, I would."

There was another pregnant pause throughout the bedroom before they realized they were about to embark on the adventure of a lifetime. Once it was settled, Palmer clapped her hands together. "This is crazy, but we are going to do this!"

Dillyn wanted to feel the hot flame of excitement but was

still too numb. "I'm so down."

Cat was hesitant but could also feel the same electrical charge of excitement emanating from Palmer. "I'm in!"

Dillyn grabbed what was left of the bottle of Merlot and lifted it. Cat lifted her glass, and so did Palmer. The three of them clinked their glasses together.

"Oh, my God." Palmer held in a scream. "This is going to be so great for all of us!" She pointed to Dillyn. "And you can hook up with that handsome cowboy you met without any guilt!"

Chapter 4

Two Years Prior . . .

"Why am I always the one who has to drive?" Dillyn maneuvered her rented SUV down a long and winding road toward the Steele Orchard Ranch.

Palmer glanced back at Cat, who was sitting in the rear seat with a conspiratorial grin. "You're better at it than us."

Cat coughed to cover up her laughter. "Yeah. That's it."

Dillyn didn't believe them for a second. She suspected her friends thought she might be a bit of a passenger-side driver, plus those heffas liked to drink . . . a lot. Dillyn was almost always the designated driver since she was more of an occasional wine drinker. This weekend she planned to change that. Dillyn wanted, no, needed to forget about her problems with Steven for just a little while. Nothing she did lately made him happy, and their relationship only seemed to be getting worse. Dillyn just wanted to relax and recharge. She was surprised that Palmer and Cat hadn't already started drinking. After all, it was five o'clock somewhere.

"Plus, something I ate on the plane has upset my stomach," Palmer added. "We need to get to the ranch quick so I can get to a bathroom."

"You too?" Cat asked. "I thought it was just me. I wonder if it was the seafood salad."

"I didn't eat that," Dillyn replied. As they drove closer to the B&B, their chatter started to die down, and a slight frown appeared on Dillyn's face. "Um . . . Cat? This house doesn't look like the image on the website."

"No. It doesn't," was all Cat could say as she stared at

the house coming into view.

"Oh, God. What in the world?" Palmer echoed Dillyn's sentiments. "Cat, this place doesn't look anything like the website. Well, maybe twenty years ago."

"I planned this girl's trip from Paris. I did the best I could, okay. Either one of you could have done it."

"Girl! Yo ass is from Chicago." Palmer reminded her. "Don't act brand new, like you don't know your way around the internet or the good old U.S. of A. You couldn't have found us a nice spa?"

"You asked for fresh air and mountains. At least you got that!" Cat couldn't help but notice the peeling paint and missing shutters. "Anyway, the house might look a little in disrepair on the outside, but I'm sure the inside will be pleasant."

Dillyn pulled the car up and parked. Both she and Palmer turned around and glared at Cat with expressions that said it had better be.

An older gentleman in overalls and a young woman, who looked to be in her early twenties, came out onto the porch, wearing big smiles. "Afternoon, ladies. I'm Gavin Steele, and this is my daughter, Amber. Welcome to the Steele Orchard."

Dillyn, Palmer, and Cat responded warmly in unison, "Hello!"

Gavin walked down the stairs. "Let me grab your bags, and Amber can show you to your rooms."

"It's such a pleasure to have you in our home." Amber's southern twang was strong. As they walked inside the house, Dillyn noticed that it wasn't much better looking than the outside. Outdated floral-patterned wallpaper, turned pale from both the sun and time, was plastered throughout. The furniture had also seen better days . . . years ago. Dillyn did like all of the floor-to-

ceiling windows. They ran throughout the lower level too. It allowed lots of sun to come inside, and she could use the light to boost her mood.

Dillyn sighed inwardly. The place was clean, and the Steeles seemed nice enough. At least they didn't appear to be axe murderers or sex traffickers.

Amber settled Cat and Palmer, showing Dillyn to her room last. "This is a really nice suite," *Amber said.* "We call it the yellow room." *She opened the door.*

Dillyn's eyes widened in amazement. She did her best not to laugh. Were they serious? *Her room was a throwback to* Little House on the Prairie, *and* yellow *was an understatement. Nope, Laura Ingalls Wilder had a better decorator.*

Did they do this on purpose? *The walls, the floors, the curtains, and the bed coverings were all some version of that ghastly yellow color. It wasn't short on frills, lace, and floral patterns either.* Whoever decorated this house must have hated the place to do it such an injustice. *It was too bad because the home, or at least the parts Dillyn had seen, was structurally beautiful.*

"Please let me know if you need anything." Amber continued to smile brightly.

Dillyn did her best to mask her thoughts as she returned her smile. Wine. I'm starting now. Please bring lots and lots of it. *With a straight face, Dillyn managed to ask about dinner and refreshments.* "Thank you so much for your hospitality. What time should we be down for dinner? And is it possible to get something to drink?"

"Dinner is in a couple of hours. We're preparing a nice little barbecue for you and your friends in the backyard. And I just made a fresh batch of lemonade and sweet tea. Which would you prefer?"

"Dinner sounds great. Refreshment-wise," Dillyn brought her thumb and forefinger close together but not touching, *"I was thinking of something a wee bit stronger than that."*

"Got it." Amber's grin widened. *"My dad makes the best wine from our peach trees. I can bring you a glass of that."*

Peach wine? Like a wine cooler? *Again, Dillyn kept a straight face. "Peach wine. That . . . would be fantastic. Thank you."*

"Perfect. I'll be right back." Amber left and closed the door behind her.

Dillyn made sure to lock the door behind Amber and made a mental note of how solid it was. She then went and sat on the edge of the queen-sized canopy bed. "At least it's comfortable," she said to herself. Dillyn continued to check out the room. It also had several large floor-to-ceiling windows and one of the most incredible views Dillyn had ever seen. It was so picturesque that the burnt-orange-colored sky and the majesty of the mountains didn't even look real. "Well, we did ask for a peaceful environment and fresh air. Cat delivered on that." However, Dillyn took pleasure in knowing that the only alcohol on the premises was essentially peach schnapps. That was a great punishment for Cat half-assing the planning of their trip. Dillyn burst into laughter as she fell back on the bed and was swallowed up by the softness of the mattress.

*****

"Thanks for coming over." Gavin waved to Ben. *"Not sure what happened with the stove. It blew up just as our guests were arriving."*

"No problem. All you've done for our family, it's the least I can do." Gavin had been a good friend to Ben's dad. Ben could see that he had been struggling to maintain his property. He hated

32

that Gavin even had to open it up to strangers just to pay the bills. "We can set up a barbecue pit in the backyard, and I'll have my sister whip up a few side dishes."

"That would be great. I have a young fella working on the stove now. It should be fixed tonight but not in time for dinner. Can I repay you with a bottle of wine? I made it about ten years ago. It's pretty good if I have to say so myself."

"Thank you, but it's not necessary. I'd hate to waste it since I'm not really a wine kind of guy. However, I do love a good bottle of whiskey." Ben had heard rumors that Gavin made a great moonshine.

Gavin chuckled. "Well, between you and me, I've got a few bottles of the good stuff hidden in the shed."

"I'll definitely take that." Although, he would have helped Gavin for nothing, Ben understood that folks didn't like to feel as if you were giving them a handout. He accepted the bottle as payment.

"How long are you here for?" Gavin asked.

"I fly back to Chicago on Sunday."

"I know your family must be glad to see you. It's been a while since you've been home."

It had been a while. Lana hadn't been up for traveling much these days, not with a two-year-old. It was a valid excuse. But, if Ben were honest, Lana hadn't been up for much of anything over the past few years. He could blame it on her being postpartum, but the truth was he and Lana were having problems well before the pregnancy. It had only gotten worse since Rylee was born. It wasn't really Lana's fault. Still, it was tough.

Gavin ran his hand over his stubbled chin. "Have you seen those gals that are staying here from New York?"

"I can't say that I've had the pleasure."

33

"Woowee. They are quite stunning. All three of them. I think I saw a ring on one of 'em's finger." Gavin turned his head toward the house, a wistful look in his eyes. "If I were a few years younger . . ."

Ben laughed. "If you were a few years younger, they wouldn't stand a chance."

"You got that right!"

Ben tried to suppress a grin as he shook his head. "Let me run back to my house. I'll grab a few things and be back before you know it."

Chapter 5

When Dillyn arrived at the patio, it seemed as if she was the first to arrive, except for the guy working the grill. She couldn't get a good look at him because his back was to her, but it wasn't hard to notice his height. He was very tall and muscular. Not the hulking kind, but he easily dwarfed Dillyn in size. She thought about making a beeline back to her room until her friends arrived but realized she was being ridiculous. Dillyn Anderson-Havenhurst, stop acting paranoid. Everyone will be down soon. *Dillyn took a deep breath before announcing herself. "Hi."*

Ben half-turned only to have the wind knocked out of him at the very sight of the Dillyn. Gavin hadn't been lying. The woman standing before him was stunning. She was downright gorgeous, and her smile was sinful.

Dillyn hoped to appear friendly. "I think I'm the first one down."

Ben found his voice. He wiped his hands down the front of his jeans before extending it out to her as he walked over. "Hi, I'm Ben Cash."

Dillyn looked at his hand but didn't shake it. She had a thing about touching, especially men. Instead, she glanced down at her feet. "Sorry, I'm a bit of a germaphobe."

His intense gaze made Dillyn uncomfortable. She hated feeling like a lab rat but hated more that her phobias were front and center.

Ben sensed her unease. He dropped his hand and glanced away, hoping it would make her more comfortable. "Got it. Well, the others should be down shortly, and dinner is almost ready." That was strange, *he thought as he walked back toward the grill.*

Not wanting to make Ben think he'd done anything wrong, Dillyn tried to make light conversation. "Whatever you're cooking smells delicious."

"Thanks. I hope you and your friends enjoy it."

Where are Cat and Palmer? They should have been down by now.

Ben's back was still to her as he stood over the grill. Her mouth watered, and Dillyn's stomach growled at the smell and sound of the sizzling steaks on the grill.

Amber Steele appeared out of nowhere. "Hey, Ben! Thank you so much for helping out tonight." She clapped her hands together as she walked down the pathway toward them. "I see you've met Dillyn."

"Ah . . . that's her name." Ben turned slightly.

Dillyn blushed. "Um . . . yes. I'm . . ." She glanced from Ben to Amber and back to Ben. She'd always been socially awkward, but this was ridiculous. "I'm Dillyn."

Ben got caught up staring at Dillyn's mouth and eyes again as he responded to Amber. "I guess now we've met." He caught himself and tried to pretend he wasn't affected by Dillyn's beauty. He shouldn't have been since he was a married man, but Ben wasn't blind either.

Dillyn felt his eyes on her, and they were friendly enough. Her thoughts immediately went to Steven. He hadn't even given her friendly looks lately. He'd been so busy with work that they had become virtually roommates. They weren't even friends with benefits, which was fine with Dillyn. She wasn't good at sex and didn't particularly enjoy it anyway.

Ben noticed the size of Dillyn's rock on her left finger when she moved a wayward curl behind her ear. She must have been who Galvin was referring to—the married one.

"Dillyn, I've known Ben forever. He lives a couple of ranches over. We were having some troubles with our kitchen, and he volunteered to help us out."

"Oh, you don't work here?" Dillyn asked, surprised.

"No, ma'am. I do not," he responded.

Amber giggled. "Oh, gosh, no. Ben's a—"

"Just a friend helping out." Ben cut Amber off before she could finish her sentence.

Amber smirked, getting the message loud and clear. "Well, too bad you won't get to meet our other two guests, Palmer and Cat. They won't be joining us tonight."

"What?" Dillyn was both surprised and confused.

"They both seem to be suffering from some sort of upset stomach."

Dillyn vaguely remembered them talking about it on the drive over to the ranch. She received text messages from both Palmer and Cat just as Amber was informing her of the absence.

"I'm sorry." Amber genuinely felt bad. "It's such a beautiful night, and I hate that they are going to miss the barbeque. If you like, I can cancel my plans and have dinner with you."

Dillyn waved her off. "Absolutely, not. Please don't do that on account of me. I'll just take dinner in my room."

Amber gave Ben the eye, pleading with him to help. Ben initially ignored her because he was not in the mood to entertain, and second, if his instincts were correct, Dillyn didn't really want his company.

Dillyn looked away toward the darkening sky. "It is getting dark. It's not a problem to eat in my room."

Amber took the opportunity to put her hands together as if in prayer, begging Ben to have dinner with Dillyn. She silently mouthed the words, "Please, please, please."

Ben rolled his head around his neck. Shit. This is not how I planned to spend my night. *He'd finally finished up his business and, for the next couple of days, could just enjoy his family. Only tonight, his brothers and sister were out for the evening, so* technically, *he would have been home alone anyway.*

With a look of defeat, Ben mouthed back. "Fine! You owe me."

"Anything for you," Amber mouthed and winked.

Ben rubbed the back of his neck. "Um. . . Dillyn, I'm actually pretty hungry. There's a lot of food here. If you don't mind, we could have dinner together, so the food doesn't go to waste."

Slowly, Dillyn turned in his direction but wouldn't look him in the eyes. "It's not necessary."

"I insist!" Amber said. "Part of the experience of this ranch is the barbeque around the fire. It should have been tomorrow night, but we had to switch it because of the kitchen."

"I promise. I'm not an axe murderer," Ben said, only semi-joking.

Dillyn's eyes jerked up to his. They almost blew Ben away. He was utterly transfixed.

Dillyn stuttered, "N-no. Of course, not." She was being irrational and her usual socially awkward self. It was a beautiful night, and Ben was trying to be friendly. "Are you sure you don't mind?"

He lifted a shoulder in a small shrug. "Not at all."

"Great!" Amber clapped her hands together in relief. "Then, I'll leave you to it." Amber turned toward Ben. "Dad won't admit it, but he's not feeling the best either. I'll be back in a few hours, so if you need anything, call me on my cell." Amber could tell Dillyn was antsy, so like the wind, Amber was gone be-

fore she could change her mind, leaving Ben and Dillyn completely alone.

Nervously, Dillyn glanced around.

His immediate attraction to Dillyn caught Ben off guard. It was the first time something like that had ever happened, and he needed to nip it in the bud. The saving grace came at the sound of his cell. He pulled it out of his back pocket. "Sorry, I've got to take this. It's home. If you want to have a seat in front of the fire, I'll bring you a glass of wine. Supper should be ready in another few minutes." Ben stepped away and went back to tending the grill.

Dillyn hugged herself as she did what Ben had asked and took a seat on something that resembled a large wooden log. She wasn't trying to eavesdrop but could hear Ben talking on the phone.

"Is everything okay?"

Dillyn looked around, stood, stamped her feet, sat back down, and scooted farther down the log. Still, she could hear his side of the conversation.

"Where's Lana?" he asked the person he was talking to before releasing a heavy sigh. The irritation in his voice was unmistakable.

"Maybe I can sing to her? That usually helps."

Seconds later, Dillyn heard the deep dulcet tones of Ben singing the Stevie Wonder classic "Isn't She Lovely" with a country twist. Surprisingly, Ben had a great voice. He sang with so much love. Dillyn wasn't sure she had ever witnessed anything so pure in her life. She had no idea a man could give that kind of care to another human being, even she was soothed.

Ben continued to sing for a few more minutes before whoever he was speaking with came back on the line. "I'll be home on Sunday, but if Rylee gets fussy, just call me day or night."

Dillyn didn't even realize it, but she had a goofy smile on her face as she watched him.

Ben disconnected the call and returned his cell to his back pocket. He blew out another long breath before taking the steaks off the grill to let them rest. Dillyn could tell by the set of his shoulders that Ben might have soothed Rylee, *but the call had the opposite effect on him. He picked up a couple of glasses and a bottle of wine before turning and walking toward her.*

"Was that your daughter?" Dillyn knew it was nosy, but she couldn't help but ask.

His face softened. "Yeah. Her name is Rylee. She's two. She was having a little trouble getting to sleep." Ben handed Dillyn a glass.

"Did it work?"

"For now." He cracked a small smile. "Is Merlot okay?"

Dillyn held back a little laugh. "You mean it's not peach wine?"

Ben laughed too. He whispered conspiratorially, "Are they still serving that?"

"They are. Actually, it's not that bad."

"Okay. Then let me run to the kitchen to grab a bottle."

"No! Please. I mean . . ." Dillyn bit her lower lip in embarrassment. Then covered her mouth to keep from laughing.

This time Ben's laughter came from his gut. "Yeah, that's what I thought. Don't worry. I'll keep your secret." He liked the way her eyes sparkled when they weren't so guarded.

Dillyn's stomach growled. She quickly placed her hand there to calm it.

"Hungry?"

Dillyn was embarrassed Ben had heard it. She had been

40

on a continuous diet but planned to break it this weekend. "I haven't eaten today." She smiled cheekily. "Whatever you're making smells divine."

"Thanks." Ben thought Dillyn was a little slip of a woman. With her comment about not eating, he assumed she was on a diet but by no means needed to be on one. Maybe it was a New York thing. "I grilled the steaks, but my sister made you ladies some corn-on-the-cob, baked potatoes, and a fresh salad."

Dillyn briefly closed her eyes and moaned. "Mmm . . ." Her reaction sounded sexual even to her own ears. Shocked, Dillyn stiffened and glanced away from Ben. Her eyes flitted around the property. She couldn't look at him.

Ben pretended as if Dillyn hadn't just made his cock jerk. "Steaks should be done resting by now." He got up and walked away, thinking about the indigestion he was going to have by breaking the world's record for scarfing down his food so he could get the hell out of dodge.

Dillyn took a large gulp of wine. She couldn't have created a more perfect cowboy. One who seemed to be both rugged and thoughtful, seeing how he'd said nothing about her indecent moan.

A few minutes later, Ben was back with two mouth-watering plates.

"My goodness! That looks so good." Dillyn's voice was much too loud. Ben made her nervous. Cat and Palmer would have known how to play it cool, but Dillyn didn't have that skill.

"I hope you enjoy it." Ben took a seat next to Dillyn but not too close.

Dillyn pushed her food around, trying to think of something mundane to say. "You didn't have to give up your night to babysit me."

41

"It's your first time in Summer, right?"

Dillyn nodded.

"Amber's right. It's so beautiful this time of year. It would be a shame to waste a night like tonight." His wife flashed through his mind. Ben wished he could share a quiet evening like this with Lana, but she hated the outdoors.

Dillyn pointed at his ring more so as a reminder to herself that they were both off-limits. "How long have you been married?"

Ben glanced down at it. "Five years. You?"

"Eleven together but six years married."

"Wow. That's a long time. He's a lucky guy."

Dillyn wasn't so sure Steven felt that way. She distracted herself from that statement by cutting into her steak. The knife went through it like butter. What better way to not answer a question than eating? Dillyn put a small piece into her mouth. Her eyes widened then rolled into the back of her head. "This is so good."

"Thank you."

"I saved all of my calories for this weekend."

Ben had noticed Dillyn was thin. He couldn't help it. But now, up close, he also saw she was very curvy. Her jeans fit nice. Real nice. He coughed into his drink. "So . . . um . . . what brings you here?" Keep it cool, cowboy.

Dillyn tried to speak between chews. "My friends and I try to get together once a year for a carefree weekend."

"Carefree, huh?" Don't go there.

"Yep."

Ben was grateful that Dillyn missed his unintended innuendo.

"We're all so busy that we don't have a lot of time to hang

42

out. Cat found this place on the internet. So, here we are." Dillyn shook her head. "I can't believe they got sick."

Ben caught himself staring at her mouth and quickly looked into the flames as they crackled and danced. "Summer is a great place. I miss it."

"Miss it?" Dillyn asked.

"Yeah, I grew up here, but my life is now in Chicago."

"By the tone in your voice, I'd wager a guess that you don't like the Windy City?"

"It's okay. I would prefer to raise kids here. Fresh, clean air. Lots of land for them to run and play, and the people are great."

Children had been a sore spot between Dillyn and Steven. They had been trying to conceive but hadn't been successful. "It does seem like a great place to raise a family. Your wife disagrees?"

"Not really." Ben didn't want to put Lana in a bad light, so he quickly changed the subject. "How about you? Do you have any children?"

"Not yet." Dillyn put her plate down. "We've been trying for a while." She hadn't meant to share that bit of information. Dillyn hadn't even shared it with her friends.

Ben could see a brief glimpse of sadness wash over her. "Everything always happens when it's supposed to."

"Being a parent just seems so scary. It keeps me awake at night, worrying I might screw a kid up. You seem to be great with Rylee, though."

"I'm learning and doing my best. But I did hit the lottery with my parents. They were incredible. I had great role models."

Dillyn wouldn't know what that looked like. She took another sip of her wine. Her voice softened. "You lost them?"

43

"Yeah. About six years ago now. It was hard, but my family came together."

Dillyn wondered what it must have been like to have a family you could count on.

"As far as children, don't stress it. I can tell you one thing for sure; your heart will expand in ways you never thought possible."

"Hmm." Dillyn looked thoughtful. "Not sure that happens for all parents," she said, imagining her own.

It didn't take much for Ben to put two and two together. "You had a tough time growing up?"

"Understatement of the year. I have so many isms and phobias because of them. I don't want to pass that stuff on to my child. Just being here with you tonight is a testament to years of therapy." Dillyn didn't know why she revealed all of that to Ben. Maybe it was because he seemed so calm, and it left her feeling . . . comfortable. He was also a stranger that she would never have to see again.

"Being here with me?"

Dillyn put up a single finger. "Hold on." She took a long sip of wine. Might as well exercise these demons. "I'm sure you can tell that I'm a bit socially awkward."

He smiled. "I wouldn't say awkward, but I can say I've never actually met a genuine germaphobe before."

Dillyn wasn't a germaphobe, but she wasn't going to admit that part. "I've just never really been good meeting people. It's always been difficult."

"You seem fine now."

"Probably because you showed me a side of yourself that you rarely see in people."

"I did? When?" Ben was confused. He had no idea what

44

Dillyn was talking about.

"Yes. When you sang to your daughter, do you know how amazing that was? I could hear the love you have for her in your voice. Any person who has that type of love inside of them can't be too bad."

"I don't know about that, but that little girl owns my heart. She has me wrapped around all of her fingers. This is my first trip away from her since she was born, and I miss her like crazy."

"I'm sure both Rylee and your wife miss you something crazy too."

"I hope so."

Dillyn thought that was a strange response. She went to take another sip of wine and realized it was gone. "Oh."

"Would you like more?"

"I would love another glass. Thank you."

Ben poured Dillyn more wine. "Just say when." He waited and waited until her glass was almost filled to the rim.

"Okay." Dillyn giggled.

Her smile was like gold. Damn. Their eyes locked and held for longer than three seconds. Ben was the first to glance away and up into stars. "They're so bright." Ben had never cheated on Lana and didn't plan to tonight. Lust and love were two entirely different things. He wouldn't make the mistake of confusing the two again.

For a moment, Dillyn thought maybe Ben was attracted to her, but she couldn't tell. She'd always been terrible at gauging a man's interest. Not that it mattered. They were both married. Dillyn decided to just go with the flow and enjoy his company instead of overthinking everything like she always did. She glanced up too. "It is and so peaceful."

45

"Peace. That thing can be elusive, can't it?" Ben returned his gaze to her. He couldn't help staring at the slender column of her neck. What the fuck, man? *Again, Ben turned away when he realized what he was doing. He was getting aggravated at himself. What was his problem? Sex-starved? Definitely, but he was a man. He could control his base instincts.*

Dillyn hadn't noticed him watching her. She sighed wistfully. "It sure can."

Ben got the feeling Dillyn wasn't very happy in her marriage. In all honesty, neither was he. At the moment, and considering how physically attracted he was to Dillyn, it wasn't good information to know. Ben reminded himself that he had said vows, and that meant something. No matter how bad it got between him and Lana, he wouldn't break them.

Ben moved the conversation to something safer. "So, Ms. Dillyn. What do you do?"

She tore her eyes away from the stars. "Excuse me?"

"What do you do? For like, work?"

"Oh. I'm in IT security. You?"

"Agriculture."

"Agriculture? Like farming?"

Ben laughed. "No. Nothing like that. I experiment with sustainable agriculture."

Dillyn nodded her head up and down, then side to side. "I have no idea what that means." She laughed.

Her laugh was infectious. "Most people don't. I'm just doing my part to try to save the planet and make sure folks don't go hungry."

"That's admirable." The wine was making Dillyn loosen up. "You really are a good guy, huh?"

Ben shrugged. "It's just what I do."

Handsome and modest. Dillyn would be deaf, dumb, and blind not to notice that Ben was more than a little attractive, not that it mattered. She glanced at the ring on her left hand.

Two hours went by like two minutes as Ben and Dillyn simply enjoyed each other's company. When Amber returned, she found them still in front of the fire and surprisingly laughing.

"I hope you enjoyed your dinner," Amber said, meaning it. She and her father could use the money from a return visit and any potential referrals.

Dillyn glanced up. "Dinner was amazing. Thank you." She turned to Ben, and her eyes softened. "Thank you for the company."

Ben hadn't realized that time had gotten away from them. Dillyn was sweet and easy to talk to. He'd enjoyed spending time with her. If things were different, he would ask her out. But they weren't, so there was that.

"I should probably get to my room," Dillyn said.

Like a true gentleman, Ben stood and helped Dillyn up. This time, Dillyn didn't complain about being a germaphobe. His hands were warm to the touch on her chilled arms. As they stood face-to-face, the energy between them changed from friendly to something else. Seemingly unable to pull away, Dillyn held her breath as her heart raced. Ohmygod. Is he going to kiss me? What the hell should I do?

Ben swallowed as he tucked some loose strands of hair behind Dillyn's ear. In the process, the tips of his fingers skimmed her face.

Initially, Dillyn hadn't recognized the signs, but something was simmering between them all evening, and that pull was strong. They'd both ignored it, but this time, with Ben holding her gaze hostage, it was hard to pretend that there wasn't something

47

in the air.

Amber glanced away, then cleared her throat, reminding them both that they weren't alone.

Dillyn was grateful for the reminder. Her smile was shaky from nerves. "Again, thank you both. I had a great evening. It was really nice to meet you, Ben."

"You too." He refused to say, "I hope we meet again," because being alone with Dillyn might be dangerous for both of them.

Dillyn nodded, then almost ran-walked to her bedroom.

Ben had been almost certain that he wouldn't have made a move, but the look in Dillyn's eyes gave him second thoughts. It was a good thing she had left when she did. Neither of them wanted to find out what would have happened if they had spent a little more time together.

Chapter 6

Dillyn opened the door and got out of her car. It had been an exhausting day. She just wanted to crawl into bed and snuggle underneath the covers. Instead, she'd allowed her friends to pressure her into going out. "I can't believe I let y'all talk me into coming to a bar."

Palmer grinned. "One of the guys working on the house suggested it. Did you just say *y'all*? Look at you. You're already adapting to our new environment."

"She is!" Cat laughed. "C'mon, Dillyn. Don't be a fun sponge. We've just bought a vineyard and spent our first week moving into our new home. We need to celebrate that! We shouldn't feel guilty about wanting to cut loose."

"Exactly!" Palmer's dark eyes glittered with excitement. "Look at all these cars. We'll definitely meet some locals tonight. Hell, we might even find some good trouble to get into. Maybe you'll run into that cowboy you met a couple of years ago while we're here."

"A, he was married, and B, I've already told you, I'm not looking for anything or anyone." Dillyn wasn't the least bit interested in getting into any *trouble*. She'd sworn off men and relationships in general but kept that to herself. There was no need to share her disdain for the opposite sex with Cat and Palmer, who were both single and still looking for Prince Charming. Dillyn didn't have the heart to tell them that marriage, commitment, loyalty, and Prince Charming didn't exist. That most men were complete monsters. *Yeah, I'm bitter.* It was all utter bullshit. *I won't be*

49

the one to crush their dreams, though. As Dillyn looked about, she had to admit that Palmer might have a fairly decent shot of at least finding someone to hook up with. *Sex. That was always on the table.* Then Dillyn remembered who she was thinking about and suppressed a smile. Palmer talked mad trash, but she wasn't the one-night-stand kind of girl. She was a woman waiting for the fairytale.

There were quite a few cars and pick-up trucks in the parking lot, considering the town's size. As of last week, there were about twenty-five hundred people. When they moved into the property formerly known as Steele's Orchard Ranch, that number increased by three.

It seemed all of the residents of Summer, Tennessee chose tonight to show up at Frank's.

Dillyn needed to snap out of her funk. She didn't want to be a *fun sponge,* as Cat so eloquently put it. While she'd rather have been at home, she'd been convinced to get all glammed up and figured she might as well make the most of it. Palmer made her wear a little black mini dress and a pair of matching strappy heels. Jeans and a t-shirt wouldn't have captured the energy those two wanted to project. Cat and Palmer took their look a step further.

Palmer was the most confident full-figured woman Dillyn had ever met. She was more than a little comfortable in her own skin and oozed sex appeal. Tonight, her five-foot-nine-inch frame was dressed in a curve-hugging, bright yellow dress. She wore her hair pulled back and away from her face in a bone-straight phony-pony that was so long it touched the back of her knees. That yellow against her smooth mocha-colored skin was hot. But it was her large, almond-shaped eyes that were her most striking feature. Those things were lethal and were Palmer's superpower.

Dillyn wasn't sure why she hadn't used them to snag a husband if she really wanted one. Palmer was just gorgeous. Cat was too. Physically, Cat was as different from Palmer as night and day. Aside from height, they were mirror opposites.

Cat had a fairer complexion. She would burn in the sun. Her greenish-gray eyes were diamond-like and could cut you deep. She wore her dark brown hair with honey blonde highlights in a pixie cut. Tonight, she'd gone with a smoky eye and hot pink lipstick for dramatic effect. Cat was society's standard of beauty. Her friends were not only supermodel gorgeous, but they were also good people. They valued both inner and outer beauty. If men had any sense, both of them would have already been off the market. Neither had a problem attracting a man's attention, but some men couldn't seem to handle Cat's and Palmer's independent natures. At least that was what Dillyn thought about Palmer. Dillyn had another theory when it came to Cat. Dillyn wasn't one hundred percent sure she wanted to get married. Cat had a restlessness about her that was hard to calm. She was down for a one-night stand. When Cat lasered in on someone, the guy usually didn't have a chance.

Dillyn got out of her head and tried to be present in the moment. Maybe even try to have some fun. She had been down in the dumps since she discovered Steven's affair, even more so since they finalized their divorce.

Dillyn shook off the doom and gloom. She straightened her back, pasted on a smile, walked up to the door of the bar, and opened it. After only a few steps into the building, Dillyn stopped dead in her tracks, causing Palmer and Cat to bump into her back.

"Holy shit," Dillyn whispered.

"What?" Cat looked around Dillyn. Her smile froze. "Oh."

Palmer pushed her friends farther into the bar. "What's wrong?"

It was like stepping into a time warp and a western movie. Dillyn didn't think she had ever seen so many Stetsons, cowboy boots, jeans, and t-shirts all in one place. She glanced down at her outfit. "Um. I think we might be a little overdressed."

Cat nodded and agreed. She responded sarcastically. "You think?"

Palmer squinted in the dimly lit bar, trying to get a better look. "Are they line dancing?"

"Yep," Dillyn confirmed as their heads all simultaneously tilted to the right. "I guess we should have expected something like this."

"Y'all's first time here?" A petite blond-haired woman asked while balancing a tray full of empty bottles and glasses. She was wearing a Frank's t-shirt, a pair of ripped jeans, and bright red cowboy boots.

Dillyn smiled warmly and answered for the group since her friends still seemed entranced by the atmosphere. "That obvious?"

The waitress grinned cheekily. "A little."

"Of course." Dillyn couldn't help but laugh. "If possible, we'd love a table where we can hide and not stand out like the obvious outsiders we are." It was a Herculean ask, considering their style of dress, and they were probably the only Black women in the place.

They followed the waitress to a table, but Cat kept her eyes on the dance floor.

"Is this alright?" the waitress asked.

"Perfect." They took their seats. "Those moves are kind of like the Cha-Cha slide, aren't they?" Cat asked as she stared out onto the dance floor.

"Yeah, I guess it is a lot like it," the waitress answered. "By the way, I'm Selah. I'll be serving y'all tonight."

"Thanks, Selah," Dillyn said.

"Y'all just bought Mr. Steele's Orchard, didn'cha?"

"We did. We moved in this week." Palmer was curious. "How did you know?"

"Small town. Word travels fast. Plus, a few of our ranch hands have been talking about getting possible side work with y'all."

"We are not in New York anymore." Palmer had to remember that.

"My goodness. No, it's not. Far from it." Selah giggled. "What can I get you, ladies?"

"A round of shots!" Palmer was quick to answer.

Cat wrinkled up her nose. "Shots? You're going to kill my palate."

"Now, who's a fun sponge?" Dillyn shouted above the crowd as she glanced at her friend. "A round of Uncle Nearest, please!"

Palmer and Cat looked a Dillyn as if she'd lost her mind.

"What?" Dillyn said. "I did my research on the vineyards *and* distilleries in Tennessee."

"You don't drink whiskey," Cat said matter-of-factly.

"Well . . . I am tonight." The resolute look on Dillyn's face made Cat and Palmer laugh.

"Okay. Uncle Nearest it is!" Selah was excited to finally meet the ladies who had been the talk of the town. Their energy was contagious. "Coming right up!" Selah had never stepped foot outside her hometown. The closest she'd ever gotten to the city was sitting right in front of her. She made a beeline for the ladies the second she'd seen them walk through the door. Selah planned to make the most of her opportunity.

Chapter 7

"On three, ladies," Palmer said as she elevated her voice over the music. She put up a finger. "One."

Dillyn rolled her head around her shoulders in preparation. If she was going to be at a bar, she might as well have a drink—or several. It had been a while.

"Two." Grinning from ear to ear, Palmer lifted a second finger.

Cat frowned. She hated whiskey, but tonight was going to go with the flow.

"Three!"

They threw their shots back.

Cat coughed and fanned herself. "Ugh! Woo . . ."

"Lightweight," Palmer teased.

Dillyn inhaled and slowly exhaled. The burn of the alcohol as it went down her throat had the effect of thawing the internal chill she'd been carrying around for the past year. *Maybe a few more of these, and I won't feel anything.* Dillyn waved to Selah and yelled, "Another round please!"

Both Cat and Palmer were more than a little surprised. Dillyn wasn't a big drinker, and they practically had to kidnap her just to get her out of the house. One of them would have to keep a keen eye on Dillyn if she were drinking. When she turned her head, Cat and Palmer rock, papered, scissored underneath the table. "Dammit!" Palmer mouthed the words when she lost.

It didn't take long before Selah returned with their drinks. "Here ya go!"

Palmer glanced around the bar. Looking Selah over, Palmer thought she was young but might have some insight into the dating scene. "What is the dating life like around here?"

Selah lifted a shoulder in a half-shrug. "Pickins are slim for people my age, I'm twenty-two, but there are a few guys around town folks consider eligible." Selah laughed. "You're going to have to jujitsu through some women to make a good impression. There are way more single ladies than men."

Palmer took a sip of her drink. "Unfortunately, that's nothing new."

Selah continued, "I don't know, but some of the stunts women do to get noticed by my brothers are ridiculous."

Cat perked up. "You have brothers?"

Selah nodded proudly. "Yep. Three overprotective and overbearing brothers—Ben, Lucas, and Wyatt Cash."

"Did you say, Ben Cash?" Dillyn asked.

Selah nodded. "Yeah. He's the oldest. Women flock to him like he's some kind of rock star."

It couldn't be him. That Ben is married, and I think lives in Chicago. "It must be nice to have brothers looking out for you." Dillyn couldn't imagine what that must be like, given she was an only child. Maybe Steven wouldn't have been such a douche if he knew she had brothers who would beat the shit out of him if he stepped out of line. Then again, probably, not.

"Tuh?!" Selah wrinkled up her nose. "*Nice?* No way. I started working here on Friday and Saturday nights just so guys could ask me out. Frank's has become my escape."

Curious, Palmer joked—*sort of.* "Did it work? If so, maybe I'll ask Frank for a job too."

"At first, it did. Not so much now. Everyone recognizes me as the little sister of the Cash brothers. Not a guy within a hundred miles will ask me out because of them. Thank God for the internet."

56

Cat frowned. "I hate online dating."

Selah agreed. "You do meet a lot of strange folks, but after a few hundred interactions, I think I've finally found someone. I can't wait to meet him."

A few hundred! Dillyn wanted no parts of that. She sipped her drink, hoping this conversation didn't kill her vibe.

Dillyn noticed that something had caught Cat's eye. She had that familiar twinkle when she was interested in something . . . or someone. Dillyn glanced over her shoulder to look in the direction of her gaze. *Of course.* A bowlegged, tight Levi-clad cowboy was headed their way.

He sauntered up to them, and his southern drawl was strong. "I hope you don't mind, but I saw a table full of pretty little ladies and thought I'd come by to introduce myself. I'm Paul Winston."

Palmer over-exaggeratedly batted her lashes while Cat smiled seductively.

Dillyn rolled her eyes. She had just started to loosen up and have fun. This was supposed to be a girl's night. *Men always ruin everything.*

He asked, "Can I buy y'all a round?"

Dillyn wasn't surprised when Palmer spoke for the group. "Of course you can, Paul." She had that *hell, yes, free drinks* look.

Selah widened her smile. "Great! I'll be right back."

Mr. Cowboy was one of many guys who sent over drinks during the next couple of hours, keeping Selah busy. Being new in town seemingly had its perks, but Dillyn didn't like all the attention.

After her third shot, Dillyn was done. She had reached her limit. It seemed like once she stopped drinking, Palmer got going.

Even if she wanted another drink, Dillyn was the designated driver, and her friends were getting completely wasted.

Cat had been eyeing the dance floor since the moment they arrived. After several more shots of liquid courage, she was ready. "Let's go mix it up with the locals, ladies!"

Chapter 8

Frank's was packed when Ben and Lucas walked inside. They were so close to people they were almost shoulder to shoulder and, in some cases, had to turn sideways just to maneuver through the crowd.

"Who the hell are all these folks?" Ben directed the question more so to himself than Lucas.

He could see his brother's mouth moving but couldn't hear him, not with the music blaring so loud. He cupped his ear. "What?"

Ben shook his head. "Never mind." He recognized some of the regulars who frequented the place on Friday nights, but there were quite a few faces he couldn't place. Ben heard that there were new people in town due to a roadway and bridge being built in the next city over, but he hadn't seen too many of them. More strangers meant more *men* lurking around their sister. But where else would they go? Frank's was the only place in a twenty-mile radius where people could come and unwind from a long week. That also meant he and Lucas would be on-site to make sure Selah made it home safely. She might see it as being overprotective and unnecessary, but whether Selah wanted their protection or not, she was going to get it.

Lucas yelled over to Ben. "We're going to have a helluva time trying to locate Selah."

"Yeah, looks like it. Her shift should be ending soon. Hopefully, we'll get lucky and snag her so we can get the hell out of here."

The bartender recognized them immediately as they inched their way toward the bar. He threw up a hand and waved them over. "Yo, Ben. Lucas. What's up?"

Both men acknowledged Cliven with a smile and a nod as they glanced about the place. Ben said, "Busy tonight."

"Yeah. Almost too busy." Cliven laughed. "Tips are good, though. How about a couple of drinks? They're on the house." He'd known Ben and Lucas since childhood and knew their favorite drinks. He passed each of them a shot of whiskey. "Looking forward to the barbecue on Sunday."

"Thanks, man. Looking forward to it too," Ben lied as he tossed back his drink. "Should be a good time. You seen Selah?"

"I had her in my sights most of the night, but it's been crazy. She was serving those ladies who just bought the old Steele Orchard a little bit ago."

Lucas perked up and joined the conversation. "I heard about them. You meet 'em yet?"

"Not face-to-face, but I got a good look at them from a distance."

"What do you think?"

Cliven whistled. "I ain't gonna lie. They're hot. All three of 'em, but they're also like what you'd expect someone from New York to be at a place like Frank's." He laughed. "Fish out of water."

"You said they were hot, though?" Lucas asked again.

"Yeah. They are definitely good-looking women. If they're single, they won't be for long. Every guy in the place has tried to hit on them."

"Really? It's like that?" Lucas was intrigued. "Don't hold out on me, man. Point 'em out."

"Can't. Saw 'em make it over there during the line dancin.'" Cliven lifted his chin in the direction of the large circular hardwood floor. "My guess is they are somewhere in the middle of that melee. Selah's probably close around the edge watchin. We put her on their table, so she didn't cause no fights. No disrespect, but Selah attracts the guys like bees to honey too."

When did Selah become hot? Ben decided to ignore that part. Instead, he thanked his old high school buddy. "Good looking out and putting her on a table full of women." Ben reached out his fist and bumped it against Cliven's.

"I know how it is. I've got three sisters. Keeping them out of harm's way is a full-time job."

"They resent you too?" Ben asked.

Cliven laughed. "You know it. But I don't care. I'm their brother." He shrugged. "It is what it is. Anyway, Selah is still on the clock for another ten, fifteen minutes. I'm sure Baker's got his sights on her."

Ben pushed his empty glass back to Cliven. "Thanks for keeping an eye out." Lucas thanked him too.

"No problem. She's like a fourth sister." A customer walked up, and Cliven had to get back to work. *That* was the problem. Cliven and Baker couldn't keep watch over Selah at all times. Not when they had work to do too.

Lucas turned around and looked out at the crowd of people. "I think I might see her." He pointed in Selah's direction.

Ben turned and followed where Lucas was pointing. He nodded. "We should probably stay put until her shift is over. You know how she gets."

"Nuh-uh." Lucas plastered on a sly grin. "If you're going to *watch the purses*, I'll check out the scene." Lucas was the brother with all the charm. Ben had about as much of that as a bull in a china shop. He slapped Ben on the back and walked away.

As soon as Lucas was gone, Ben heard an all too familiar

sultry voice. "Hey there, cowboy."

Ben cussed underneath his breath before turning around to find a woman staring at him, flashing a wide smile and wearing bright red lipstick. Bits stuck to her teeth. *Dammit. Virginia Reddington.* Ben tried to ignore the smeared red on her unnaturally white teeth, but it was impossible. Ben also couldn't help but notice her big ass silicone tits about to spill out of one of those black bustier things. He did not think it was sexy. Ben preferred a more natural type of woman.

Ben wasn't sure if he had the patience to deal with Virginia tonight. It had been a long week, and he was exhausted. Despite his misgivings, she sidled up close, thrusting her chest in his face while making sure to place a hand on his forearm. "Third weekend in a row that we've bumped into one another. We need to stop meeting like this and go on a real date."

Ben was used to aggressive women, but Virginia took it to a whole other level. Not only was he not interested, neither was his cock. It was just as flaccid as it had been while talking to Cliven. Still, Ben tried to turn on the Cash charm. He gave her a lopsided grin. "Tempting as your offer might be, I'm going to have to save you from yourself."

Virginia glanced down at the massive bulge between his thighs, then slowly returned her eyes back to his pale blue ones. "In all honesty, we could skip the date part and just get a room."

Ben could appreciate a woman who knew what she wanted and went after it, but he just wasn't into Virginia.

"I wish, but duty calls, and I've got an early morning tomorrow."

Virginia pouted. "Well, if you ever get lonely. You've got my address and an open invitation."

Ben couldn't imagine having sex with Virginia in this life

or the next. However, he didn't reveal his true thoughts when he responded. "I'll make sure to keep that in mind." It was time to exit stage left. Ben called out to Cliven. "Thanks again for the drink." He tipped his Stetson to Virginia and walked off.

Ben wasn't ready to start dating again. He wasn't sure if he'd ever be, but he wasn't the one-night stand kind of guy and never had been. In general, people exhausted him, and women like Virginia wanted to make him shoot himself right between the eyes.

This is the shit that keeps me home at night.

*****

The energy at Frank's was electric. Selah was almost positive that it was due to Dillyn, Palmer, and Cat. She stood at a distance with her arms folded, watching them dance. There were so many guys surrounding them, each vying for their attention. It was crazy. Selah hadn't ever seen anything like it.

Her shift was just about over, but she wasn't ready to leave. Selah hadn't been sure when she would get an opportunity to meet the new owners of Mr. Steele's old place, but she was glad it was sooner rather than later. The only gossip she'd had been able to get before their arrival was that they were from New York. That was all Selah needed to hear to pique her interest.

She would be forever grateful to whoever suggested they come to Frank's. Selah laughed a little. *Where else were they going to go?* It wasn't like there were very many options.

As she continued to observe, Selah concluded that Cat and Palmer were a little more adventurous than Dillyn. She was much more reserved. However, she did move pretty well on the dance floor. Unlike many women in town, they were way more sophisticated. All three appeared super fun, and she wanted to get to know them better. *I've got to figure out a way to get them to the barbeque on Sunday.*

Selah turned her head slightly. She saw them before they saw her. "Oh. Shit." Selah said under her breath. *What are they doing here?* Her brothers were scanning the room. No doubt looking for her. *Please, God. Don't let them embarrass me.* She made a beeline for them before they could get to her.

Though Lucas had thought he'd spotted Selah earlier, he'd been wrong. The commotion on the dance floor made it impossible to find anyone. Lucas had tried to get closer to the new owners of Steele's Orchard but hadn't been able to penetrate the crowd and returned to his brother. Ben couldn't see them either since there were too many people obscuring his view. But there was a moment when everyone moved out of the way, and he could see clearly. It was definitely a trio of women who seemed to be the reason for most of the excitement on the dance floor.

Ben squinted. "It couldn't be her. Could it?"

There was a woman on the dance floor who stood out. She reminded him of the woman he'd met two years ago, a woman who'd he'd thought about often. Her back was to him, so he couldn't know for sure. Ben's gaze lingered on her as she seemed to be swaying to her own beat. Her arms were in the air, and she was rolling her hips. *It really couldn't be.* This woman was much too carefree to be her. That woman had a shy-like quality to her. Still, Ben's feet were rooted to the floor, and he was barely breathing, waiting for her to turn around. Even though the music was blaring, Ben didn't hear a thing. He didn't even blink, afraid he might miss the big moment. As if in slow motion, she turned. She wasn't smiling like the other two. Her eyes were closed as she wiggled her little ass. She was in a world all of her own. *Well, I'll be damned.* It was Dillyn. *Socially awkward, my ass.*

Ben was about to step forward when he was blocked by a

petite woman, trying to make herself as tall as him. Lucas had caught up with them too. Selah was spittin' mad. Her baby blue eyes narrowed, and her nostrils flared as she stared up at her brothers. "What are you two doing here?!" For a second, Ben had forgotten about everything and everyone—until the voice of his little sister cut through his thoughts.

"What are you two doing here?!" Selah asked again more forcefully.

Ben and Lucas towered over Selah. Both of them stood over six feet tall and weighed at least two hundred pounds of solid muscle, not the bulky kind, but lean and chiseled. Barring the height, it was uncanny how they all resembled one another. The sun-kissed blond hair, the baby blue eyes, and deep dimples were all trademarks of the Cash family. The only difference between Selah and her brothers was the angular jawline. Selah, being a woman, lacked the sharpness. Her features were softer. Lucas was clean-shaven, but Ben was scruffier. He had that haven't shaved in a couple of days look. Sexiness oozed off them without even trying.

Lucas smiled mischievously. "Same reason as everybody else. We came for a drink." Lucas had convinced Ben to come to Frank's. Ben wasn't up for it until Lucas suggested it was a good way to keep an eye on their sister.

"Lucas Cash, you're a liar." She glanced between her brothers. "You promised you would give me space. I don't need you two babysitting me."

Lucas waved off her concern. "Calm down. I told you, we came for a drink. Right, Ben?"

Ben had a hard time keeping his eyes off Dillyn. He continued to glance between the dance floor and his sister. He didn't answer the question. Ben didn't like to lie, big or small, especially when they were undoubtedly there to make sure Selah got home safely.

Lucas tipped his chin toward the dance floor as he changed the subject. "Who's that? Are those the ladies everybody's been talkin' about?"

All of Selah's anger drained from her body as she swiveled around. Her attention fully focused on the women she hoped would become her new best friends. Selah couldn't contain her excitement. "Yep. I met them tonight!"

Ben could see the excitement on her face. Selah was damn near levitating. He didn't like it. City women were nothing but trouble with a capital T. *Why didn't she understand that?* He knew that Selah wanted more than country living. She wanted to be like those women who had had the town's folks wagging their tongues for weeks. *Where had the time gone?* It seemed like Selah was learning how to ride a bike just a few years ago. She had grown up right before his eyes, and he wasn't exactly equipped to handle it.

Ben was studying Selah when she suddenly reached out and grabbed their hands, leading both her brothers onto the dance floor. Somehow, she muscled them between the ladies.

Ben was not in the mood to party, and the dance area was even more crowded than it looked. He would have liked to get Dillyn alone and take her to a quiet place which was probably a terrible idea considering she was married. Still, Ben allowed Selah to pull him in Dillyn's direction. His mouth turned to sandpaper the closer he came to Dillyn.

It was as if he were watching himself outside of himself. The last time Ben saw Dillyn, she'd been wearing a pair of jeans and a t-shirt. Not that she wasn't sexiness personified in jeans, but tonight, she was dolled up in a dress that made his whole being

66

come alive. Dillyn was more stunning than even he remembered.

It was like a scene from a movie. Slowly, Dillyn's eyes opened, and they landed squarely on Ben. Dillyn wasn't sure if she imagined him or if she'd subconsciously conjured him up. Nope. It *was* Ben. Her handsome and gallant cowboy from a night so long ago. How cliché that she could only see his face in a room full of people. Given her stance on men and relationships in general, it was a mystery that he could cause such an extreme physical reaction. Dillyn couldn't move a single muscle. "Ben? Is that really you?"

It was as if time had gone back to before all the shitty things had happened. The heaviness that was with Ben daily had disappeared.

Dillyn felt the same. For a moment, she'd forgotten that she had given up altogether on the male species. A spark of electricity flowed through her entire body. She was buzzing, and it wasn't from the alcohol.

It was too loud to hear her, but Ben could read the words coming out of her mouth. A slow grin spread across his face. "It's the only name I've ever had. So, yeah. It's me."

He moved a little closer to her until they stood mere inches apart. Ben couldn't pull his eyes away, and neither could Dillyn.

Dillyn had thought about him in passing over the past couple of years. *Since faithfulness wasn't a hallmark in my marriage, I should have pushed the envelope that night.* Then Dillyn remembered how she felt after discovering Steven's affair with Sam. She couldn't do that to another woman. Her train of thought immediately took her to look at his ring finger. *Is he still married? Probably. The good ones usually are—except for my raggedy ex-husband.* Dillyn couldn't see his hand because it was tucked inside his jean's front pocket. *I better tread carefully.*

The music changed to a slower song. Ben held out his other hand, silently asking for a dance. In a moment of indecision, Dillyn pressed her lips together. *It's just a dance, right?* She tilted her head to the side in a gesture of acceptance. Ben stepped closer and pulled her body into his. He placed his hand on the small of her back as they began to sway to the music. *Dear God, this man smells so good. Why on earth would you send him my way knowing I'm absolutely done with men?*

Dillyn snaked her arms around his neck.

Ben was the first to break their silence. He placed his mouth close to her ear. "I didn't think I'd ever see you again."

The heat from his breath on her skin made Dillyn tingle in places she didn't think was possible. "Neither did I."

"You're a resident now." Ben didn't pose it as a question.

"I am." *Good Lord, help me.* "You're home for a visit?"

"Moved back."

Shit. That could be a problem. Dillyn didn't do one-night stands and had no idea how casual sex worked. *Okay. That's it. Dancing with him is a bad idea.* She pulled back slightly. "I'm suddenly feeling a little lightheaded."

Ben looked at her with concern. He was just about to suggest stepping outside for some fresh air when Dillyn fell hard into his chest. Everything happened lightning fast. One minute a guy was dancing with one of Dillyn's friends while another tried to get her attention. The next, Dillyn was being shoved into Ben's chest. Ben turned, searching for Lucas, who was standing close by. They nodded at one another, a silent communication, but before they could stop the shenanigans, things escalated to a full-on brawl.

Ben held Dillyn in his arms as he looked around for Selah.

68

Once Lucas realized the shit had hit the fan, he started looking for her too. His only concern was making sure his sister was safe. Lucas's head turned like it was on a swivel looking for Selah until he spotted her. Waving a hand in the air, Lucas managed to get Ben's attention and pointed toward her. Selah stood close enough for Lucas to grab her by the hand as all hell broke loose.

Chapter 9

One minute everyone was dancing and having a good time, and the next, it was chaos. Dillyn was being shoved about like a rag doll. She didn't have time to appreciate being in Ben's arms.

Ben saw that Lucas had Selah and had moved them right next to him and Dillyn. Ben began to pull Dillyn away from all the action, and she held on to his hand for dear life.

In the process of trying to get away from the madness, Dillyn dropped her phone on the floor. "Wait! I dropped my cell!"

"I've got it." Dillyn couldn't see a face but heard her voice. She knew it was Selah. Seconds later, a loud boom sounded almost like an explosion, and everyone scattered out of the building.

Ben was knocked on his ass from the blast. It was hard to see through all the white smoke and debris. He sat up, trying to shake off his disorientation. That's when Ben realized he'd been separated from everyone. Quickly, he got up on his feet and yelled out for them. "Dillyn! Selah! Lucas!"

"We're here!"

Ben could hear Lucas's voice but still had a tough time seeing them. "I can't see you. Keep talking. I'll follow your voice."

Lucas and Selah did as asked while simultaneously moving toward Ben. Within moments, they connected.

"Y'all okay?" Ben asked as they moved away from the building and people running in every direction.

Lucas was out of breath. "Yeah. We're good."

Ben looked around them. "Did y'all see the lady I was

dancing with? We got split up."

"N-no." Selah turned, looking for her too. "She was right behind you. I'm sure she got out safely because we were close to the door right before the shit hit the fan."

"What in the actual fuck was that?" Lucas asked as the three of them turned to see Frank's in a huge orange blaze.

*****

The blast knocked Dillyn flat on her back. She was slow to get up. She turned around in circles looking for Ben and her friends. She'd lost them.

Dillyn was freaking out. "I did not move my ass clear across the country from New York for this!" She yelled, "Ben! Cat! Palmer!"

Dillyn screamed out for them until her voice was hoarse. Her eyes started to water from all the smoke. The problem was everyone was screaming and yelling. It was hard to hear over the other voices.

Dillyn backed away from the building. The further away she moved into the parking lot, the clearer the building became . . . or what was left of it. "Oh. My. Gawd!" Dillyn couldn't believe that only seconds prior, she'd been inside that burning inferno. "Please, God. Don't let my friends still be in there!" Frantically, Dillyn continued to call out to them until she heard the faint sounds of a familiar voice. *Is that Cat?*

"Dillyn! Over here! We are over here." Cat was standing on the hood of their truck, frantically waving her arms in the air.

Relief washed over her when she spotted them. Dillyn took off her one remaining shoe and sprinted over to them. Once they were together, they wrapped each other in a tight hug. "What happened?"

"Girl! I have no idea. A couple of guys started acting

71

crazy, pushing and shoving. So, Palmer and I immediately started moving to get off the dance floor. The next thing we knew, everyone started running. You know how we do when people start running. We run and ask questions later."

Dillyn nodded. "That's what we did too. But just as we got to the door, the building exploded."

"We had already made it to the door when that happened. We're just thankful you got out safely," Palmer said.

Dillyn was still worried about Ben and Selah. "Did you guys see Selah and her brother?"

Cat and Palmer both shook their heads no. "It's a madhouse out here. We were lucky to find you." Palmer's worry was apparent.

They turned and watched in horror as the remnants of Frank's burned to the ground. Dillyn said a silent prayer. "I hope everyone got out of there."

"I hope so too, but . . .there were a lot of people in there." Palmer expressed what they were all thinking. The likelihood was everyone didn't get out safely.

First responders from neighboring cities, as well as Summer, started arriving. They began asking people via bullhorn to make way for the emergency workers.

Dillyn looked up and, by chance, spotted Ben at the same time that he saw her. "Be right back."

"Girl, where are you going? We just found your ass!" Cat asked as she watched her friend walk away.

Both Dillyn and Ben had to dodge several people before finally coming face-to-face. "You okay?" he asked.

"About as well as a person can be who just escaped an explosion. You? Selah?"

"She's shaken up, but we're all fine. Your friends?"

Dillyn glanced over her shoulder back toward them. "They're fine."

Ben looked down at her feet. "You're not wearing any shoes." Ben took off his jacket and wrapped it around Dillyn's shoulders. "You're going to have to get over your germaphobia."

"What?" Dillyn had forgotten she'd told him that. "You don't have to give me your jacket. I'm not cold."

"You're shaking like a leaf."

Dillyn hadn't even realized it. Still, she took it off and gave it back. Ben was showing too much care, and so was she. Dillyn needed to nip whatever fatal attraction this was in the bud. "Thank you, but it's okay. I just wanted to make sure you guys were safe."

"Please. If you are uninjured and can leave the area, please do so. We need the room for our emergency vehicles." The words from the bullhorn were loud and clear.

"Did you drive?" Ben should not have been, but he was concerned. "Do you need a ride home? Our truck is in good working order."

"Fortunately, our truck is also fine." Dillyn turned toward it. "We're just going to head home and try to decompress."

Ben realized that Dillyn was stubborn. She was shaking and barefoot. He did what any reasonable man would do. He bent low and swept her up into his arms.

"Ohmygod!" Dillyn was in a whole panic. "What are you doing?"

Ben didn't miss a step. "Taking you to your truck. You're barefoot. The parking lot is littered with glass and debris. You're clearly too foolhardy to accept my help. So, I'm not asking."

Before Dillyn could argue, Ben was standing next to the driver's side door. "Ladies." He tipped his head to both Cat and

73

Palmer. Cat smiled mischievously, then quickly opened the driver's side door, and Ben deposited Dillyn into her seat. He made sure she was secured then closed the door before walking away as if he hadn't done anything.

Quickly, her friends opened the truck doors and slid into their seats. The doors were barely closed before Palmer began to grill Dillyn. "Ms. Anderson, we don't even have to ask who that was, do we? That was your cowboy, wasn't it?"

"I don't have a cowboy." Dillyn pressed the ignition button, starting the truck. Slowly, she maneuvered around the parking lot. They moved at a snail's pace. "Dammit! Can this night get any shittier? Selah has my phone."

"Interesting." Cat smirked. "Now you'll have to drop by and pick it up, huh?"

Dillyn rolled her eyes. "You know how important my phone is to me. I don't even know where they live."

"It's a small town. Someone does. Ben? What's his last name again?" Palmer couldn't remember.. She was going to google his ass.

"Selah said it but I don't remember. There can't be too many Bens and Selahs in Summer, right?" Cat asked conspiratorially.

Palmer laughed out loud. "Girl . . . we are in Hicksville, USA. Every third person is named Ben and maybe even Selah."

Dillyn knew his last name but didn't want them to look him up. So, she remained quiet. However, secretly, she was both excited and dreading the possibility of seeing Ben again.

Palmer started laughing sarcastically once they could pull out of the parking lot and onto the main road. Seconds later so did Cat.

"You two must still be drunk because I don't see anything

funny about this situation!" Dillyn's heart was still racing.

"It's not funny. We all know that some people died in there tonight," Cat said. "There's nothing funny about this shit. It's just ironic. I've lived all over the world. Spent a lot of my youth in the hardest parts of Chicago, and this is the first time I've ever been in a place that exploded. The building *exploded* in the backwoods of Tennessee. You've got to admit this is freaking crazy."

Palmer agreed. "I know we hauled ass up outta there. I haven't seen any of us move like that in years. I know I haven't."

Dillyn looked at her friends as if they'd lost their minds. She listened to them talk and talk until, finally, almost twenty minutes into their drive, they quieted. Dillyn glanced over and found them knocked out cold, sound asleep. She shook her head slightly and thanked God they were okay. Dillyn didn't know what she would do if anything were to ever happen to either of them. She pulled onto the road leading to their property, feeling a profound sense of relief.

If I were going to die, at least I would have been with my sisters. They are crazy, but I love them.

Chapter 10

Selah stood just outside the horse's stall, watching her eldest brother brush down one of the most incredible horses she'd ever seen. She was a beauty—a Turkmenistan. Most horses were different shades of black, brown, gray, and even white. Not Whisper. She was otherworldly. It wasn't so impossible to believe that she was magical. Her body was slender and had an incredible metallic golden sheen to her coat.

Ben and Whisper had a special bond. Their spirits were both unsettled, but they seemed to calm one another.

Selah didn't want to intrude but hadn't gotten up at the butt crack of dawn for nothing. She needed to talk to Ben, and the best time was just after the sun came up. He was surly on a good day but a little less so in the mornings. After going back and forth in her mind, even after everything that happened at Frank's the night before, Selah decided now was the time to have a much-needed conversation. She sucked in a breath. *Here goes nothing.*

Ben typically rose just before the sun every morning to tend to Whisper. It had become his new normal. There were ranch hands who could manage her but taking care of his horse gave Ben a sense of peace. It was akin to therapy. Today was especially difficult. After their experience at Frank's, he was triggered and needed solitude.

Selah startled when he spoke before she could get her words together.

"How long are you going to stand there?" His tone was gruff. "I'm almost done brushing Whisper down, and we want to go for a ride."

Selah straightened her spine and walked further into the stall. "Y-y-you knew I was here?"

Ben didn't bother to answer. Of course he knew. He sensed her just like he could sense something had been on her mind these past few days, even before the craziness of the night before. Ben figured he'd give her some time to work it out before approaching her with his concerns.

He looked over his shoulder and his gaze locked onto hers.

Selah had had this conversation before with the rest of her family, and the results were always the same. A big fat no. After last night, she wasn't sure if this was a suitable time but felt compelled to at least try. Maybe a different tactic from all of her other attempts might just do the trick. If she could convince Ben, then everyone else would fall in line. They all listened to him. He'd become the de facto leader of the Cash family ever since the untimely death of their parents. "*Sooo* . . . last night was crazy, huh?"

"Crazy and sad. We lost seven people. Not that it matters, but none of them were from Summer."

"Yeah, I know."

A bar was no place for Selah to work anyway. Little did she know, but last night would have been her final one at Frank's. There were too many strangers lurking around, and Ben couldn't keep an eye on her like he needed to. Selah could have gotten hurt or worse. For now, Ben would keep those thoughts to himself.

Selah cracked a small smile that probably looked more like a grimace while walking closer to her brother.

Ben didn't return it. Impatience was written all over him.

Selah pushed on. "Did you see Lucas get dumbstruck by Palmer?"

"Palmer?"

"Yes. That's the woman who left him gaping like a fool. It was a thing of beauty. Something I've never seen before. It's usually the other way around."

He responded with disinterest. "Hmm. I must have missed it."

You missed it because you were doing the same thing with Dillyn. Selah could see his patience was wearing thin. Ben had never been particularly good at small talk, but he was being purposefully ornery.

Ben was irritated at the pace of their conversation but tried not to show it. Selah was his baby sister. He loved her more than life and did his best to be patient, especially since they lost their parents. "Well, now you can finally agree that Frank's is, was, dangerous."

It was not dangerous! "Frank's has been around forever, and save for an occasional bar fight, the people there are pretty harmless. Nothing like this has ever happened before. Do they know what caused it?"

"Haven't heard yet."

Selah shook her head. There was nothing more to say about the explosion. She'd beat around the bush as long as she could. *Here goes.* "Before all that craziness started, did you see how excited everyone was to meet Dillyn, Palmer, and Cat?"

Ben had no idea what direction their conversation was going. "Yep." Ben kept his answer short and sweet. She had no idea that Ben had already met Dillyn before. He decided to keep that bit to himself.

Selah's eyes sparkled. "They're awesome." Her words began to tumble out of her mouth. "They are so smart and funny.

My goodness, are they funny." It was clear Ben was losing interest. Selah rushed on. "Dillyn does something with computers. I've never even heard of it before. Palmer is some kind of fancy-schmancy real estate broker, and Cat is a master sommelier. She's like one of just a few in the entire world! Together, they plan to turn that old orchard on Mr. Steele's property into a profitable winery. My goodness, they have this energy that is so contagious. It's hard to believe they would want to move here from New York."

Shit. That's what this conversation is about. "No."

Irritated, Selah placed her hands on her hips. "But I haven't even asked you anything yet."

"No reason to ask when the answer is no."

"Ben, I'm twenty-two!" She stomped her booted foot. "I'm not a child."

It almost made him laugh. "No. You're not, but you are also not spending the summer in New York."

"It's not fair. You, Lucas, and Wyatt have all left to do other things."

"New York is not a place for a young girl." She had no idea how a city like that could eat a person up and spit them out.

"First, I'm a young woman. And second, that's so sexist! I can't prove that I can handle myself if y'all don't let me. I have to find my own way."

"You can figure things out right here." Ben knew that Selah was restless. She was clamoring to explore the world. She was ready to fly the coop and make her own mistakes, just like the rest of them. He just wasn't ready. *When did she fuckin' grow up?* It was a question he kept asking himself but never received an answer.

"How can I figure things out when y'all hover so much? I

can't even do the simplest things like date?! You know darn well that you and Lucas weren't at Frank's last night for a beer."

"You're right. I was there for whiskey. But it's a pretty good thing we were, though, wasn't it?"

Selah refused to answer. "My *point* is that the guys around here are too afraid to ask me out."

Good! We're doing our job. Ben turned to pat Whisper on her head but mostly so Selah wouldn't see his grin. "The right one will be brave enough to ask."

Her voice was shaky from frustration and unshed tears. "You guys are smothering me."

The brokenness in her voice made him turn to face her. Her glassy eyes hit him right in the chest. "Selah . . ."

Ben didn't have a chance to finish his sentence. Selah ran out of the stable. It was probably best. He didn't know what he'd say anyway. Ben knew that he had to figure something out. He understood more than anyone the damage holding onto someone too tight and too long could do.

*****

Dillyn drove her classic 1967 red convertible mustang down the winding road to the Cash Ranch. Usually, she would've taken the Mercedes truck she acquired from Steven in the divorce, but the day was so beautiful. She couldn't pass up an opportunity to take the mustang out.

The ranch was lush and tucked high up in the mountains hidden by mature trees. Their own ranch wasn't even a third of its size. Cash Ranch was unlike any place she'd ever seen. Except, maybe Southfork from that old eighties television show Dallas with more mountains and trees.

The warm breeze caressed Dillyn's skin as the wind blew through her hair. She hadn't bothered to tie it up. It was days like this that removed any doubt about making the move.

Dillyn could see the house coming into view. It was just as grand as the property.

Lucas stood on the wraparound porch and called out to Ben, who was approaching the house. "Who is that?"

After taking Whisper out for a ride, Ben spent the morning working with their ranch hands and contemplating how to resolve the situation with Selah. She was frustrated, and he was frustrated too. Ben had too much going on inside his head. He had to figure out how to deal with it all without losing his shit.

It was close to lunchtime when he returned to the house, and he was hot as hell, so he had taken off his shirt. He was using it to wipe the sweat from his forehead when he turned to see who Lucas was talking about. Ben hadn't recognized the red car speeding toward them, leaving a trail of dust behind it.

As Dillyn drove closer, she could see Ben, and she assumed his brother, standing outside. Ben looked like he stepped right off the pages of a cowboy magazine—down to his Wrangler jeans that hung low on his narrow hips and Tecovas boots. Every sweaty muscle on his body was visible and glistened in the sun. *Damn.* The man was sculpted. Shielded by his Stetson, Dillyn couldn't see his face. However, she could still make out that magical V. Even though it disappeared in his jeans, he had it. Ben was definitely a ten out of ten. Dillyn was glad she was wearing a pair of dark sunglasses. Nobody would know she'd just given him a full inspection.

Dillyn leaned her head out of the car. "Is it okay to park here?"

Lucas flashed his megawatt smile. "Absolutely."

Dillyn was amazed at how much Lucas and Ben resembled one another. Fully clothed and up close, Lucas seemed equally rugged and handsome, but Ben had something else. Something she couldn't put her finger on.

I know my hair is all over my head in the most unsexy way. Good. He won't be interested. Dillyn had made up her mind that she was out of the relationship business. That meant Ben could only be a friend—especially if he were still married.

Dillyn got out of her car. She looked a whole entire mess and hoped it would serve as protection from any possible advances. Still, her stomach did a little flip, and she couldn't help but offer Ben a smile. "Hey."

Ben remained stoned-faced. "Hey."

Dillyn was confused. His demeanor was so different from the night before when he had held her in his arms. "Last night was pretty crazy, huh?"

"Yep."

Not only did Ben still not offer a smile, but his tone was also curt. Dillyn had no idea why. The warmth he'd often shown was absent. Well, if he wasn't offering a reason, she wasn't going to dig for an answer. "Okay. Is Selah home?"

"Yeah."

He didn't say it, but Dillyn could hear the "why do you want to know?" lingering in his response. His usual easygoing manner was non-existent. *How do I know the easygoing manner was his usual?*

Selah was right on the money when describing her brothers last night. *Protective much?* Dillyn sighed inwardly and made another attempt to be friendly. Whatever reason Ben was surly couldn't possibly have anything to do with her. "Can I speak with her?"

Selah had been on Ben's mind all morning. He had been trying to figure out a way to assuage her restlessness and protect her. *How can you protect Selah when you couldn't protect Rylee?* The words popped into his brain out of nowhere—not exactly nowhere. Rylee was always on his mind, but this weekend more than usual. With those thoughts stirring in his head, Ben was probably terser with Dillyn than necessary. "What do you want with my sister?"

Why is Ben pulling a Dr. Jekyll and Mr. Hyde? This was the man who so tenderly carried me to my truck, so I didn't hurt my feet? Talk about whiplash. So much for southern hospitality. Dillyn was out of her element and trying to be all neighborly, and clearly, Ben was not. Dillyn wasn't sure what changed, but she wasn't going to give it any energy. "Selah has my cell. I dropped it on the floor at Frank's, and she grabbed it as we were running for our lives."

Ben nodded. "I'll go ask her. If she has it, I'll bring it to you."

He *was* overbearing. Dillyn didn't like it. She notched her chin up slightly. "I'd prefer to speak to her myself. Is she here?"

"Dillyn!" She heard her name being called from behind him, and a smiling Selah came bounding down the steps.

Dillyn shifted from Ben to the young girl who had called out to her. "It's good to see you're okay."

"You too! Last night was just so crazy. I was going to call, but I didn't have your number, and I couldn't for the life of me figure out how to unlock your phone."

Dillyn glanced down at the ground and smirked. *It should be.* "The encryption is pretty tough."

Something was off. Selah could feel the tension in the air as she looked between Dillyn and her warden wannabes. "I see you've met my brothers, Ben and Lucas." Selah turned toward Ben. "This is Dillyn Anderson."

Ben responded. "We've already met." His voice was still rough.

What was his problem? Dillyn was ready to get her ass back to her own slice of heaven. It was clear Ben wanted her gone, and Lucas seemed to be taking his cues from his brother. "I just came over to get my phone."

"Oh, sure! It's in the house." Selah glared at Ben and Lucas. "My goodness. It's so hot out. Why don't you come inside for some lemonade, and I'll get it?" Selah was dying for some female company, especially with someone as worldly as Dillyn.

"Thank you, but I've got to get going." Dillyn politely declined. "If you could just grab it, that would be great." Dillyn glanced over at Lucas. He tipped his head and almost gave her a smile. Ben remained stone-faced and would *not* grant her even a hint of a smile.

"Make sure you wash it off," Ben said, remembering Dillyn was a germaphobe.

Dillyn frowned at him. Why was Ben being an asshole? She didn't understand it.

Selah's shoulder drooped in disappointment. "O-ok . . . okay. Sure." She rolled her eyes at her brothers as she went inside, leaving Dillyn alone with them.

Nobody said a word. *This is Awkward.*

Fortunately, Selah was only gone a few moments. "Are you sure you don't want to come inside for a glass of lemonade?"

Not even if the grounds opened and hell swallowed me whole. Dillyn smiled. "Thanks so much for asking. We just have a lot on our agenda for today but feel free to drop by *our* place anytime. You have an open invitation."

"Really?" Selah asked.

"She's just being polite," Ben said.

84

A sense of rebelliousness rose in Dillyn. "Actually, I'm being *neighborly*." She smiled at Selah. "We'd love to get to know our neighbors. You're welcome to visit anytime you feel the need for some girl time." Dillyn's smile vanished the second she turned away from Selah and toward her brothers. "*Gentleman*." It was weird that Ben was acting like anything but. *Whatever. Don't give it another thought.* Dillyn straightened her spine and got into her car. She revved the engine before backing up and speeding off.

Selah was pissed. She turned fiery eyes toward her brothers. "What was that? Why are you two always acting like jerks?!"

Lucas shrugged. He was following Ben's lead, figuring Ben had a good reason to be an asshole, so he just went with it.

Ben waved off her irritation. "Women like her are too nickel slick for their own good." He knew Dillyn was anything but, yet those words still came out of his mouth.

"How do you know what she's like? You only met her five minutes ago," Selah asked.

"I told you we already met."

"Wait a minute. Before last night? When? Where?" Lucas was genuinely curious.

"It doesn't matter," Ben responded. "After our conversation this morning, I don't want anyone filling your head with the joys of living in the city."

"Selah knows she's not moving to the city." Lucas had the good sense to be a little embarrassed. "And if you're not going to tell me what Dillyn did to deserve us acting like jerks, then we should apologize."

"You don't know any such thing, Lucas Cash! I've had it up to here with y'all's bullshit!"

"Hey! Watch your mouth." Ben's eyes went wide, equal

parts appalled and amused by his sister's outburst.

Selah ignored him. "I have dreams that are bigger than this farm. One day, you, Ben, and Wyatt are going to wake up, and I'm just going to be gone!" Selah stormed off toward the house, leaving Ben and Lucas staring after her.

Ben released an exasperated sigh.

"If we don't figure something out, Selah is going to make good on that promise," Lucas said matter-of-factly.

Ben knew Lucas was right. Lately, he couldn't seem to get it right with Selah. Begrudgingly, he agreed, "Yeah, I know. I've been trying to work out a solution all morning." If he were honest, Ben hadn't been able to work out his confusing emotions about Dillyn either.

Lucas was thoughtful. "I might have an idea."

"Good. Because short of locking her up, I've got nothing."

"I think we should pay those ladies over at Mr. Steele's old place a visit."

Lifting his right hand, Ben grasped the back of his neck, massaging his neck and rotating his head. "For what? Is this plan for you or Selah? She told me you were eyeballing Dillyn's friend."

"Nuh-uh, big bro. You were the one sweeping women up off their feet and then freaking out over it."

Ben remained silent because Lucas wasn't too far off from the truth.

"We might be able to kill two birds with one stone. Maybe we can convince them to hire Selah for something, and she'll have an opportunity to spend a little time with the types of women she seemingly wants to become."

Ben was about to protest.

"It'll help prepare her for all those guys trying to paw at

86

her. We're not blind. Selah's attractive. She could probably use their influence."

Lucas had a point. A big point.

"They moved here for a reason," Lucas continued. "Apparently, the city ain't all it's cracked up to be; otherwise, they would still be there. Maybe whatever Selah is itching for is over at their place."

"We could keep an eye on her," Ben said almost to himself.

"Yep. We could."

"You sure going over to that ranch ain't about the woman who had you drooling before all hell broke loose?"

Lucas played it cool. "Ain't no woman ever made me drool."

Ben laughed. "Is that right? Selah made it seem like you needed a whole beach towel to clean up after you."

Lucas thought it was nice to see his brother almost laugh. It had been a while.

Ben knew that Lucas had a solid idea. "Do we have a bottle of hot sauce?"

Lucas was confused. "Hot sauce?"

"I'll need it when we go to visit the ladies. I heard it goes down good with crow." They cracked up, laughing even harder as they headed into the house.

As their laughter died down, Lucas decided to test out a theory. "Dillyn is kinda hot."

Ben tried to remain nonchalant. He shrugged. "I guess if you're into skinny women. She had nice boots."

"You seemed pretty into her last night." Lucas chuckled. "And she is curvy in all the right places. For the record, I like all women. Skinny or thick, it doesn't much matter to me."

Ben shook his head. Most women liked Lucas too. Unlike Ben, Lucas was a playboy, and Ben didn't see that changing anytime soon.

"A walking and talking siren just walked onto our property, and even you had to notice. I refuse to believe the only thing that stood out about Dillyn were her boots." Ben's silence caused Lucas to laugh out loud. "Okay, man."

Ben had noticed, and that was the source of the problem. He had enjoyed the brief time they'd spent together the night they first met. Dillyn had him thinking about crossing a line that was way out of his character. That was also the weekend his life blew up. He'd felt guilty about that night ever since. When Ben saw Dillyn at Frank's, he felt drawn to her in ways he'd never felt with Lana. That made Ben feel even guiltier.

"Maybe when we go over there, you can turn on some of that Cash charm? Ask her out." Lucas knew better, but it was worth a shot. His brother was out of sorts and needed to get back in the game.

Ben turned serious. "You know I'm not ready for that."

Lucas sobered up too. "I know, but it's been two years."

"I said I'm not ready."

Lucas wasn't trying to be pushy, but he saw the way Ben looked at Dillyn. Maybe she could help him heal. "You're never going to be ready. You just have to do it."

"Are you trying to pimp me out?"

Lucas's face softened into an expression of care. "Nah' man. I just want to see you happy again. If not Dillyn, maybe Virginia, but you got to get back out there." Lucas would never say it aloud, but Lana never made his brother happy.

Ben's throat felt a little thick, so he cleared it. "You don't have to worry about me. When I'm ready to date, I'll date. In the meantime, I'm good." Ben couldn't hold Lucas's gaze, so he glanced around. It was the perfect time to get gone. He had no desire to dredge up the past. Ben plastered on a smile. Ben walked past Lucas as he went into the house. "I'm gonna go grab a shower."

Lucas watched as his brother walked away. He could only hope that Ben would one day find his way back to himself.

Chapter 11

Ben had some time to think about his conversation with Lucas regarding Selah *and* Dillyn. He was having second thoughts about their plan. Selah was smart. She had a good head on her shoulders and had never given them any real problems. She was responsible. Maybe they should just give her a little more space. If she needed them, they would be there.

A glimmer from the sun came through his bedroom window and caught the locket hanging around his neck at just the right angle. It twinkled in the mirror as he gazed at his reflection.

Ben caressed it as if it were the most precious thing on earth. Everyone who ever told him the pain would lessen with time, and things would get easier *lied*. Ben closed his eyes, drew in a deep breath, then slowly let it out.

He took a moment to gather himself. After the wave of emotion passed, Ben continued to dress. He put on a fresh black t-shirt, pair of jeans, and boots, then headed out to meet up with his brother.

Lucas was standing impatiently on the porch, waiting. He'd put on a crisp white button-up and held several bunches of flowers in his hands. A frown appeared on his face as he watched Ben approach. "Dude, you ain't wearing that. We're trying to woo a bunch of ladies. You might be the ugliest Cash brother, so ya gotta put in a little more effort."

Ben wasn't amused. "You of all people know that I'm not trying to woo anybody." Ben ran a hand through his damp hair. Lines creased his forehead. "This isn't just a bad idea. It ain't right."

"So, you're cool with letting Selah go off to New York by

90

herself cause she's going to be on the first thing smokin' if we don't take action."

"Of course I'm not cool with it," Ben said, his voice a growl. "I'm also not okay with manipulating this situation. Who do we know in New York that we can trust?"

"Not a damn soul." Lucas reached into his back pocket and removed his cell. He was animated as he held it up to Ben. "Might as well dial up American Airlines."

"Shit." Neither of them was in a position to go with Selah, and Wyatt wouldn't be home till the end of the month. He would not be interested in spending an entire summer in the city. He hated it just as much as they did.

"Exactly. Change your shirt," Lucas said.

"I'm good. No reason to change." Ben was adamant.

"Dude, you're stubborn. From what I've gathered, those women won't be bowled over by a shot of whiskey and our charm—in your case, the lack of. We're going to have to put in some work."

"You're the lover-boy in the family. I ain't pimpin' myself out to anybody for any reason. Matter-of-fact, let's go before I change my mind." Ben jogged down the stairs and headed toward his pick-up truck.

Chapter 12

The ranch needed a lot of work, but it was also the perfect place for a fresh start. It sat on more than two hundred acres. The grounds were rich, and the soil was just right for The Chicks Vineyard. The crown jewel was the main house. It was close to five thousand square feet and sat on the property's highest point, overlooking the rest of the grounds. The views of the mountains were spectacular. The mornings were so incredible Dillyn thought God himself was present.

The property also had four other separate living quarters. All were in disrepair and the main reason Palmer was able to negotiate a purchase price well under value.

The main house was livable but still needed a lot of TLC. They decided to fix it up first since it was where they were living. They hired a few handymen to oversee the plumbing and electrical issues. They would refurbish the other properties once the main house was finished.

By the time Dillyn returned from the Cash Ranch, Palmer and Cat were already in the process of tackling the painting of the parlor. Dillyn figured they would have slept well past the afternoon given everything that happened the night before, but no. They seemed bright-eyed and raring to go.

Dillyn walked into the room, and Cat noticed her first. "Hey, girl! Where did you rush off to this morning?" She stood on a ladder, pouring paint into a tray.

Dillyn held up her phone. "I went to get my cell."

"At Selah's?" Palmer asked as she adjusted her coveralls and baseball cap.

"Yep."

"Ooh. How did you find out where they lived? Did you meet her other two brothers?" Palmer's curiosity wasn't casual. She had her reasons for being interested. "Are they good-looking as she made them seem?"

Dillyn shrugged. "I googled it, and yes, I met two of them. Selah's brothers are assholes."

"Are you talking about the guy who carried you to your car?" Palmer asked. "He's an *asshole*?"

Cat and Palmer exchanged a glance. They knew Dillyn's judgment was, at best, *off,* so they didn't take her too seriously. Still, Cat asked the obvious question. "What happened?"

"Selah's characterization of her brothers was an understatement. As I said, I went to get my phone, and it was the strangest thing. Ben acted like he'd never met me. He was so cold."

"Huh? That's odd." Cat wrinkled up her nose. "Did you greet them as the sweet Dillyn we all know and love, or the *I hate all men because they are trash* Dillyn?"

"Is there a difference?" Dillyn asked.

Hell, yes! Palmer bit her lower lip to prevent herself from blurting out her thoughts.

"If you were your incredibly charismatic self, why do you think they would have behaved that way? Did you do something?"

"No!" Dillyn was slightly offended.

Cat went for the low-hanging fruit. "Well, some people might not take too kindly to outsiders who also happen to be *Black women* buying this property. You know Randy? Our electrician? He stopped by this morning because he forgot a few things, but word on the curb is they are handling the situation at Frank's last night as arson. Somebody purposely blew it up."

"Are you serious?" Dillyn asked.

"Yep," Cat confirmed. "I wouldn't be surprised if cops showed up at our door asking questions. You know they'll probably be looking at us."

"Arson?" Dillyn found that hard to believe. "Who would want to blow up Frank's? I mean . . ." She stopped her train of thought. It was silly. Summer didn't even come up on a map. She was tired. "Look, I moved here because it's peaceful, and I can escape most of the bullshit this world has to offer. I don't even want to imagine what you're saying can be true."

Palmer looked at Dillyn with concern. Anger and pain radiated off her. "But . . . we didn't move here to escape. We moved here for a fresh start."

"Right. A fresh start. Escape. It's all the same. That means I can live my life in peace without any messy entanglements."

"Messy entanglements?" A lightbulb switched on for Cat. "Are we still talking about Frank's? Isn't that kind of like life? It's full of all kinds of messiness."

Talk to me after you've been publicly humiliated by a philandering ex-husband and suffered through two miscarriages. Dillyn didn't want to argue. "Look . . . I've lived the so-called *dream*." She used her fingers to put her words in air quotes. "I've built a successful business and married *the man of my dreams* only to realize it's all bullshit. At this point, I just want to shed the things that don't make me happy and focus on the things that do. That list is very short. Fortunately, you two are on it. Making our venture work is right up there too. I'm not interested in anything else."

Cat spoke softly. "Dillyn, I know you're still healing after everything that happened between you and Steven, but you can't let him change who you are."

Dillyn suddenly felt hot. Her chest started to tighten, and her throat felt like it was going to close up. Her emotions were too close to the surface as she blinked back tears. *Where did those come from? Cry? I don't cry.* Dillyn whispered, "I don't want to talk about Steven. I don't need a man. From birth until now, men have only hurt me." The room suddenly became much too small. Dillyn had to get out before she broke down in front of her friends. "Look, we are supposed to be painting, not analyzing my life. Let me go get changed, and I'll be back." Dillyn rushed out of the room.

Palmer released a breath. "Is it me, or does Dillyn seem really sensitive today?"

"She's triggered by Ben, but I get the feeling something else set her off."

"People heal at their own pace. But it's been almost a year since Dillyn discovered the Steven fiasco, but I get the feeling you're absolutely right."

Cat knew exactly where Palmer was going. "There is no timetable to get over someone, but Dillyn doesn't seem to be getting better."

Palmer agreed. "We have to help her find her way. The problem is Dillyn has layers of shit I don't think she's ever dealt with, and Steven is just the tip of the iceberg."

"You would know since y'all met in the ninth grade," Cat said.

Palmer had figured out a few things, but Dillyn was always tight-lipped about that time in her life. "We've all been through a lot, but Dillyn has gone through more than most. None of us grew up in the best of situations, but Dillyn was raised by heathens."

"Dillyn said Steven anchored her. She told me that he was

the first guy ever to give a damn. I find that hard to believe."

"Steven was different and the same in college. He was a narcissist and rebellious and cloaked it in the appearance of care. He was also very controlling where Dillyn was concerned. I hated the way he groomed her." Palmer sighed. "I've often wondered if Dillyn mistook his narcissism for love and if she understood the difference between love and loyalty."

Cat wasn't sure either. She hunched her shoulders. "I don't know, but Steven breaking her trust hit her differently than when guys we've dated broke ours. That's where she and I are different. I don't trust a man as far as I can throw them. Most are only good for sex. I don't have the inclination to figure out which ones are bums and which aren't, especially since most are bums. That's why I'm not interested in a relationship."

Palmer was confused. "Isn't that kind of the same as what Dillyn's going through?"

"Not at all. I've never felt the need to have a man in my life to feel complete. Dillyn wanted that with Steven. You saw her. She went to the ends of the earth to make him happy. He never seemed to do the same for her. So, while I get the part about her feeling like she doesn't need a man, it should be her choice. Not because Steven broke her heart. No man can break my heart because I'll never give it away."

"That sounds like bullshit." Palmer laughed. "This is where we part ways, friend. I want the husband, the house with the white picket fence, the two point five kids, the damn dog, and a cat!"

Cat shrugged. "Husbands. I don't want one of those. Kids either. Maybe a cat." She smirked. "Now *sex*. That's different. That I can't live without." Cat placed the paint roller on the wall and rolled it up, stretching as tall as she could. Paint dripped onto her face. "And I'm deprived! It's been almost three months since I've had sex. My body is like . . . *what in the entire hell*?"

Palmer giggled as she picked up the paint gun and began to spray it on the wall. "I know, Cat! You're the nympho of the group. I was surprised you didn't find someone to hook up with at Frank's."

"I was looking, but it blew up." Cat flicked paint over onto Palmer. "Plus, I had way too many drinks to give consent even before the place turned into a burning inferno."

"Your ass sobered up real quick when they started fighting on the dance floor." Palmer laughed.

"They were fighting over you!" Cat reminded her.

"Maybe." Palmer had a glint in her eye. "Did you just hit me with paint?"

"I sure did." Cat lifted the corner of her lips into a devious smile. "You called me a hoe on the sly."

There was a silent stare down between them before Palmer directed the sprayer at Cat and proceeded to press the button, sending paint shooting across the room.

Cat could see what was about to happen before it did but couldn't get out of the way fast enough. It was as if everything moved in slow motion until the cold, wet liquid splattered all over her body. "Oh shit! No, you didn't!" Cat was quick to retaliate. She climbed down the ladder, holding her can of paint as Palmer continued to laugh hysterically while targeting her with the sprayer.

The floor was slippery from the plastic covering it and the excess paint. Cat slid, trying to get to Palmer. They were laughing uncontrollably. Still, she got close enough to rear the bucket back and toss most of the contents onto Palmer.

Palmer could barely talk through her laughter. "You get

paint in my hair, and you're going to wash it out! You damn well know they don't have a good stylist within twenty miles of here."

Cat wasn't deterred. "You're wearing a baseball cap!"

Dillyn walked into the parlor to see her friends making the biggest mess. Their light-heartedness brought a small smile to her face. She placed her hands on her hips like a stern mother. "What in the world is going on?"

They froze. Cat and Palmer were covered from head to toe in paint. Cat was breathless. "Um . . . we're . . . um . . . working!"

Cat and Palmer exchanged a conspiratorial glance.

Dillyn saw it in their eyes. "Oh, no, you don't!" Before she got the words out, her friends sprayed and doused Dillyn with what was left of their paint. Screaming, Dillyn joined the fray. "Oh, my gaaaaawd!" She made a mad dash for one of the extra paint cans sitting next to a wall; however, the floor was slippery. Dillyn tripped and slid across the room like a bowling ball rolling down an alley. When she finally stopped moving, Dillyn lay sprawled out on her side. She was wet and completely covered in white.

"Dillyn! Are you alright?" Palmer yelled. The room grew quiet again as Cat and Palmer waited for her to answer. They didn't think she was hurt but waited for her to give them a sign.

Dillyn flipped over onto her back and started to giggle. Her giggles turned into a hearty laugh until she was hysterical. Palmer and Cat began to laugh, too, as they walked over and joined her on the floor. They dropped down and lay on their backs, staring up at the ceiling as they continued to crack up.

They weren't sure how long their bout of hysteria lasted, but at some point, Dillyn's laughter faded out. It turned into something else—more like a guttural wail. Tears streamed down the sides of her face.

Surprise was an understatement, even for Dillyn herself. It was the first time she'd truly cried since finding out about Steven's affair. Dillyn never allowed people to see this side of her. Her emotions must have become too much to bear. Cat and Palmer remained still and gave Dillyn the space she needed to release her pain.

Slowly, Palmer linked her fingers together with her friends. It was their way of saying *we've got you*. After some time, Dillyn's sobs began to subside. She sniffled and sighed. "I have no idea where that came from."

Palmer turned her head slightly and smiled at the woman who was like a sister. "I'm no expert, but it's probably a good thing to finally get it out."

Cat remained silent, keeping her thoughts to herself. *Steven doesn't deserve your tears.*

"You know what pisses me off the most?" Dillyn didn't wait for an answer. "He just let me go as if I never meant anything. Why do people who claim to love you do that? As if all those years we shared didn't happen, and I imagined it all. Not a phone call, a text, an email, or even an *I'm sorry*. I hate Steven and would never want him back, yet I still miss his touch. Even the way he smells. I can't wait to get his toxic ass out of my system."

"Fuck him," Cat said.

Dillyn groaned. "I did for thirteen years!"

Cat frowned. "Girl, thirteen years with Steven? He probably sucked, and you wouldn't even have known it since he was the only man you've ever been with. Boy, do you have a lot of lost time to make up for."

That wasn't exactly true, but Dillyn didn't feel the need to correct her.

Palmer lifted her head above Dillyn's so only Cat could see her glare and mouthed, "That is not helping!"

Dillyn missed her friend's silent communication. "Sex is not important to me. I've said this before, but I'm done. I mean done done done with men." Ben's face flashed into her mind. He was just like all the rest, hot one minute and cold the next. Literally, all men were the same.

Her words hung in the air for a bit, each woman lost in their own thoughts. Dillyn angrily wiped away the wetness from her face, leaving large white streaks behind.

After a few more moments, the three of them sat up and looked at one another. Only Palmer and Cat's eyes were visible. Some parts of Dillyn could still be seen, but they all looked a hot mess. Dillyn was the first to say what they were thinking. "We're going to need to hire someone to paint."

"Thank *gaawd* you said it." Dillyn's statement mirrored Cat's thoughts. "I'm down to my last bit of savings, but I'm willing to part with it to get a professional to do this shit."

"Excuse me." The deep voice of a man surprised them.

Palmer, Dillyn, and Cat all turned toward its direction.

"We rang the bell and knocked, but nobody answered. We heard voices, so I hope you don't mind that we let ourselves in."

"Oh, my," Palmer said under her breath. *Damn, he's finer today than last night.* Even Cat was rendered speechless at the fineness that greeted them. Ben was hot, but he was off-limits. He was Dillyn's, even if she didn't know it. Now, the other brother? He was probably off-limits too, but Cat was hoping it was the third brother. If so, she might have a shot.

Palmer scrambled to her feet. "N-no. Of course not. Please come inside. I'm sorry we didn't hear you." She greeted them with a warm smile.

100

Dillyn watched Cat stretch like her namesake. That girl could turn on the sex appeal like most people blinked. It was second nature. It was also hard to believe, looking the way they looked and covered almost head to toe in paint, that Cat could still make getting off the floor look sexy.

Inwardly, Dillyn rolled her eyes as she sat up. *Men.* They were the root cause of basically every problem known to man. They probably orchestrated the original sin and blamed Eve for it. They'd definitely ruined this private moment and gave her another reason never to want to see them again.

Dillyn took her sweet time rising. Palmer and Cat were being much too friendly. After her morning with the Cash brothers, Dillyn couldn't imagine what they wanted.

Ben had a brief moment to study the ladies before they announced themselves. He couldn't put his finger on it, but something about Dillyn captured his interest the same as two years ago and the night before. It wasn't the beauty of her large brown eyes that intrigued him. Dillyn was attractive, but it was more than that that made him curious. The problem was Ben didn't want to be curious. He wasn't free to be interested. Ben had way too much stuff to work out. Still, he couldn't help but notice in Dillyn's unguarded moments there was something about her that he recognized immediately. It was something he saw in himself.

She was broken.

Dillyn felt Ben studying her. His face was a blank canvas, but his eyes were intense, and it left Dillyn feeling uncomfortable. It was as if he could see into parts of her that she preferred no one see. *Why were he and Lucas here?* The sooner they found out, the sooner they could leave.

Dillyn raised her chin and challenged his gaze. Ben held it to let her know he knew what she was doing.

Lucas spoke to Dillyn but couldn't seem to keep his eyes off Palmer. "I'm afraid Ben and I may have gotten off on the wrong foot with you this morning, Ms. Anderson. My brother and I brought flowers to make amends." Lucas handed Palmer and Cat each a bouquet. When Ben didn't give Dillyn the flowers he held, Lucas elbowed him and smiled to cover up his brother's rudeness.

Ben forgot he'd been holding them. He extended his arm and pushed the purple and white magnolias toward Dillyn.

Dillyn stared at the flowers but didn't take them. It was clear to her Ben was being forced. After a few awkward moments, Palmer had to nudge her as well. She spoke into the weird silence as Dillyn begrudgingly accepted the flowers from Ben. "Well, thank you both kindly. They're beautiful."

Cat agreed as she lowered her head to breathe in the scent. "They are lovely and smell wonderful. Don't they, Dillyn?"

Dillyn directed her words to Lucas. "Gorgeous. Thanks, and I accept your apology." She then returned her gaze to Ben. "Life is too short for bullshit. If you didn't want to give me flowers or apologize for being an ass, then don't. Excuse me. I have some things to do." Dillyn turned and walked out of the room.

Cat and Palmer were both floored. They'd never seen Dillyn act like this. Embarrassed, Palmer almost choked. "W-w-well, that happened."

This is going to be a heavy haul. Lucas's lips tightened as he pushed Ben in the direction Dillyn had stormed off. His face clearly said, *Fix this shit.* Lucas had never seen his brother be this rude.

Ben looked slightly embarrassed. "Sorry, ladies. It's been a long morning. I apologize for my rudeness."

Finally hearing his voice, Cat and Palmer would later

agree that his baritone was smooth like a fine brandy. They both smiled at him and waited.

Ben took a deep breath and headed in the direction that Dillyn had gone. He found her outside on the porch angrily, pacing back and forth.

"You're going to wear a hole in the floor," he said lamely.

Dillyn sighed loudly. "Why are you here? Clearly, you don't want to be, and I didn't invite you? So, what do you want? The sooner we find out, the sooner everyone can get on with their day?"

"Damn. Straight to the point. I can respect that. So, I will get to it. My brother thinks you ladies can help my sister, Selah."

Dillyn's face softened at the mention of her name. "Help her?" She had to remember to be angry as she folded her arms across her chest. "Unlike her brothers, Selah seems to be the only Cash I've met with her head on straight."

"Do you always say what you think?" Ben asked.

I've lived too many years not fully expressing myself. Not anymore. "Yes, I do." She was resolute. "Is Selah in some kind of trouble?"

Ben appreciated what appeared to be genuine concern. "No. She's a good kid."

Dillyn was losing patience. "I don't understand."

"Selah wants to be a big-time event planner. She wants to move to New York this summer to pursue her dream."

"Let me guess. You don't want her to?"

"Pursue her dream? Yes. Go to New York by herself? No. It's not safe for a girl as young and naive as she is."

"I can't argue with that but sheltering her isn't going to help. Still, I don't know what we can do."

Ben could admit that Dillyn had a point. "Lucas heard that

103

y'all are hiring. Maybe you can give her a job. If Selah has an opportunity to learn from successful New Yorkers, maybe that will curb her appetite for leaving Summer for a while."

Dillyn was touched by how much they loved their sister. "Do I need to tell you how controlling this sounds? Most young women her age are already exploring the world."

Ben agreed, it wasn't one of their best ideas, but they didn't have any others. "It sounded like a good idea at the time."

Dillyn couldn't seem to help herself and had to ask the question that had been gnawing at her. "Can't your wife help?"

Ben glanced away, but before he turned his focus elsewhere, Dillyn caught a flash of pain in his eyes. Ben didn't completely answer her question. "I think your influence might be more helpful."

"I see." Why did she basically ask if Ben was still married when she didn't care? Dillyn decided to stay on topic and focus on what mattered. Then she veered off, asking another question that she shouldn't have. "Why were you so rude today?"

Ben appreciated her honestly. Most women fawned all over him. He sighed. "The truth is, today is a tough one. More so than usual."

Dillyn wondered why today was so tough and why more so than usual but decided not to ask. If Ben wanted her to know, he would have told her.

There was an uncomfortable silence between them before Ben turned soft blue eyes back to Dillyn's. "I apologize for my behavior earlier."

He seemed sincere, but Dillyn had already proven that she was a poor judge of character. Still, she mumbled, "Apology accepted."

Lucas, Cat, and Palmer stepped out onto the porch just in

time to hear Ben apologize and Dillyn accept. Lucas' shoulders relaxed. He was glad they hadn't killed each other because Dillyn looked as if she was going to hurt Ben.

"Great to see things are working themselves out between you two." He breathed a sigh of relief. "Ben and I should have come by sooner to see if we could be of any help."

Dillyn spoke before Palmer or Cat could. "Thank you, but we have everything covered."

"Don't hesitate to call us if you need anything. We know most of the people in the area. That kind of info might be beneficial." Lucas pasted on a cocky grin as he focused his attention on Palmer. "Don't forget, the barbecue is tomorrow at two o'clock."

Surprised, Ben turned to Lucas. His eyes said it all. *Why did you invite them?* Lucas shrugged. A big smile spread across his face from ear to ear.

Ben shook his head. He hadn't had time to reconcile his attraction to Dillyn with his feelings for Lana. Not that he planned on acting on them, but damn, he still felt guilty. And now, he was being forced to socialize with her . . . again.

"We'll be there!" Palmer responded.

Ben tipped his hat, sighing in resignation. "Ladies. I guess we'll see you tomorrow."

Chapter 13

Selah had been buzzing around all morning, making sure everything was ready for the barbecue. It was an event her family threw every year to show their appreciation to their employees for their hard work. Meaning they ate good food, partied hard, and received nice big fat bonus checks. Her family was all about sharing the profits from their successful cattle business. Her dad, the late, great Willy Cash, always said people worked hardest when they felt like they were a part of something special. He took pride in knowing everything about the people who worked with him. He actually cared about their wellbeing. Ben was a lot like his dad. He had a big heart. At least Ben did until everything changed. He hadn't been the same since Lana. She almost destroyed him. Selah knew this weekend was going to be difficult for Ben. She could only hope that he wouldn't think about *it* too hard.

Selah shook off those feelings. Instead, she thought of her mom as she walked around the house doing a final check. It was something Linda Cash used to do when Selah was young. Selah had tagged along, not realizing she was in training. If her father was the hard power of the family, her mom was definitely the soft power. Initially, Linda's idea was to throw an end-of-summer party for the workers and their families. Willy made it his business to know his employees, but Linda knew the personal stuff like who was about to have a baby or if so-and-so was about to have surgery. They made a dynamic team, which was why folks loved to work for them. They had employees whose kids had grown up and now worked for them too. Over the years, the Cash barbecue had grown into a big celebration that almost all the people in Summer would attend.

The barbecue was a tradition that she and her brothers vowed to keep alive even after the death of their parents. Planning took almost a year in advance. It meant a lot to Selah to follow in her mother's footsteps. They were big shoes to fill, but she was determined to try. This was the first barbecue her brother Wyatt wouldn't be able to attend. He was off gallivanting around the world.

Selah's cell vibrated. She pulled it out of the back pocket of her jeans. A slow grin spread across her entire face as she read a text.

Ben walked into the foyer just in time to see her beaming. He frowned. "Who's that?"

Selah glanced up nervously. "W-what? Who's who?"

He pointed to her phone. "The person who put that goofy smile on your face." Apparently, they hadn't scared off everybody.

"Oh." She shrugged innocently. "Nobody you would know."

"He's coming to the barbecue?" Ben asked.

"First, how do you know it's a *he*? And, second, how on earth did you get Dillyn, Palmer, and Cat to come considering you were so mean to Dillyn yesterday."

"I wasn't mean." Ben wasn't about to give her the whole conversation—just the Cliff's notes version. "I may have been a little gruff. We just needed to apologize and make amends. So, Lucas and I extended an invite."

"*We* as in Lucas?" *Mission accomplished.* Selah had distracted Ben from her phone call and stuffed her cell into her back pocket.

He smirked. "We as in . . . they're coming, so it doesn't matter." Ben glanced around. "It looks great in here." He turned serious. "Mom would be proud."

The joy Selah felt could be seen in the blush creeping up her face. "Thanks, Ben. That means a lot." She wrapped her arms around his waist and hugged him tightly. "They would be proud of you too." Selah stepped back and hoped to lighten the mood. "Everyone should have a good time. Oh . . ." She snapped her finger. "Let someone else win the bull riding contest today, okay?"

Ben cleared the thickness from his throat. "Nobody wants to be given a win. I'm not throwing a contest."

Selah placed a hand on her hip. "Then don't ride. Did you forget this party is for our employees and their families?"

In that moment, Selah reminded him so much of their mother.

"Of course he forgot." Lucas joined them in the foyer. "You know how competitive he is."

"It's more about self-preservation," Ben said, pushing his hands into his pockets. "Unlike you, I don't enjoy women hanging all over me. If I'm busy riding bulls, I don't have to entertain the bullshit."

"You're such a romantic," Selah said sarcastically.

It was Ben's turn to change the subject. "Talked to Wyatt. He's good and sends his love."

"Is he still on track to come home in a couple of weeks?" Lucas asked.

"Yeah," Ben responded.

"I can't wait to see him." Selah loved all of her brothers, but she and Wyatt had a special bond. It could have something to do with both being the youngest. She being the youngest child and him being the youngest son. "Anyhoo . . ." She pointed to

Ben and Lucas. "Go get dressed. Wear something nice. Ben, that means you. No t-shirts today!"

*****

Dillyn pulled up onto the Cash property and was directed by someone, telling them where to park. She was having flashbacks of Frank's. There was a sea of cars. Dillyn maneuvered her car into its spot.

"Why do I always have to drive?" Dillyn asked. "I feel like I'm getting the short end of the stick."

"Because you don't drink, and we do." Palmer laughed.

"I should take it up as a hobby. Why did you convince me to come again?" Dillyn asked.

"We are being neighborly," Palmer said cheekily.

"Are we being neighborly, or are you trying to get with Lucas?"

"Yep!" Palmer laughed heartily.

"I ain't mad. No point in putting my hat in the ring." Cat sighed. "It's obvious that he is locked and loaded on you."

"You think?" Palmer asked.

"Yep," Cat confirmed. "And the search for me continues."

"What about Ben? You could ask him out," Palmer asked, mainly to see what Dillyn's response would be. *Nothing.* Palmer got absolutely nothing.

Cat responded. "I don't think he's available."

Palmer blurted out. "He's single! I asked Lucas."

He's single? Dillyn was surprised. He hadn't mentioned that.

"I think Ben might be interested in Dillyn," Cat responded.

Dillyn whipped her head around. "He is not!"

"Yes, he is." Palmer and Cat said at the same time. Palmer

continued to push her point home. "Selah said there are three Cash brothers. Cat can have the other one."

"What if he's ugly?" Cat asked. "I haven't even seen him."

"I'm going to go out on a limb and say he probably looks like the rest of his family," Palmer said.

Dillyn chimed in. "Okay, ladies. Didn't we just discuss this not even twenty-four hours ago? I'm not here to get with Ben. I'm here because you forced me and because I like Selah." Dillyn got out of the car and planted her booted feet firmly on the gravel. "I'm just glad this time I wore the right shoes. So, if the shit hits the fan, I can run my ass off."

They had learned their lesson and were all dressed more appropriately. The thought of Friday night had the three of them on edge.

*****

The barbecue had been in full swing for several hours. As expected, Lucas was surrounded by women all vying to lock him down. He typically loved the attention, but for some odd reason, Lucas wasn't fully present. He smiled when appropriate but hadn't been able to keep track of any of the conversations. Instead, he kept glancing over toward the entrance.

Ben was in almost the same situation. It took every bit of his energy to mingle with his single female guests. Most of them were seeking a lot more than just his attention. It was hard to know who really wanted him for him and who just wanted the money and status that would come with being married into his family. He'd chosen once and had chosen wrong. It almost ended him. Ben would never have what his parents had, and he'd made peace with it—sort of. There was a better chance of hell freezing over.

Ben saw them as soon as they walked into the backyard. Dillyn, Palmer, and Cat were instantly greeted by guests hoping to have a conversation with the ladies from New York.

Selah was chatting it up with several girls her own age when she saw them arrive. From her vantage point, Selah had a bird's eye view of everything and everyone, including her brothers. They were entertaining two separate groups of people, but their heads lifted at the exact same time. She turned to see what was drawing their attention and there stood Dillyn, Palmer, and Cat.

Selah wasn't surprised to see that three beautiful women had caught the attention of Lucas. But Ben? That was a surprise, considering his previous experience. Selah excused herself from her friends and walked over to Ben. She managed to sneak up on him while he was still staring at her new friends. Selah stood up on tiptoe and whispered into his ear, "She is very beautiful, isn't she?"

Ben quickly turned away as if caught with his hand in a candy jar. Speaking through a faux smile only Selah could hear, he asked, "Who?"

"You know who." She looked up at him while smiling and batting her eyelashes.

"Excuse me, ladies. Can I borrow my brother?" Selah grabbed Ben by the arm and led him away. "You should go say hi."

He frowned. "Thanks for rescuing me from that pack, but I'm good." Ben maneuvered out of her grasp, tipping his hat. "I've got a bull that needs riding." He walked away in the opposite direction.

Selah could only watch him leave. She wondered if her brother would ever open up to love again.

Ben spent the rest of the afternoon mingling with the guests. It was weird, but he could feel her. It was strange that he seemed to know exactly where Dillyn was at all times. She had separated from her friends and was walking around on her own.

She didn't lack for male attention. She seemed to nod and smile a lot, but he couldn't tell if she was enjoying herself.

Lucas caught up with him. "Yo! I've been looking for you. It's time to go to the booth."

Ben rolled his eyes. "That booth is a stupid idea."

Lucas slapped him on the back. "Stupid or not. You agreed, so bring ya ass. We've got women to kiss."

Chapter 14

"C'mon, Dillyn. It's for a worthy cause." Palmer pleaded as she pulled her toward the kissing booth.

"Nope. No way, I'm not putting my lips on a stranger. You know I'm a germaphobe."

"First, they are not strangers per se. They are our neighbors, and it's no tongue involved, and second, that's a lie. You are not a germaphobe." Palmer admonished her. "You should stop using that as an excuse not to do something."

Cat waved a thin slip of paper in the air. "I've got my ticket. Never thought I would be attracted to a cowboy, but my goodness, they're sexy. Wonder which one I'll get."

Dillyn shook her head. "I'm going to sit this one out and watch you two enjoy yourselves."

Palmer turned to Cat. "If it's Lucas, you better move on to the next guy."

"Aren't we territorial? He's not even yours—yet." Cat's giggle was more like a purr, sexy, feminine, and feline.

Palmer wiggled her brows up and down. "*Yet* is the operative word."

Dillyn shook her head. She found a bench and sat down. The lines for everything were much too long, but the kissing booths were insane. No way would she stand in that. Instead, Dillyn watched as her friends waited patiently for their turn. It was a spectacle. Seemingly, every woman in Summer, Tennessee wanted a chance to kiss the ten eligible bachelors on display. It was a round-robin of sorts. No one knew exactly who they would get until it was their turn for a kiss.

Some guys were really into it and were doing the absolute

most. Cat finally made it up to the front. She was lucky the guy she was paired with wasn't Lucas. Palmer truly had set her sights on him. She might just strangle Cat if she broke girl code and went after him. Cat would never do something like that, though. None of them would.

The second Cat handed in her ticket, her cowboy appeared. She thought he was kind of cute. He leaned in and planted one on her. Dillyn laughed at the ridiculousness of it. It happened so fast Cat was caught off guard. It only lasted a second, but it was clear from her facial expression that her kiss was a bust. There weren't any sparks.

A roar of hoots and hollers went up from the crowd as they had for every person who was kissed. Cat smiled politely and started making her way back toward Dillyn.

"Was it everything you hoped it would be?" Dillyn asked when she made it.

"Shit. I don't even know. It happened so fast I didn't even realize I'd been kissed until it was over." Cat folded her arms across her chest. "I think I want my money back, a do-over, or something."

"Look," Dillyn pointed. "Palmer is next. Mmm . . . she's going to be so disappointed. That's not Lucas."

Palmer stood in line, trying to play it cool. She was hoping and praying that Lucas Cash would be her guy. Palmer glanced around to see all the other women standing in line. Selah wasn't lying when she described the men to women ratio. They were all probably hoping Lucas would kiss them too. Finally, after what felt like forever, it was Palmer's turn.

She stepped up to the booth.

Of course, it wasn't him.

Palmer did her best not to show her disappointment and

plastered on a big smile. The guy was cute. Not Lucas Cash cute. *Oh well, maybe I'll get to shoot my shot later on today.* She extended her hand to give him her ticket in exchange for a kiss.

Out of nowhere, Lucas stepped into the booth. "Excuse me. I think I've got this one." Keith Jones, a ranch hand who had been thanking his lucky stars that he'd get to kiss Palmer, begrudgingly moved over to another booth.

Lucas kept his eyes trained on her. "I hope you don't mind?"

A hush fell over the group.

"Depends on how well you kiss," Palmer said playfully. She handed him her ticket. He clasped her hand in his and slowly pulled Palmer forward, kissing her. Most of the kisses had lasted no more than three seconds, but Lucas lost count of time with Palmer.

Someone coughed several times, bringing Palmer and Lucas out of their haze. Lucas stepped back. A lopsided grin appeared on his face. His voice was deep. "Was that good enough for you?"

Palmer typically would have had a snappy comeback, but his kiss had knocked the wind out of her. She couldn't form one coherent thought. Instead, she just smiled, turned, and walked away.

Dillyn and Cat glanced at each other.

She seemed to be mesmerized still when she returned to her friends. "That was the most intense kiss I've ever had."

"Your turn!" Selah popped out of nowhere. She placed a ticket in the palm of Dillyn's hands and started pushing her toward the booths.

Dillyn protested. "Oh, no, I'm not. I can't."

"It's for a great cause." Selah gently pushed and prodded.

"No, really. I can't. I have a phobia."

Selah immediately stopped prodding Dillyn until Palmer and Cat spoke simultaneously, "No, she doesn't."

Selah began to pull Dillyn's arm gently. "C'mon. Summer's Angels Foster Home could use the money."

It was a good cause. Shit. Dillyn had to kiss for the cause. Didn't she? As Dillyn stepped up to the booth to see her cowboy, her stomach dropped. She had avoided him most of the day. *Just my luck.* Dillyn stood face-to-face with Ben Cash.

For a split second, Dillyn could see the surprise on his face before it returned to a blank mask.

Dillyn was sure he didn't want to kiss her just as much as she didn't want to be kissed. *What am I supposed to do?* The entire town was watching. Dillyn wanted to drop in the nearest hole. *Maybe it won't be so bad.* She hated being the center of attention. She preferred to blend into the background. Instead, Dillyn stood in front of Ben, frozen and full of anxiety, wondering what to do with her hands.

Ben frowned. Dillyn did not want to kiss him. It was a slight hit to his ego, especially when *he* didn't want to kiss *her*.

He spoke quietly so that she was the only person who could hear. "I'll make this quick."

Her eyes widened as she swallowed hard.

Ben leaned forward.

Dillyn's heart was already beating fast, and now it was about to burst out of her chest. Her face was flushed, and her body became as rigid as a board. Dillyn's hands clenched into fists at her sides. She felt as if she were about to have a full-on panic attack.

Dillyn felt the heat of his breath tickle her upper lip as it hovered close but not yet touching.

116

Ben frowned. He realized something else was going on other than her displeasure at not wanting to kiss him. Then Ben remembered her phobia. He spoke softly as if talking to Whisper. "I'm going to kiss you now."

Dillyn nodded before Ben pressed his lips gently against hers. All the breath left her body as her eyes fluttered closed.

His lips were warm and soft, gentle. Ben and Dillyn's kiss lasted no longer than three seconds. It was the opposite of Palmer and Lucas.

Ben pulled back. Concern was evident in his eyes. "You're okay." It wasn't a question. It was a statement.

Dillyn could barely hear him over the roar from the audience. She was so embarrassed. Dillyn cleared her throat and stepped back. "I-I'm fine." Her emotions were scattered everywhere. Dillyn quickly pivoted and navigated her way through the crowd and back to her friends.

As Ben watched Dillyn almost run away, he wondered what ghosts were chasing her.

Chapter 15

Dillyn wanted to go home. She walked back toward her friends with her arms wrapped tightly around her body. "Are you ladies ready to go?"

"How was it?" Cat asked.

"What?" Dillyn played dumb. She didn't have an answer.

"His kiss? How was Ben's kiss?" Palmer pushed.

Dillyn shrugged. "I don't know." She tried to keep it light. "Aren't all kisses the same?" Dillyn didn't want to sort through the emotions roiling within her.

Palmer was disappointed. She had hoped there were some sparks between them. Cat was also disappointed. She wanted to see her friend wake up from the nightmare of her marriage to Steven.

"I'm ready to leave." Dillyn was emotionally drained. "We've been here long enough. We've most certainly given everyone something to talk about."

"Before we go, we made a promise." Palmer reminded her. "We still have to talk to Selah about a job. Are we all still in agreement about making her our assistant?"

Dillyn ran her hands up and down her arms. "Umm . . . yes. Of course. Let's get this over with. Where is she?"

"Buzzing around. To be honest, I'm pretty impressed with her skills." Cat glanced about. "She might be a real asset."

"I'm sure she had some help, but this is a big party. It's well organized." Palmer agreed. "We can't leave until we have that conversation."

"She has done an incredible job," Dillyn said softly. She needed a minute alone. There were too many people, and it was much too loud. She wanted some privacy to process why she almost had a whole panic attack. *It was just a kiss.*

"I'm going to walk around a bit." Dillyn told her friends, "I'll be right back. If you find her before I return, offer her the job without me."

*****

Ben was emotionally spent. He had smiled so much his face hurt. He'd also kissed way too many babies and women. The women's kisses seemed to blend into each other except for one. Although Dillyn's kiss wasn't passionate, it bothered him that it was the most memorable. It was soft and tender even though she didn't enjoy it. With her issue, why did she even do it? *Why couldn't I have just written a damn check for the charity?*

Ben managed to escape from hosting duties and into his bedroom. He massaged the muscles around his neck as he walked over toward the window. It was getting close to dusk. Still, he could see everything around for miles, and that's when she caught his eye.

Dillyn was standing next to the stream by the stables with her arms wrapped tightly around her body. He could tell by her stance that she was still tense. She seemed so alone and disconnected. Not just from the party but people. He noticed that about her when he had gone over to her place. It was something Ben understood, except he was much better at hiding it. He could be in a room full of people and still feel all by himself. That same energy radiated off her, drawing him like a moth to a flame. As if on autopilot, he decided to make his way down to that stream.

Everyone seemed to want a word with him as he made his way to her. Several people stopped him, but Ben managed to extricate himself from any lengthy conversations. Dillyn was elusive and could easily be gone if he didn't get there in a hurry.

Dillyn's back was turned away when Ben walked up. "Not enjoying the barbecue?" She jumped slightly at the sound of his voice.

Dillyn turned halfway. *Why on God's green earth does this man keep finding me?* He was the last person she wanted to run into. Dillyn released a soft sigh into the gentle breeze. "Selah has outdone herself. It's a pretty great party."

"Then why are you out here by yourself?"

"Nosy much?"

Ben half-grinned. "Well, kinda. It's my house and party too. It's my job to make sure all the guests are having a good time."

"Then count yourself successful. I'm having a great time." Her words rang hollow.

She still hadn't made eye contact with him. "A great time, huh? So then, what brought on your anxiety attack?"

Dillyn didn't know how to answer. She was so embarrassed that he noticed. "W-w-what?"

"Your panic attack." Ben repeated himself, but he was quite sure Dillyn heard him the first time. "Was it your phobia?" He also wasn't so sure she had one since Dillyn hadn't exhibited any other signs of it. Her phobia almost exclusively seemed to be targeted against him.

"I wouldn't call it that exactly." It was one of the reasons she was staring at the stream and trying to focus on the peacefulness of the water flowing through it.

Ben stared at her profile. She looked soft–delicate even. "What would you call it?"

Maybe if you just answer him, he'll go away. Only Dillyn didn't have an answer. In this case, the truth was all she could give. "I have no idea."

"I remember the first time I had an episode. I thought it was a heart attack."

That piqued her interest. Dillyn finally gave him her full attention. She was genuinely curious. "The first time?"

"Past couple of years have been . . ." he paused, "let's just say difficult, and I started having panic attacks. I don't have them too much anymore."

Dillyn mulled over his words. "I didn't feel as if I were having an actual heart attack, but," she released a heavy sigh, "lately, I've just been a jumble of emotions. Depending on morning, noon, or night, any one of them can make an unexpected appearance."

Dillyn gave off vibes of needing to be in control. She was behaving like a newborn foal that was completely out of her element and struggling. Ben decided to use the same tactic with Dillyn as he would on a filly when they were spooked.

He took small steps toward her as they spoke before finally standing shoulder to shoulder. "I understand that feeling of being all over the damn place."

Dillyn cut her eyes to the side, catching Ben in her peripheral. "Yeah?"

"Yeah."

"You mentioned the past couple of years has been hard. Is that why you're out here stalking me? Or did you just need a break from all the *ladies*?" Dillyn asked somewhat jokingly.

A deep chuckle escaped his lips. "I am thrilled that the fundraising part of this shindig is over."

"That's surprising."

"What?"

"That it doesn't sound like you enjoyed making out with all those beautiful women."

Ben lifted a brow. "Would that surprise you?"

"If I'm honest, yes." Dillyn returned her gaze to the stream. "I thought all men loved to be loved by women."

"Hmm." *Somebody hurt this woman.* "Selah talked me into it. The money we raise will go to a great cause. But that's not why I came out here. I saw you from my window."

"Oh. So, you *were* stalking me." Dillyn glanced up at his home. She wasn't sure which window he may have seen her from. "You purposely sought me out?"

He shrugged nonchalantly. "I guess you could say that."

Dillyn needed to set the record straight. "Look, I know we kissed, but it wasn't my idea. It was kind of forced on me by my friends. Unlike some of the women here, I'm not after you. I'm not interested in you like that."

Ben released a hearty laugh. The tail on Ben's laugh died down as he bent low to pick up a rock. He threw it, and the rock skipped across the stream several times. "Wow. Not sure if I've ever been shot down before I even made a move. Rest assured, Dillyn. I'm not interested in you like that either. I just wanted to make sure you were okay."

Dillyn should have been relieved, but his words had the opposite effect. "Good. Just so we're clear."

"Ma'am, we are clear." Turning back, Ben pierced her with his gorgeous blue eyes. "So? How are you? Are you really good?"

Dillyn sighed deeply. "I'm fine."

She didn't sound like it, but Ben thought it best to let it go for now. "What brought you to Summer? Were you running away or toward something?"

Dillyn rolled his words around in her head before answering. "I don't think either."

122

"That's a nonanswer."

Dillyn fidgeted. "I don't want to talk about me. What about you? What brought you back to Summer?"

Dillyn saw a shadow of darkness fall upon his face.

Ben turned and stared straight ahead into the crystal-clear spring water. "Moved back to be close to my family."

She turned his initial question back onto him. "Were you running away from something or someone?" Dillyn could only assume he came back after his divorce.

"Neither. Summer is just home. I'm most at peace here."

Dillyn nodded as if she understood. What had given her peace wasn't a place; it was a person. Steven had been that. "Peace." Dillyn sighed. "Not sure why it's so elusive. It's what I hoped to find when we moved here."

"You haven't?"

"We've only been here a little over a week." Dillyn took a deep breath, held it for a moment, and let it go on a long sigh. "I've had moments where I think so, but it's fleeting."

"You've experienced a recent trauma." Ben wasn't asking.

"Why would you say that?"

"Just a guess."

Dillyn took a minute to answer. "My whole life but most recently a divorce."

He lifted his head in understanding. "Ah. How long has it been?"

"Officially, six months. But . . ."

He waited patiently for her to finish.

"Our marriage was over long before that."

It was now obvious why Dillyn was so adamant about her interest in him, or better yet, lack of. "What about the rest of your family? Have they been supportive?"

123

Dillyn lifted her head to the heavens. She spoke quietly. "Not really."

Ben could feel her pain. He connected with it on a level Dillyn would never understand. He should probably mind his own business, but for some reason, he couldn't.

An idea came to Ben. Maybe he could help in some small way. He extended his hand to her. "Come with me. Let me show you something."

Dillyn was hesitant at first and just stared at his hand.

"This again?" Dillyn glanced up at Ben through thick lashes before deciding to follow him. Slowly, she placed her hand in his and allowed him to lead her.

"Just so we're clear, you're not really a germaphobe, are you?" he asked.

"No." Dillyn bit her bottom lip and cast her eyes down, having the good sense to feel bad about lying.

"The kiss I understand, but what was the big deal about shaking my hand?"

"I didn't know you." Dillyn might as well be honest. "We were alone, and I may have overreacted a little."

"What about now?" he asked.

"We've shared a meal, a dance, and a fight. While I don't know you well, I don't have *stranger danger* bells going off in my head."

"Don't forget a kiss."

"What?"

"We shared a kiss too."

Her brown eyes looked deeply into his. Dillyn took a furtive glance over her shoulder back toward the party and all the people.

Ben regretted the words almost as soon as he said them. "I

promise. You're safe with me."

Ben didn't *feel* threatening. "You're not a serial killer, are you?" Dillyn was only half-joking as they started to walk over a short distance over to the stables.

"It's a little late to ask me that, but no, I'm not." It wasn't long before they stopped in front of Whisper's stall. Ben clicked his tongue a couple of times, and the head of the most beautiful golden beast peeked out.

"Oh, my God." Dillyn's eyes widened. Her hand went to her chest. "I've never seen anything so incredible in my life!"

Ben beamed with pride. "She is pretty magnificent." He released Dillyn's hand and caressed Whisper's head. "This is my favorite girl in the whole world—next to Selah. She is not only beautiful, but she has a calming force that's unmatched. Whisper has done more for me than tens of thousands of dollars in therapy was ever able to do. Whisper, meet Dillyn. Dillyn, meet Whisper." He reached for Dillyn's hand and placed it on his horse. "Here, touch her."

Dillyn had never been around horses. She didn't even know they could look like the one standing in front of her. She was slightly intimidated. "Ben, I'm a computer geek. This animal is huge. I'm somewhat nervous."

He appreciated her honesty. "She won't hurt you. Quite the opposite. Here. We'll do it together." He linked her hand with his then slowly ran it up and down Whisper's head.

Whisper could sense the unease in Dillyn but remained calm.

As Dillyn slowly glided her hand up and down Whisper's head, she suddenly felt more at ease than ever before—even peaceful—as if Whisper had a secret magical healing power. Shocked, her eyes jerked up into his.

He smiled knowingly. "I know. If you think this is something, you can't even imagine what it's like to ride her at full gallop with the wind blowing in your face. For a little while, Whisper can make you forget everything. That's what she does for me every morning between five and six a.m."

Dillyn was curious. "Every morning?"

"Yep."

"I wish I knew how to ride." She would give anything to have that experience.

"You mean it?" Ben was somewhat surprised to hear Dillyn say that, considering she was a city girl.

"I'd give my left kidney for five minutes of what you've just described."

"A kidney is a hot commodity. At least make it an hour ride." Ben laughed. "If you're serious, maybe I can take you out sometime."

"You'd take me out?"

Against his better judgment, Ben nodded. "Yeah. If you want to go." Honestly, Dillyn was able to get under his skin without even trying. His invitation was meant to be helpful. At least, that is what he kept telling himself. "I only want to help. Figure it's the least I could do considering I was an ass yesterday."

Dillyn nodded in agreement. "Yeah. I do wonder if this is the real you. That night, when Amber had plans and my friends were sick, and we had dinner, and when we met again at Frank's are completely at odds with what happened yesterday."

"In my defense, I've been an ass to most people in general lately, so I hope you don't take it to heart."

Dillyn asked softly, "Why?"

"The situation with Selah was stressing me out, and I'm dealing with something else I'm not quite sure how to handle."

"I'm sorry. Want to talk about it?"

"Nope. Not really."

"Okay, then." Dillyn changed the subject. "Can Whisper really do all that stuff you claim?" She returned her attention back to the amazing mare in front of her. She hadn't realized her hand was still linked to Ben's until she tried to caress Whisper again.

Ben had seen plenty of sadness in Dillyn, but he'd bet his life that Whisper could help both of them. Dillyn seemed entirely captivated by her. He'd never seen her eyes look so alive. There was even a hint of excitement. Maybe even a twinkle. It made him feel . . . useful.

"That and more," he responded.

Dillyn couldn't keep the excitement out of her voice. "How about tomorrow? Can we ride tomorrow?"

"Tomorrow?"

Dillyn mistook his surprise for something else. "If you didn't mean it or are too busy, that's okay."

Ben was a man of his word. He would never have asked if he didn't mean it. "I'm never too busy to ride. So, if you're serious, we can go tomorrow."

Dillyn's eyes danced as she bobbed her head up and down with the enthusiasm of a child. "Yes. I'm serious."

Ben had hoped that Whisper could work her magic, and seemingly she had. "Okay. I usually make my way to these stables every morning at five. If you're here by six . . . we ride." Ben thought of his sister, Selah, and how long it took her to get ready. "Not six o'one. If you're even a minute late, your ass is going to get left."

"Got it." Dillyn moved to unlink her hand from his. Immediately, she missed the warmth and comfort. She shook that feeling off and saluted as if she were in the military. "I'll be here."

Dillyn touched Whisper's forehead with her own and spoke softly. "See you in the morning, Beautiful."

Whisper neighed. Dillyn would take that as a sign that she was happy with the idea. "I better get back. I've been gone for too long. Cat and Palmer have probably already called out a search party." Dillyn backed out of the stall wearing a genuine smile. She was excited for the first time in too long to remember.

Chapter 16

It was still dark when Dillyn woke and left the house. It was also a little chilly, so she threw on a parka. Dillyn did not want to be late and miss the opportunity to ride Whisper. Of course, it had nothing to do with Ben. *Nothing at all.* At least, that is what she kept telling herself.

On the drive over, Dillyn couldn't get Ben off her mind. She didn't know what to make of him. He was such a contradiction. Their first meeting was almost flirty and fun. When they danced at Frank's, for a split second, Dillyn thought she might be attracted to him. More than anything, Dillyn didn't feel threatened either emotionally or physically. Dillyn wondered what was causing his mood swings. How was Ben so comforting and charming one minute and overbearing and controlling the next.

Dillyn wasn't completely blind. He was in pain and trying hard to bury it. Clearly, his divorce was hard on him too. *Could that be why there seemed to be a connection between them?* As much as Palmer and Cat loved and supported her, they didn't get it. There were a lot of reasons for that. It was a breath of fresh air to be around someone who didn't look at her as if she were going to break at any moment. A person who didn't feel as if her emotions should be turned on and off like a switch. Dillyn decided it was best not to ask Ben about his demons. Whatever was going on seemed to be more about him than her.

Dillyn checked her phone when she arrived. *4:55 a.m.* She walked over toward the stall and waited. Dawn still hadn't broken through the darkness. Dillyn hoped Ben hadn't forgotten or was too tired for an early morning ride. She figured the barbecue had probably ended just a few hours ago.

At precisely five a.m., Ben strolled around the corner of the stable. He stopped short. He was somewhat surprised to see her. "How long have you been here?"

Dillyn was relieved to see him. "Just a few minutes. You weren't kidding when you said five a.m. on the dot."

"I thought you'd be here at six." He sounded irritated. "Not five."

"Good morning to you too," Dillyn said with as much cheer as she could muster while holding back a biting response. *The man and his mood swings!* Mostly to herself, she said, "Not a morning person, huh?"

"What?" he asked as he walked into the stable.

I hope he snaps out of this. "Nothing. Um." Dillyn thought if she were helpful, maybe Ben wouldn't mind sharing his space. "You said we ride out at six, right?"

"Yep."

Dillyn placed her hands on her hips as she glanced around. "That means you must do something for an hour until you gallop out of here." Everything in the place looked foreign. "What can I help you with?"

Ben wasn't a hundred percent sure Dillyn was even going to show up. He especially didn't expect her to come this early. He used this time to gather himself, and he especially needed it today. Ben hadn't slept a wink. It was impossible. He was more irritated with himself than Dillyn for inviting her into his space. It seemed the right thing to do at the time. Now he was rethinking the whole Gandhi approach. His voice was gruff. "You can muck out the stalls."

Dillyn was confused. "Muck out?"

Ben grabbed a shovel, which hung on the wall, and held it out to her. "Yep. Scoop up the shit and toss it over there."

130

"Oh." Dillyn wasn't dressed to shovel shit, so she was a bit hesitant as she reached for the shovel. "Sure. No problem."

She didn't turn tail and run in her designer clothes. For the most part, Dillyn accepted his request without putting up too much of a fuss. He knew damn well her pretty little self didn't even know what to do.

Dillyn stood rooted to the floor staring at the shovel. Confusion was written all over her.

"Never mind, I'll do it." He moved to take it back. "Wouldn't want you to mess up your new boots."

Why is he being such a jerk, again? For some reason, Dillyn didn't want Ben to think she was soft or that she was useless. She decided to stick it out. "Wait." She reminded herself that whatever was eating him had nothing to do with her. "If you show me how to do it once or twice, I'll get it."

Ben stared at her for a long moment as if contemplating something. "Are you serious?"

"I wouldn't have said it if I wasn't serious." Ben was giving Dillyn whiplash. "It's what you asked, right?"

"A city girl like you is willing to clean up horse shit?"

Dillyn's patience was quickly running out. Her lips tightened. *I got up early for this?* "You're acting like the Ben I met on Saturday and not the dude I spoke with yesterday. And, for the record, that's the second time you've called me a city girl. A . . . I'm a woman and B . . . Do you have something against women from the city?"

Ben was taking his frustrations out on Dillyn. He had invited her for a ride. It wasn't the other way around. He shouldn't have been directing his bad attitude at her.

He took a deep breath as he scratched his forehead with his thumb. "Look, I've been told I'm not a morning person."

Dillyn placed a hand on her hip. "Clearly, you are not. Anyway, is that your version of an apology?"

"Something like that." His head tilted slightly. "You accept?"

Dillyn thought about it for a second. "I don't know. Maybe if you promise to stop being hot one damn minute and cold the next."

"Okay."

"And . . . answer a question for me."

Ben wasn't up to answering any questions but figured he owed it to her. "Okay."

"What do you have against city women?"

Dillyn had no idea why that question was a powder keg. He wouldn't maintain eye contact. "I don't."

Dillyn didn't believe him. "Yeah, you do. Contrary to what you may think, we are the same as any other woman."

He half snorted and laughed. "No. You're definitely not."

"Oh really? Please explain that, Mr. Cowboy."

"For starters," he smirked, "women from Tennessee would already know how to muck out a stall."

Instead of taking her ass back home, Dillyn snatched the shovel from him and headed over toward the stall Ben had initially pointed to. She almost shoveled the shit at him instead of the pile. Why she felt the need to prove him wrong was beyond her.

Ben was impressed by the steel in her spine. He yelled out after her, "The sooner you finish, the sooner we can go for that ride."

*****

Dillyn's back was killing her. She didn't even know how she got herself in this situation. Why did she let Benjamin Cash goad her into shoveling horse shit? Her two-thousand-dollar boots were ruined, and she planned to send him the bill to replace them.

Ben was leaning up against the doorframe of the stall with his legs crossed at the ankles, watching. Dillyn's back was to him. She was working hard. He hadn't heard a peep out of her in almost an hour. Dillyn was so focused on her task that Ben didn't think she even knew he was there.

Dillyn was going to need a long hot bath with Epsom salt along with several pain meds from all the bending over, shoveling, and tossing of horse crap. Her anger was starting to rise. *What am I doing? Why am I doing this? I don't have anything to prove. Yet here I am, falling into similar patterns. Why do I need or want his approval? He's getting nothing but joy watching me be completely out of my element.*

Dillyn stopped and stood up straight. She took a deep calming breath.

Ben could see that Dillyn had reached her limit. He cleared his throat to announce himself and pushed off the doorframe. "You ready?" After uttering those words, he had no idea what was about to hit him.

Dillyn turned, face flushed from both arduous work and a slow simmering rage, which had built up over the past hour.

She held his gaze and took slow, deliberate steps toward him.

He could see the fury in her eyes.

Dillyn slammed the handle of the shovel into his palm. "I'm done." Angrily, she stalked away.

"Wait . . . I thought you wanted to ride?"

Dillyn stopped. She pivoted and took a few steps back toward him. They were face-to-chest since Dillyn wasn't as tall as Ben. "I did when I thought there might be some good in you. That you wanted to help me. It's taken almost an hour to realize you're a fuckin' masochist! I've had enough of those kinds of men in my life." Dillyn glanced heavenward. "Here I am doing the same shit I always do. Someone pretends as if they care, and I eat it up!" She brought her gaze back to his and narrowed her eyes. "I'm shoveling SHIT! For what? For your approval?" Dillyn jabbed him in the chest as she enunciated each word that came out of her mouth. "Who are you that I need it?"

She had every right to be angry. Ben felt like a world-class jerk. He hadn't meant to take his frustrations out on her. The guilt would eat him alive if he didn't do something to fix it. Dillyn was going through a rough time, and he added to it. He lifted his hands as if surrendering. "You're right. Let me try to make things right."

"Tuh?!" Dillyn rolled her eyes. "For five seconds, I forgot that you're a man. Your gender is only good for tearing things down. You have no idea how to build something up!" Again, she turned away and headed for the exit doors.

Dillyn's words hit him hard. Ben felt if she walked out of that door, she would be proof that there was no redemption for him. Quickly, he followed behind. "You're right! For the past couple of years, I've destroyed everything in my path. I was already in a bad mood when I came into the stables. It had nothing to do with you. I am sorry. You shouldn't have had to bear the brunt of it."

"Why? What is it with you?" Dillyn asked.

Ben looked toward the heavens. "My daughter's birthday is tomorrow, and it's killing me that I can't be with her."

Instantly, the anger left her body. Dillyn remembered how he had sang to her over the phone. It was clear that Rylee was his pride and joy. "I'm sorry." Dillyn was glad that she and Steven never had a child. She was sure he would use a baby as a weapon, much like she figured Ben's ex was doing.

Ben ran a frustrated hand through his hair. "You have nothing to be sorry for. You shouldn't be enduring me feeling shitty. It's me who should be apologizing to you."

Whisper made a noise. She was restless. It was more than likely brought on by the energy bouncing between them. When she poked her head out of the stall, it was clear Whisper was ready for her ride.

Ben repeated himself. "Let me make it right." He already had Whisper saddled up for their ride. He opened the stall, and she trotted out—tall, beautiful, and magnificent.

Ben had no doubt that Dillyn could say no to him but to Whisper? She seemed mesmerized by the mare. Ben reached out to touch Dillyn's shoulder. "Why don't we ride and, for a little while, forget all of our problems?"

Chapter 17

Dillyn nodded and allowed Ben to pull her body close. He placed his hands on each side of her waist before hoisting her onto the saddle.

Dillyn's lips parted. She released a small gasp. A whole gang of butterflies started swarming the pit of her stomach. She hadn't been expecting *that* reaction from his touch. Dillyn was grateful that Ben hadn't seemed to notice.

Ben couldn't get over how light Dillyn was. She weighed hardly anything and was even smaller than she appeared. While Dillyn had him thinking of her in ways he shouldn't, if Dillyn were Ben's, he'd make sure she added a little more meat on her body.

Dillyn worked hard to slow her breathing. Even though she wanted to blame it on never being on a horse, she couldn't. Whisper wasn't the only reason her pulse was racing. Dillyn did her best to push those thoughts out of her head by focusing her attention on Whisper. Even though Ben was making her body tingle, sitting astride Whisper made her feel powerful. It had been a long time since Dillyn had felt that way.

Ben made sure Dillyn was settled and secured before hoisting himself up and getting on. He positioned himself behind her. Dillyn's body melded perfectly to his as if she were always meant to be wrapped between his arms.

Ben hadn't been this close to a woman in a while, and Dillyn felt damn good. She stirred emotions within him that should stay buried. Ben couldn't allow himself to be attracted to her or anyone. Yet, he found his attraction to her impossible to ignore.

Ben lowered his head and placed his lips close to her ear.

"Hold on tight."

Dillyn trembled. She wasn't sure if her reaction was due to nerves or the heat of Ben's breath tickling the skin just behind her ear. Her mouth went dry. She didn't trust her voice not to crack. Dillyn nodded her consent.

They left the stable at a slow trot. Once outside, Dillyn bore witness to the most amazing sunrise she'd ever seen. "Whoa," she whispered. A blush crept up over the mountains, turning to blood orange. After a few seconds, the sky exploded into a flash of gold as the sun ascended the ridge. Rose gold tones merged with amethyst, and the blue above was sapphire clear. It was truly a remarkable sight.

Ben didn't need to wonder about Dillyn's reaction. He understood it all too well. He continued to speak into her ear. "Yeah. It still takes my breath away too." He tightened his arm around her waist and spurred Whisper on. "Let's go."

*****

Whisper wanted to run, but she sensed her riders needed something else. They'd covered quite a bit of Ben's property, but there were thousands of acres to go. Dillyn knew that the Cashes owned a lot of land, but she couldn't imagine how much. There was no way they could cover it all in one day or three, even on a horse.

Ben was right. Thousands of dollars' worth of therapy couldn't touch the beauty of nature. Dillyn had calmed down considerably since their fight earlier.

Ben maneuvered Whisper to a high point on the mountain, which was more like a ledge that jutted out from the earth. There was nothing but blue skies above and ahead of them. Lush green trees crowded the enormous mountainsides. "This is my favorite spot. I always come here to think."

137

Dillyn glanced around. She was in awe. "I can see why." She leaned back into the hard wall of his chest. For the briefest of moments, Dillyn basked in how safe she felt in his arms. She could even feel the steady beat of his heart through his shirt. The second Dillyn realized what she was doing, her eyes popped open.

Ben could no longer ignore the way her body felt nestled against his. He needed to put some space between them.

"Whisper could probably use a break." He moved to dismount and got down, then held his arms out for her.

Dillyn also worked quickly to shut down whatever feelings were trying to bubble up to the surface. She thought it best to put some distance between them too. Dillyn gave Ben a small smile, then leaned over into his waiting arms so that he could help her down. Dillyn fell into him, causing the front of her body to come crashing into his chest.

"I've got you." Ben caught Dillyn and held on tight as if she were precious cargo.

Dillyn gripped his shoulders tightly to keep from falling. Once she was sure she wasn't about to face-plant onto the grass, Dillyn looked up into Ben's face and their eyes locked. She swallowed hard, knowing her breasts were pressed against his chest.

Her nipples hardened, and her insides went from tingling to a dull throb as she slowly slid down the length of his body until her feet touched the ground. Dillyn was shocked at her reaction. She had been with Steven for thirteen years and never had this type of physical response.

Ben released Dillyn as soon as he knew she was down safely. *She can't look at me like that.* His eyes darted away.

Dillyn nibbled on her lower lip. "Umm . . . thank you."

"You're welcome." Ben backed up a few steps as he

looked around at everything but her. "No problem."

Dillyn took the tiniest moment to steal a glance at him. She couldn't quite figure him out. Was Ben attracted to her or not? One minute she could swear maybe he was, and then the next, there would be nothing more than curiosity in his eyes. She was probably a novelty to him. If Dillyn was truly giving up on relationships, why did it matter what Ben thought? She decided to push those thoughts away and enjoy her excursion without over-analyzing everything.

The silence between them was a little awkward. Dillyn wasn't good at idle chatter, and it appeared neither was Ben. Dillyn figured now was a good a time as any to give it a try. "You said you come here every morning?"

Ben finally felt in control enough to look at her again. "Mmhmm . . . rain or shine."

"That's dedication."

"It chases away the ghosts, even if only for a little while."

"Ghosts?"

He shrugged. "We all have them."

Dillyn's head tilted slightly. "You do?" She was skeptical. "What are some of yours?"

Ben wondered how much if any of his demons he wanted to share.

Dillyn could see him thinking. She wasn't sure if he was going to tell her anything other than about the beautiful place he'd brought her to.

"Having a difficult time dealing with missing my baby girl. It's been a little over two years since I've seen her."

"I'm sorry. That has to be hard."

"Feels unbeliatiful," Ben said quietly.

Dillyn knew better than anyone how devastating divorces

139

could be. She thought back on the timing of their first meeting and realized he'd probably gotten divorced shortly after.

"I wish you had said something earlier, but now I understand why you wanted to be alone this morning. We can go back if you want."

"It's nice to have the distraction."

"Distractions are amazing. The only drawback is they don't last forever."

"Agreed"

Instead of prying and asking about the details of his divorce, Dillyn decided to make him smile. "Well, remember you do have Whisper. She's magical, and if you're not careful, she might come up missing."

The sadness in his voice went away slightly. "I'll know exactly where to look if she does." Ben decided to take his cues from Dillyn. He shook off his negative feelings. "How about we go explore? It would be a shame if you didn't get to become one with nature up here."

"Become one with nature," Dillyn said as if pondering his words. "Okay. Well, these boots are made for walkin' . . ." Dillyn sang, poorly and off-key.

Ben cracked a small smile and shook his head. "Not those boots. We won't be doing much walking in those."

"Why?"

"They're cute. Not functional."

Dillyn glanced down at her feet. "Oh." She began to walk alongside him. "They *are* cute, though, aren't they? At least they *were* until someone made me muck out a stall. I'll be sending you a bill."

Ben shook his head. Dillyn had a way of making Ben smile like a crazy teenager. "C'mon. Let's go." As they went on a short walk, he got a kick out of watching Dillyn experience the joys of nature for the first time. She smiled a lot. Some of them reached her eyes. She was like a little kid discovering all the new things around her. Her reactions were sweet and innocent. Again, Ben found himself grinning like a fool. They were easy to come by around Dillyn. She was much too tempting. *I need to focus on something else. Anything else.* Ben looked away, but his eyes kept drifting back toward Dillyn.

She had been studying some kind of flower, and it had been quiet for so long that Ben was surprised to hear her voice.

"My husband cheated on me with a good friend of mine." Dillyn wasn't sure why she blurted it out. Maybe because Ben had shared with her.

Ben didn't skip a beat in his response. "He's a fool."

"It almost destroyed me."

"But you're still standing."

"Some days. I've been thinking a lot about why it almost destroyed me."

"Did you find any answers?"

Dillyn hesitated. "I'm only telling you this because I think you might understand."

Ben nodded but didn't say anything.

"I trusted him."

"I would hope so. He was your husband."

"No. Steven was more than that. He was my everything. Before our divorce, there were only three people that I knew I could ever count on—Cat, Palmer, and Steven."

"Not your family?" Ben wasn't sure he should have asked that question by the look on her face. He had a feeling it was like opening Pandora's box.

Dillyn glanced down at the ground and kicked at the dirt.

141

"Definitely not my family. They are nothing like yours. In a lot of ways, Steven was my family. He took care of me. He was the father I never had and the friend I always needed. We met in college. I was there on scholarship and didn't have very much support. He helped make things easier. Steven made sure I had food to eat, decent clothes to wear . . . stuff like that."

Ben listened intently.

"Honestly, I would have understood if he had just told me that we had grown apart and that he wanted a divorce. It would have been heartbreaking, but I could make sense of that."

"Instead, he betrayed your trust. He's a bastard." Ben was one to talk. Hadn't he betrayed Lana's trust? Though Lana never knew, Ben had been attracted to another woman and spent time with said woman instead of going home to take care of Lana and protect Rylee.

"So much more than that." Dillyn wrapped her arms around her body. "I allowed him to shape me into the person he needed. I lost myself. Then little by little—when the marriage was over but before I left him—he chipped away at my self-esteem. He would make everything wrong in his life my fault, and I allowed Steven to use that to tear away the tiniest bits of my self-confidence. For a long time, I believed it." Dillyn's eyes misted, but she blinked back the tears.

Now Ben understood her overly independent stance and why she was adamant about not dating. Dillyn was metaphorically fighting for her life. Ben was so angry that a man could do that to her. It was apparent she was a good person and didn't deserve all the hurt and betrayal she'd suffered. He felt a strong urge to comfort her but didn't think he should. Who was he to comfort her when he wasn't there for the people who needed him the most? Ben's throat thickened as his own guilt ate away at him.

142

Ben just remained quiet and listened.

Dillyn's voice was soft. "I have so much to figure out. My life is one big shit show. Summer is where I planned to try to put the pieces back together."

Ben felt like crap for being difficult earlier. "This is a great place to figure things out, and anytime you need Whisper." Ben gave Dillyn a lopsided grin, lending him a boyish charm to him she'd not seen before. "She'll be here for ya."

Dillyn rolled her head around her neck. "Ugggggggggh. I know you don't want to hear me moan and groan about my life. You're dealing with so much."

"Actually, it's nice *not* to have to think about me for a change." Ben tried to lighten the mood. "But, if you want to send me a check for this session, you have my address."

"Less the money for my boots?" Dillyn laughed sadly. "You're not running for the hills away from the trainwreck that is me?"

Ben turned serious as he held her gaze. "I don't run from difficult situations. Ever. I may not make the best decisions, but I'm determined to try to be there for those who need me." *Especially after messing up with Lana and Rylee.*

It was nice to hear him say those words, but only time would tell. So many people often promised one thing and did another. Dillyn hoped he wasn't one of those people.

"We better get moving. There is still so much to see." They walked back to the clearing where they had tied Whisper to a tree, and Ben helped Dillyn get up and onto her. "You ready?"

Ben understood Dillyn's need to have a clear mind and worked hard to make it happen. It was what they both needed, and she seemed appreciative. "There's more? Another special place?"

143

"All of it is special to me, but I have a couple more spots I'd like to show you."

"If you're willing, then I guess I'm riding."

Ben climbed onto Whisper. This time he decided to sit in front of Dillyn. He thought it was much safer that way and quickly had a change of heart the second she wrapped her arms around his waist.

Dillyn held on tight, and she pressed her cheek against Ben's back. She had no real reason to trust him, but she did.

They continued to explore his family's property. He couldn't help but get caught up in her excitement. It was nice to see his family's land through Dillyn's eyes.

After spending the entire morning together, Dillyn was slightly disappointed when they finally made their way back to the stables.

Ben helped her down. "Do you do any of that fancy stuff like yoga?"

Dillyn had worked out like crazy when she was married to Steven. "A little. Why?" Her eyes narrowed. "Be careful. We've had a nice morning, and you've almost redeemed yourself. Don't ruin it."

He laughed. "This was your first real ride. Your ass is going to be sore. You might want to stretch and ice your joints and muscles. If you give me your number, I can text you the name of a cream to use that might help."

"Oh." A rosy blush crept up Dillyn's face. She hadn't thought of that. She was already feeling the effects of their morning ride. "For a minute, I thought you were checking me out." She grinned.

Dillyn's smile lit up her entire face.

Ben was grinning, too, as he basked in her attention. He

stopped immediately after realizing he'd been doing *exactly* that—checking her out. Dillyn was nowhere near ready to date, and in all honesty, neither was he. But today was a good day to start a special friendship.

Chapter 18

Dillyn walked through the front door of her house, and for the first time in a long while, she felt a little lighter. A feeling of hopefulness was expanding within her chest.

"Where have you been?" Palmer walked into the foyer with a hand on her hip and lips pressed into a firm line. She was clearly irritated.

Her voice snapped Dillyn out of her good mood. "Gee, *mom*, I went out for a ride."

"Did you forget Selah was coming over today? We were supposed to be discussing her role with us."

Dillyn had forgotten. She glanced down at her watch. "Shit. Is she here already?"

"Yes! Cat and I have spent the last hour showing her around and discussing what we'd like her to do. Wait a minute." Palmer narrowed her eyes. She noticed that Dillyn looked different. She was almost glowing. Her cheeks were indeed dewy.

Dillyn nibbled on her lower lip at the intense scrutiny. "What?"

Palmer's shrewd gaze bore into hers. "Where have you been?"

Dillyn lifted a shoulder. "I told you. I went out for a ride."

"A ride where?"

Before Palmer could respond, Selah and Cat joined them. Selah's smile was bright. "How was your ride with Ben? Whisper is amazing, isn't she?"

Cat and Palmer's expressions were nothing short of shocked.

Dillyn wouldn't look at either of her friends. She addressed Selah. "She is pretty amazing." Dillyn did her best to ignore the quizzical glances from her girls. "I'm sorry I'm late. We're all so happy you decided to help us out."

"Nuh-uh. You went riding with Ben?" Cat was not going to save her questioning until after Selah left.

"Who is Whisper?" Palmer followed-up. "Is that why you're kinda glowing?"

Dillyn had to shut this conversation down. They were not going to embarrass her in front of Ben's sister. "My gaaawd. Ladies! I went out for a ride on Ben's horse, Whisper. He just wanted to show me around."

"I knew it!" Cat didn't believe her for a second. "What happened when you kissed him? Clearly, there was more going on than we could see."

Dillyn shrugged. "I hate to disappoint you, but it was just a ride."

"Are you sure?" Selah asked. "My brother has never taken anyone out on Whisper except for . . ." Selah stopped short before she said too much. "I mean, he doesn't take anyone for rides."

Dillyn wondered if Selah was going to say Ben's wife. "I can promise you that it was just a ride."

Selah's cell phone vibrated. She pulled it out of her back pocket and looked at the screen. She smiled mischievously before glancing up to find Dillyn, Palmer, and Cat all staring at her. "Sorry. I thought it was a call from home."

"I believe you about as much as I believe Dillyn," Palmer said.

"I can admit it." Selah was all smiles. "That text was from Thomas. We're trying to schedule a time to meet up." Her expression turned sheepish. "Depending on my work schedule."

147

Dillyn was more than happy to redirect the heat from her inquiring friends. "I forgot. Is that the guy you were talking about at Frank's?"

Selah was beaming. "Actually, no. Funny coincidence. We met online after leaving Frank's. He claimed he saw me, but I didn't see him. Anyway, there was just this instant connection."

Dillyn knew her brothers would not go for her meeting with Thomas this soon. Still, she kept her thoughts to herself. She was not the one to give dating advice. Instead, Dillyn smiled warmly but did offer a little bit of caution. "I'm sure you probably already know this but be careful. I should get showered and changed. I'll be back down to go over our game plan."

*****

Ben jogged up the steps to the main house just as Lucas was walking out onto the porch. Ben seemed to have a bounce to his step. "Whoa?! What's this?" Lucas was surprised, given that Rylee's birthday was tomorrow. He didn't know exactly where Ben's head was, so Lucas was only going to mention it if Ben did.

"What?" Ben responded. He glanced about, trying to see what Lucas was referring to.

"Something about you is a little different." Lucas walked around Ben, giving him a head-to-toe inspection. "Is that a little extra pep in ya step?"

Ben shook his head. "You're an idiot," he said jokingly. "I thought something was wrong." Ben started to brush past Lucas. "I've got the same pep I've always had."

Lucas blocked his path. "Nah, bruh. You don't." His eyes narrowed. "Where are you coming from? Are you just getting home?" Lucas pretended to sniff Ben. The lightbulb popped on. "Wait a minute. Were you with a woman?"

Ben wouldn't maintain eye contact. "I went for a ride like

148

I always do."

Lucas didn't believe him for a second. Ben had always been a bad liar. "You *were* with a woman! Virginia? She finally caught you?"

"Absofuckinlutely not."

Lucas grinned as he slapped his hand on his thigh. "Damn, man. It's about time. Who is she?"

Lucas has the wrong idea. Sort of. "Dude. I told you I just went for my regular morning ride."

Lucas ignored him. "Was she at the barbecue?"

"Don't you have anything better to do than to harass the shit out of me?"

"Nope. I have nothing to do, especially since we always give the employees the day off after the barbecue. I've got nothing but time. You might as well tell me who she is because I'm going to find out."

Ben ran a hand over his face. Lucas was like a dog with a bone. He wasn't going to let it go unless Ben gave him something. "Alright! I went for a ride with Dillyn."

Lucas couldn't possibly have heard him correctly. "You took who?"

"You heard me the first time, asshole."

Lucas broke out in laughter. "Okay. You got me. Seriously. Who is she?"

Ben didn't crack a smile.

Lucas' smile froze. "You're serious." His eyebrows raised to his hairline. "Are you trying to tell me that you spent all night *and* morning with Dillyn?"

"Just the morning."

"Dillyn Anderson," Lucas repeated in disbelief.

Ben was over it. He tried to sidestep Lucas again, but his

baby brother wasn't having it. "You know that's a bad idea."

"Not that my love life is any of your business, but since you're sticking your nose into it, why is Dillyn a bad idea?"

"For one, she's now Selah's boss and for two . . ." His voice softened. "It's clear that Dillyn has some stuff going on, and I just don't want to see you get hurt."

Just like that, the heaviness Ben had managed to escape for the past several hours returned with a vengeance. Ben cleared his throat. "I appreciate your concern, but you don't have to worry. Neither of us is interested in anything other than a friendship. Look . . . I'm tired. I'm going to hit the showers and grab a quick nap." This time Ben was able to get past Lucas. His footsteps were heavy as he walked into the house.

Lucas could punch himself in the face. Ben may not have been happy, but he seemed to be something close to it, and he'd just ruined it.

Chapter 19

Ben lay in bed with his fingers linked behind his head, staring at the ceiling and thinking about Dillyn and Rylee. Should he even be thinking about Dillyn when his daughter's birthday was tomorrow, and he wouldn't get to spend it with her? Ben had surmised that the dull ache in his chest would never go away. He didn't think he'd ever be able to resolve or absolve himself of the mistakes that let his wife and daughter down. *How could I possibly be thinking about dating?*

Ben's head was a mess. Lucas had been somewhat right. Dillyn was a walking, talking emotional wreck too. At least one person in a relationship needed to be emotionally sound because he sure as hell wasn't. Ben could tell that Dillyn's hurt ran much deeper than just a divorce. Granted, he understood how devastating that could be, but Ben felt there was more. He'd only known Dillyn for a short while but couldn't imagine her ex would be enough to break her.

Just admit it. You like her. "I like her," he said aloud into the empty space of his bedroom. As much as Ben wanted to deny his attraction, he had to be honest, at least with himself. He was wholly into Dillyn and had been since the first time they'd met. Only then she was off-limits. *Shouldn't she still be off-limits?* It was part of the reason the guilt with his family sat so heavy on his heart. She'd been on his mind the weekend everything went wrong in Ben's life and why he felt so conflicted. There was no question that Dillyn was beautiful, but it extended well beyond the physical. There was a vulnerability about her she tried to hide that called to him. "Pursuing Dillyn is not sensible." Ben figured if he said it aloud, it would register with his brain.

Ben couldn't imagine opening his heart up, but when he was around Dillyn, that's precisely what happened without any effort on his part. *I've got to put a stop to this before it goes any further.* Even if Ben wanted to pursue Dillyn, it wasn't like she had shown the slightest bit of interest in him. Everything within him was saying no. Don't do it. Stay away from her. Yet Ben couldn't help but glance at his cell next to him. His heart accelerated just at the mere thought of calling her.

Shit. Ben's desire to talk to Dillyn overrode his common sense. Just like it did at Frank's when he pulled her into his arms to dance. Ben picked up the phone and dialed Dillyn's number. It rang a few times before going to voice mail. "Hi, this is Dillyn. Leave a message, and I'll get back to you as soon as possible." *Beep.*

Ben sat up. "Hey, it's me, Ben." Nervously, he rubbed the back of his neck. "I enjoyed our ride this morning. Hope you enjoyed it too. Feel free to drop by anytime. Whisper would love it." He disconnected the call. "I sounded like a young punk."

"You're just out of practice." Lucas walked into Ben's bedroom.

"So now we're eavesdroppin'?"

Lucas looked awkward as he shifted from foot to foot. "I was just on my way up to apologize."

"For what?"

"For what I said earlier. I know I'm the younger brother, but I'm protective of you." Lucas ran his hand through his hair. "It's not my place to tell you who to like or not. It's just . . . you've been through a lot . . ." Lucas let his words drift. "The bottom line is that it's good to see you happy. Dillyn's the only woman who has been able to help you smile. I'm *surprised* she is the one to do it but happy you're smiling."

"Lucas, we just went for a ride." Ben tried to downplay the importance of how Dillyn made him feel.

"Yeah, but you called her, and it sounds like you want to do it again."

"No point in denying it. I do. I'm not sure how she feels about it. I'm not sure how I feel about it. I just enjoy spending time with her."

"Then definitely, call her."

"I just did. I left her a message."

"Aw hell, man, you're a Cash." Lucas grinned. "If she doesn't call you back, show up on her doorstep. We're irresistible. And if you're interested in pursuing her, you've got the easy in."

Ben frowned. "What's that?"

"Selah. She just accepted a job as their personal assistant."

A slow grin appeared on Ben's face. "That's right. She surely did."

Chapter 20

It had taken six months for Steven to get everything set up to make his move against Dillyn. She had made it all too easy. However, Steven planned to give her one more chance. Dillyn had to provide him with access to CyberCom so that the people he worked for could execute their plan.

Steven stood outside the doors of her rundown property, waiting for someone to answer the door. He couldn't believe he'd married someone willing to waste millions on what he thought was bullshit. Steven rang the doorbell again as he looked around.

Palmer opened the door, and the smile she'd been wearing fell away. "What the hell are you doing here?"

"Gracious as always, I see. Where's Dillyn."

"Leave." Palmer started to slam the door, but Steven put his foot in the crack to keep it from closing, forcing his way inside.

"Hell, no! You can't just come up in my home like this. What is the matter with you?!" Palmer didn't have her cell phone, so she started screaming, "Cat! Call 911 NOW!"

Cat came running toward the door with her phone in hand. "What happened?"

Dillyn ran in behind Cat and froze when she saw Steven. "What are you doing here?"

"I suppose I could ask you the same thing. What are you doing *here*?" Distaste was evident on his face as he glanced about their foyer.

Dillyn refused to answer. "Steven, you need to leave before Cat calls the police."

"She could, but I'm here trying to keep you safe."

"Keep her safe? You're the bastard who hurt her." Cat turned to Palmer. "It's three of us. We should beat his ass!"

Steven's eyes never left Dillyn's. She could tell that he was serious, and a cold shiver went down her spine. "Wait. Let me talk to him."

Both Palmer and Cat began to protest, but Dillyn shook her head. "As you said, it's three of us. I'll only give him five minutes, and then after that, Steven will be out of my life forever."

He turned to her gatekeepers. "She's right. I'll be gone forever. Five minutes. That's all I need."

Palmer was pissed. She crossed her arms underneath her breasts. "Fine, but I'll be right here just in case you need backup."

"Dillyn, please. Call off your pack. I need to speak with you and you alone."

Against her better judgment, Dillyn turned to her friends and silently pleaded. "Just five minutes." Against *their* better judgment, Cat and Palmer left the room. As soon as they were gone, Dillyn turned to Steven. "It's been six months. I hope you don't think you can come crawling back—"

"Dillyn we're divorced. It's final. I'm not trying to win you back. I'm trying to save your life."

"What?" She was confused.

"I know what you do and whom you *really* work for. I've always known."

"Stop talking in riddles. You know I work for myself."

"Dillyn, I don't have time to waste playing games. I need you to get me access to this." He handed her a sheet of paper. "Or things are going to go very badly for me, you, and everyone in this house."

Dillyn glanced down at the paper. Slowly, she lifted her

155

head. Dillyn laughed in disbelief. "Steven, you've got to be kidding. Seriously, I can't get into CyberCom."

Steven ran a hand down his face. "Did you not hear me? When you went snooping into my shit, you opened yourself up to this. Now, you'll help me get inside, or we're all going to end up in tiny little pieces."

Dillyn took a deep breath. "I don't know all of the shady shit you're into, but I can't help you. I handle basic IT security and tracing digital footprints. What you're asking is impossible. You need a master hacker. That's not me."

"You hacked into my shit! I had some very sophisticated encryption codes set up by the people who run world markets and governments. There was no way you could get into some of the systems you did without having access to CyberCom systems. As I said, I know who you are. I know whom you work for."

"You keep saying that! Who? Who is this mystery person you speak of?"

"Syntax."

"Syntax?" Dillyn tried to remain calm. "Steven, did you really fly from New York to Tennessee to ask me about someone who doesn't even really exist?"

"He exists, and you know it."

Dillyn glanced heavenward. "If so, the dude is anonymous. He's a ghost, and you think I know him because you are a predictable ass and never change your passwords? A high schooler could have gotten into your devices. You've lost your mind. I thought you came here to apologize for trying to destroy my life, but you only came here to involve me in whatever crazy scheme you've got going. Truth be told, if you needed help unlocking your password to your laptop, I wouldn't help you. Your five minutes are up. You need to leave." Dillyn was about to show

Steven the door when he grabbed her by the arm.

"Did you not hear me? This is not a joke. Our lives depend on this."

Dillyn was shocked. Steven had never been violent with her, and there was real fear in his eyes. "You're hurting me." She tried to sound calm because he was starting to look unhinged.

Steven's eyes bulged. "Bitch! You're going to get me inside that system!"

He was gripping Dillyn's arm so hard that she knew it was going to leave a bruise. Not only was it evident that Steven was scared, but now, so was Dillyn. She had no idea what he had gotten himself into and what he was about to do.

*****

Ben stood on Dillyn's doorstep. He had left her a message several days ago, but she hadn't returned his call. Ben would have come sooner, but he'd been in a funk dealing with all of his emotional crap. He didn't want to bring that energy around Dillyn. Initially, Ben was going to let sleeping dogs lie when it came to her, only he felt so much better when she was around. Ben liked who he was when they were together. So, he made up his mind. Ben was now in full pursuit of Dillyn. He understood that she was just getting over a divorce and might not be ready to jump into a relationship, but he was patient. They could take things slow. Lucas wasn't right about a lot of things, but he was on point when it came to the Cash charm.

Ben raised his hand to knock on the door when he heard a man yelling. "Get me into the system, Dillyn!"

"Steven! Stop. . . I don't even know what you're talking about!"

Ben recognized Dillyn's voice, and there was genuine fear in it. He didn't waste any time. It didn't matter that the door was

157

unlocked when he rushed inside. Ben would have broken the damn thing down if he had to. Ben saw red at how Steven had Dillyn's arms in a vice grip.

Ben arrived at the same time as her friends came into the room yelling. He didn't have words for the guy manhandling Dillyn. However, when he found his voice, Ben's tone was low, almost a growl. "You clearly don't like breathing above ground."

Dillyn didn't know where Ben had come from, but she was grateful.

Steven looked up into the face of Ben Cash. "This ain't your problem, country boy. You might want to turn around and go home. This is between my wife and me."

It took two steps and one hard punch to Steven's jaw to lay him out.

Steven's knees buckled as he crumpled onto the floor, holding his mouth. "You dumb shit! You have no idea you're trying to protect a lying slut."

Ben was ready to give Steven the beat down he deserved when Dillyn stepped into his path, stopping him.

"I'm calling the police!" Cat started dialing.

"No. Don't!" Dillyn pleaded. "He's leaving. Steven, leave. GET OUT!" Tears streamed down Dillyn's face as she glanced between Ben and her friends.

Cat's and Palmer's mouths dropped open at the same time. Confusion clouded theirs and Ben's faces.

"This bastard put his hands on you!" Palmer was shocked.

Steven struggled to get up from the floor. "No. You wouldn't want them to do that, would you?"

Ben tried to get at him, but Dillyn continued to stand in his way.

Steven spit blood onto their floor. "I tried to do this the

easy way. Just know that everything that happens from here on out is your fault."

"Get. The. Fuck. Out!" Ben had a look in his eyes that said, *if you don't leave now, nothing on God's earth will keep me from tearing you apart.*

"It's fine. I'll go." Steven smoothed out his disheveled Armani suit. "I just wish we hadn't met like this, Mr. Cash, but I'm sure I'll see you again."

*****

"Dillyn, you should have let me call the cops on that bastard, or at the very least, allowed Ben to beat the crap out of him," Palmer said.

"You know TNZ would have had this entire encounter all over their website. I was trying to protect everyone."

Dillyn crossed her arms. She was right, and her friends knew it.

Dillyn walked over to Ben. She couldn't look at him. She was too embarrassed. Dillyn whispered, "I'm sorry."

"You don't have anything to be sorry for." It took some time for Ben to calm down. He was pissed for her. But what pissed him off more was that he couldn't help noticing Dillyn was much too calm. As if Steven acting violent was a regular thing.

Dillyn could see that Ben's knuckles were bleeding. She moved to lift his hand. "We should take care of this."

Palmer and Cat glanced knowingly at each other. "We're going to go back into the study. If you need us, holler."

"Thanks, Cat." Dillyn watched as her friends left the room.

After they were gone, Ben turned to Dillyn. He placed the tip of his finger underneath her chin and lifted her head until she had no choice but to face him. "Are you okay?"

Her eyes were still shimmering. "I don't know." She tried to turn away, but Ben wouldn't allow it. "I'm so embarrassed."

"You have nothing to be embarrassed about."

Dillyn couldn't stop thinking about Steven calling her a *slut* and a *liar*. How could he say such things when he knew her? Steven knew almost everything about her. Had he always felt that way? Dillyn just knew Ben had to be wondering why Steven would say such vile things. Dillyn felt ill. She was sick to her stomach.

"Your knuckles are bleeding. We should take care of that."

Dillyn was clearly out of it. She had started repeating herself. "How about I take care of you?" Ben asked. Without looking, he knew his knuckles had fared better than Dillyn's emotional state.

"I know you must have a million questions."

"Actually, just the one you never answered." Ben paused. "Are you okay?"

Dillyn hunched her shoulders. "I'm not falling apart, so that's something."

"No. You're not, and I won't let you."

"Why are you being so sweet? If you knew the real me, you would run fast and far."

Ben used the pad of his thumb to caress her cheek. "I already told you, I don't run. But I do listen. When you're ready to talk, I'll be here."

Dillyn wanted to believe him. The tenderness in his eyes told her she should. Dillyn nibbled on her inner lip. She sighed and glanced down as a tear drop spilled onto his knuckle. "Let me take care of your hand before it gets infected."

Ben just wanted to pull her into his arms and make all of

160

her pain go away. Instead, he allowed her to lead him. Ben followed Dillyn past the library, the family room, and the kitchen. He didn't ask where she was taking him until they started to climb the stairs. "Where are we going?"

"I have some peroxide and stuff in my room, and it's private. We can talk there." Watery eyes looked up into his. There was something between them, and Dillyn didn't think it was fair to let Ben get close to her if he didn't know her full story. "I want to tell you everything."

Chapter 21

Ben hadn't been in a woman's bedroom in a very long time. When he entered Dillyn's room, he wasn't surprised at what he found. Her suite suited her personality–soft and classy with a tinge of edge. The walls were something close to a pale pink. She had decorated in soft shades of grays and greens with splashes of darker shades of pink throughout. There were also candles of various sizes on almost every flat surface in the room. Everywhere Ben turned, there were freshly cut white roses. The lemony scent was fragrant but not too strong. White roses. He made a mental note of that. Ben continued to look around. He reared his head back slightly when his eyes landed on Dillyn's bed. He was more than a little surprised at the size. It was much too big for her. Ben could imagine Dillyn getting lost underneath the covers. A naked Dillyn flashed through his mind. *Pull up, Ben.* He had to fight to keep his thoughts from going to places it shouldn't have. She wanted to talk, but Ben's brain failed to pass that information on to his libido.

The energy in Dillyn's room was nothing short of soothing. Ben figured that was intentional—to create her own personal oasis.

Dillyn chewed on her lower lip, her nervousness on display, as she pointed Ben toward the sitting area. "Have a seat on the sofa while I grab the first aid kit."

Ben sat down on the sofa, looking around and taking stock of the room.

Dillyn came out of the bathroom carrying a little white box with the Red Cross. She sat next to him as she opened it.

"You know this isn't necessary, right? It's no big deal."

Ben gazed at Dillyn, but she was busying herself with the kit. She was going through a lot of trouble for basically a few scratches on his knuckles.

"You're hurt because of me, and I just want to fix it. I want to . . ." Her voice trailed off.

Ben took her hands in his. "What? What do you want to do?"

"I just want to make everything better, but I swear, I can't escape."

"I thought you'd already escaped. Summer is your own piece of heaven, remember?" Ben's smile was reassuring.

"It's not that simple. Steven's in my head."

"Kick his ass out."

"I want to, but it's hard." Dillyn couldn't look him in the eyes. "I know you heard what he called me."

"I heard a selfish prick trying to hurt you. I didn't take any of the things Steven said seriously, and you shouldn't either." Ben took the box out of her hands and placed it on the table. "I've only known you a short while, but any man who would let you go isn't very smart."

His words had a surprising effect on Dillyn. She needed to hear them. Without thinking or warning, Dillyn leaned in and kissed him.

It was clear by Ben's nonreaction that he wasn't interested. Almost immediately, Dillyn regretted her actions. "Oh, God. I'm sorry. I-I . . . I shouldn't have . . ." *Why did I go for a kiss when what I really wanted was his warmth and strength? Because the physical is your default.*

Ben held her gaze for just a moment before gently pulling her close. "I want to kiss you. I've thought about it a thousand times, but I'm not sure that's what you need right now."

163

Dillyn felt the sting of his rejection and shot up out of her seat. She started pacing and panicking. *You tell the man you're not a slut only to behave like one.* "I'm sorry. I don't know what I was thinking. I just—"

"Dillyn, it's okay." Ben got up and placed his hands on her shoulders, gently turning her around to face him. "Talk to me—or not. It's up to you. I've got nothing but time."

Dillyn looked at everything and everywhere but Ben.

Gently, he used the tips of his fingers to turn her face toward him. "I see you. The real you, and I think you're amazing."

No one had ever said anything like that to her before. Ben almost gave Dillyn the courage she needed. "You might not say that if you knew why Steven said those things to me."

"Steven and his thoughts don't matter. But if you want me to know, then tell me."

Dillyn hated to admit it, but she wanted to be loved completely, flaws and all. That meant Ben needed to know her ugly truth.

"However, I do wish you would have allowed Cat to call the police or at the very least let me whoop his ass." Ben's joke didn't have the desired effect. Dillyn was so tense he was afraid she'd pop a blood vessel.

She wrung her hands together. "Both of those things would have been problematic."

"I would have felt better." Ben chuckled. "Why didn't you let either of us do it?"

"Steven is a high-profile attorney in New York and you . . ." *Are a high-profile environmentalist.* "Can you imagine the press?"

Ben took her explanation the wrong way. "Are you still hung up on him?"

164

"No! Ohmygawd. No. It's just, you shouldn't have to suffer the public scrutiny of being associated with someone like me."

"Someone like you? Someone who is kind, thoughtful, and loyal to a fault?"

"I don't see myself that way."

"How do you see yourself?"

Dillyn shrugged. "Steven says I'm a slut and a liar."

That man was really in her head. Ben hated that for her. "I don't give a fuck about what Steven thinks. What do you think?"

"I just want to be a good person." Her eyes were watery. Dillyn had to fight to find the words. "I want to have love and give love."

Ben didn't care about her past, but he didn't understand how the woman standing in front of him was so amazing and did not know it. Ben lowered his head and allowed his lips to hover just a fraction of an inch away from hers. "I think you're a good person, and I want you to have love too." Ben couldn't help himself. He was too close. This time, he moved in for a kiss.

Just before his lips connected with hers, Dillyn whispered, "I know I kissed you first, but this can't be a good idea."

"Probably not." He knew that she was filled with too many emotions and was nervous. Hell, so was he.

Dillyn's heart started racing. She began to feel warm all over, and her anxiety levels shot through the roof. *It's only a kiss. You just kissed him! Why are you trippin? What's the difference from when you kissed him? Control. You had it. Now he has it.* Warning bells started going off in her head. *I can't do this.* Dillyn was on the verge of a full-on panic attack. She gave his chest a gentle push. Dillyn spoke his name in a breathless whisper. "Ben, I . . ."

He felt her entire body tense up. Ben was confused.

165

Hadn't she just tried to kiss me? He knew damn well he was moving too fast. *Slow down, cowboy.* Ben loosened his hold and pulled back to look at her. There was genuine fear in Dillyn's eyes. He had to fix this. Immediately, he dropped his arms to his sides. "I'm sorry. I know it's too soon, and I would never try to force you—"

"No. Gawd. That's not it." Dillyn shook her head adamantly.

"Tell me what's wrong, and I'll fix it."

Dillyn was falling for Ben fast and hard. If she had a shred of a chance of having a real relationship with him, that would mean she had to be wholly honest. She dropped her head and stared at her feet. Her words were mumbled.

Ben couldn't make out anything Dillyn was trying to say. He took her by the hand and sat back down on the couch. Ben pulled her onto his lap. Patiently, he asked once more. "Let's try this again. Tell me, what's wrong?"

Dillyn was laser focused on her hands. They were clasped together tightly in her lap. Nervously, she chewed on her lower lip. Finally, she took a deep breath and started talking. "I'm not like normal women."

Ben wanted to kill Steven. That man did his damnedest to break her. If Dillyn allowed him, Ben would do anything to build her back up. "No. You're not. You're perfect."

A tear rolled down her cheek. "I'm so far from perfect it's not even funny."

"You're not looking at the same woman that I am."

"You only see what can be seen."

Gently, he prodded. "Then tell me about the parts I can't."

"I'm not . . . I'm not very good at relationships. I'm especially not good at . . . sex."

166

"First, I find that hard to believe." He pushed a wayward strand of hair out of her face. "Second, I find that hard to believe."

"It's true. I don't physically respond right, and you might as well know that sooner rather than later. It's also the reason Steven called me a slut."

"Dillyn, I don't care what Steven—"

"I know you don't care what he thinks, but Steven's not completely wrong. He knows me better than anyone."

Ben thought about her words. "I want to take that position. I want to know you better than anyone, starting from this moment. Let's start over. Let's pretend that asshole didn't show up at your door today, and I got an opportunity to tell you why I came over."

"Ben, we can't bury our heads in the sand."

He ignored her. Ben was going to take the long road to her heart. He needed to get back to the basics. Ben asked an easier question but one he wanted an answer to. "Why didn't you return my call?"

Dillyn brought her eyes to his. "I thought about returning your call."

"Why didn't you?"

"You've got eyes. I clearly have a lot to figure out."

"That's fair." Ben could be patient. He would wait for Dillyn, but he had to know if he had a real shot at something with her. "But you did want to call me?"

She whispered, "Ben, I just kissed you five minutes ago."

"Was that really about me?"

"I want it to be about you."

"I can only imagine how difficult it is to open up your heart again. It isn't easy for me either, but I think you're worth it.

167

I hope you think I'm worth it too."

"Ben, I am so into you. And I wish . . . I wish I knew how to show you properly."

Ben caressed the side of her face. "You just did by telling me how you feel." He was trying his hardest to work out what was holding Dillyn back. He couldn't figure it out. "What am I missing?" He tried to pretend like there wasn't an elephant in the room, but he couldn't. "What did Steven do to make you feel like this?"

Dillyn glanced up, then back down. She was just too ashamed. It was impossible to answer his question and look him in the eyes. Dillyn blew out an exaggerated breath. "Steven had many faults, but he was also the first man to show me kindness and compassion. He proved that while I may never actually enjoy the intimacies that happen within a relationship, I could survive it." Dillyn didn't dare look at Ben's reaction.

He pondered her words. Ben hoped to be thoughtful and not condescending. "He missed the mark. He should have shown you that touching, kissing, or making love is about a much deeper connection than just the physical act."

Dillyn's tears started up again.

Ben hated to see her cry and wiped her tears away. "I can't explain it, but I already feel connected to you in both big and small ways. I won't put any pressure on you, and I'll wait until you're ready."

Dillyn swallowed. "What if I'm never ready? What if I can't . . ."

Ben cracked a small smile. "Damn, I guess that would mean I'd have to wait forever."

"You wouldn't."

He touched his forehead to hers. "I would."

"You don't deserve that." Dillyn swallowed the lump in her throat. "You also deserve one hundred percent of the truth."

Ben could see a vein pulsing at the base of her throat. It was beating fast. He remained quiet to allow Dillyn the space to say what she needed to get off her chest.

"Steven wasn't the first man to touch me. I was . . ." Her voice broke. "I was nine the first time I had sex."

It took Ben's brain a minute to process her words.

"My parents were addicts." Dillyn had only ever told Steven the sordid details of her childhood. She'd only told him to explain why she wasn't very passionate. Dillyn suspected that Palmer might have had her suspicions about some form of abuse, but she never said anything. Dillyn had spent years in therapy just to get to this level of healthy.

Subtly, Ben held Dillyn a little tighter. *There it is. The missing piece.* He wanted to lose his shit. He wanted to make someone pay. What kind of monster would do that? Instead of acting on his rage, Ben remained still. Dillyn needed him to keep calm. This moment was about her, not him.

Dillyn continued to tell him the story of her own personal hell. "It was only the first of many until my dad and my mom changed focus. They realized they could make a lot more money selling children than selling drugs. Drugs were actually more dangerous because my parents were addicts. They always seemed to use the product instead of selling it. When the money came up short, I was used to make up the difference." Dillyn was sobbing. "It didn't stop until they were busted for sex trafficking. I think I was about fourteen."

Ben tightened his hold. "That should have never happened to you. I'm so so sorry." Ben didn't know what to do, so he just continued to hold her while she released years upon years of pain and suffering. His shirt was soaked. It all made sense. Now he understood why she wasn't able to kiss him at the booth.

Dillyn spoke through muffled cries. "There was so much damage done to me physically. Believe it or not, I was considered one of the lucky ones. The doctors were able to repair most of it but . . . but certain parts of me just don't work. I mean, all of my lady parts work. I just have a hard time emotionally. Add to it two miscarriages, and I'm sure that's why Steven cheated. I couldn't be the wife he needed."

Ben understood how Dillyn probably had to disconnect mentally in order to get through sex. He had been naive in understanding her need for survival. While it was painful to hear and impossible to process, Ben was glad that Dillyn trusted him with her story. He lifted her head from the crook of his neck and cradled her face within his hands. "Thank you."

Dillyn still looked like a scared little girl. In some ways, Ben guessed she was. He tried to give her a reassuring smile and placed a tender kiss on the side of her head. He could tell that she was emotionally spent. "I don't know about you, but I'm exhausted. Can we get in your bed?"

Dillyn tensed somewhat. It was only slight, but Ben felt it. "I promise all we'll do is sleep. I'm just not ready to let you go."

Slowly, Dillyn nodded. She would love to be held by him.

Ben stood with her in his arms and made the short walk from the sofa to the bed. He was so careful with Dillyn. He handled her as if she were the most precious thing on earth. Gently, Ben deposited her into the center of the bed. He kicked off his shoes but left on his clothes. He climbed into bed and pulled her body close but not touching. He wasn't sure Dillyn was ready for that just yet.

Eventually, Dillyn relaxed fully. It didn't take long before

the comfort of being in Ben's arms lured her into the most peaceful sleep she'd had in years.

Chapter 22

After midnight, Dillyn woke to a heavy arm draped around her middle. She craned her head around to find Ben sound asleep. Dillyn took this time to study him. He was calm and relaxed. Dillyn didn't know when or how Ben moved them underneath the covers, but she didn't miss the fact that their bodies weren't touching. Dillyn was sure that Ben took extra care to ensure they didn't.

Dillyn flipped over onto her side and gently caressed the side of his face. It wasn't surprising that he'd considered her needs before his own. He wasn't a taker. Ben was strong, steady, consistent, and hadn't shown himself to be the type of man to run away. If anything, Ben ran toward the fire, not away from it. He was authentic, and Dillyn knew it. How she could trust him with her life and not her body was crazy. *I want to know what it's like to make love to this man.*

It was time to take a leap of faith. She whispered his name into the dark. "Ben."

It didn't take much to wake him. Ben cracked open an eye. His voice was groggy from sleep. "You good?"

Dillyn's heart was going crazy. "Can you show me?"

Ben could hear the tremble in her voice and knew what she was asking. "I meant what I said. We don't have to rush. It's enough to lie here next to you."

Ben didn't realize how loud silence could be until Dillyn finally responded.

She sat up on her elbow. "It's not enough for me."

"Dillyn—"

172

"I trust you, and I know you can show me how sex is supposed to feel."

Ben sat up too. He could hear the earnestness in her voice. "Sex with you is impossible."

Dillyn's stomach dropped. *Does he think I'm too damaged to sleep with?*

Ben could tell by the look on her face that she didn't understand what he meant. "It's hard to have sex when you're in love with someone. When we finally come together, I will show you the difference between making love and having sex. I want to replace those ghosts and make your body burn."

Dillyn hung on to his every word. "I want that too." A shy smile broadened on her face. "You're in love with me?"

"I knew you were the one after our first kiss. I denied it, but I felt something the first night we had dinner underneath the stars."

Dillyn felt the same energy that night too. She spoke softly. "I *need* you."

Ben reached out to Dillyn, gently pulling her close and lifting her face upward. He pressed his lips against hers. His kiss was full of want and need. Ben found the strength to pull back. "As much as I want you, we should take our time." Ben wanted Dillyn, but he couldn't think of himself. He had to put her first.

Dillyn got up on her knees and sandwiched Ben's face between her hands. She wanted him to know that she was serious. "Please, make love to me."

"Are you really sure?"

Dillyn was terrified, but she was sure of Ben. "I've never been more certain of anything."

Ben hadn't ever wanted a woman as much as he wanted Dillyn. He reached for her hand and placed it over his heart. It was beating fast. "This is all you. You make me feel this way. If we do this . . . you've got to promise that you'll stop me at any point you start to feel uncomfortable."

Dillyn nodded. "I promise." This wasn't the first time she'd had sex, but it felt like it. Dillyn didn't want to disappoint Ben. She didn't want to disappoint herself. But was it possible? Dillyn hoped so. Ben's willingness to be patient allowed her to make the final decision.

Ben was determined to make tonight all about her. He planned to show her that she didn't need to disconnect with him. He helped Dillyn remove her shirt and jeans. She was left wearing a silky-golden bra and panty set. The moon bathed her in its light. Dillyn had the smoothest, softest brown skin. "You're beautiful."

Her entire body blushed. "You still have your clothes on. I feel so overdressed."

"We can't have that." Ben's eyes never left hers as he quickly removed his clothing.

Dillyn sucked in a breath. She knew that Ben was fit, but his body was ridiculous. His muscles were impossibly well defined. She could trace every single ab with her fingertips. Her gaze moved lower until it stopped at his semi-erect penis.

She shivered.

Ben was well endowed. *Like really, really well endowed.* Dillyn didn't even think he was fully aroused. She was intimidated by his size and length.

The mattress dipped when Ben got back into the bed. Dillyn had to take a deep breath when she saw the intensity of his gaze. There was no denying it. Pure desire lit his eyes.

Ben watched Dillyn follow his every movement as he made his way over to her. He wanted to see her eyes change from wide-eyed and scared to just wild for him. That was Ben's singular mission, even if that meant he would deprive himself of complete sexual satisfaction.

Ben pressed Dillyn's body into his, so they touched from thigh to chest. Ben had been dying to kiss the patch of skin at the base of her neck. He wanted to love on her nipples and slide into her body all night long. Ben intended to make Dillyn his is in every possible way. He would start his takeover with her neck and wouldn't stop until his lips had touched every single inch of her body. Ben would make damn sure that Dillyn's only memory was of him.

His voice was filled with need as he leaned in close. "I'm going to kiss you here."

At a loss for words, Dillyn could only nod.

Ben placed his lips on the side of her neck.

Dillyn held her breath. Her hands felt clammy. Bees replaced the butterflies in the pit of her stomach. Her heart was already racing, but this wasn't the good kind. They were all telltale signs of her anxiety rising. *Please. Not this time. I can do this.*

Ben felt Dillyn tense up. He spoke softly as he placed gentle kisses up and down the column of her neck. "Breathe. I've got you. I've always got you."

"I-I . . ." Dillyn wasn't sure that she could.

"You're safe with me," Ben whispered. "I promise I won't hurt you." He ran the tips of his fingers up and down the length of her spine, hoping it would have a calming effect while planting little kisses against her neck.

Have faith in him. Dillyn closed her eyes and took several deep breaths, and slowly released each of them.

Ben waited as he continued to speak lovingly to her soul. "I won't go any further until you're ready." He needed Dillyn to show him a sign. Until then, he would continue to caress her back and take pleasure in tasting her heated skin.

Finally, after several agonizing moments, Ben received the signal he was looking for. Dillyn exhaled. She started to breathe. He knew this was a big step for her, and Ben would take it with her. Unfortunately, her breaths were still short and choppy.

"You want me to stop?"

Dillyn was a little breathless. "No. Please, don't stop."

That was all the encouragement Ben needed. Dillyn still wasn't relaxed enough for him but getting there. Ben dragged his mouth away from Dillyn's neck to her lips. "I'm going to kiss you." He intended to telegraph his every movement so that Dillyn could stop him at any stage where she might start to feel uncomfortable.

This time his kiss was a little different. He parted Dillyn's lips with his tongue. Ben was pleased that she let him inside. His kiss was hot, soft, and moist, maybe even a little demanding. At first, Dillyn was tentative. *We have to work on that*. If he had to make love to her mouth all night, they wouldn't move to the next step until she was able to let go and kiss him with the same intensity, want, and need that he had for her. Ben was seeking another level of closeness, and his kiss was just the start.

He spoke into their kiss. "You taste so good. I can't wait to sample the rest of you."

Dillyn trembled. His words were magical. They made her feel . . . *excited*. Dillyn refused to allow any thoughts to enter her head other than Ben. She focused on the way his skin felt underneath her hands. Dillyn breathed in the musky scent of his cologne. It was mixed with Ben's natural scent, and the combination made her body heat in ways it had never done before.

Dillyn sigh.

Ben wasn't sure if it was a sound of contentment or pleasure. Both were good. It added more fuel to Ben's fire, but it still was not enough. One thing Ben could never be accused of was not being thorough.

Ben reached behind her and unhooked her bra, then slowly pushed the straps down before wrapping Dillyn up in his arms and continuing his loving onslaught of kisses.

Dillyn was feeling dizzy. No one had ever kissed her the way Ben was kissing her, and it intoxicated her. She began to return his kisses at his same enthusiasm.

Ben's cock twitched. It was sandwiched between them and had thickened and lengthened as their bodies pressed tightly together. It was a sure sign of how much he wanted her. Ben wasn't sure how far Dillyn was ready to go, but he hoped his arousal didn't scare her away.

Dillyn wasn't in her head. She was fully present in the moment, so when pre-cum dripped from the head of Ben's cock, she was hopeful because she wasn't turned off. Not only was she not turned off, but Ben's touches, his kisses—all of it—made her body react in new ways. Dillyn was beginning to heat from her core.

"Ben . . . I'm hot."

He didn't feel her body tense like it did when she was about to have a panic attack. He murmured against her lips, "You want me to stop?" It would kill him if she did, but he would.

"No. Don't stop." Dillyn leaned deeper into their kiss, snaking her arms around Ben's neck. "Not that kind of heat but the kind that makes you wet." Dillyn pressed her thighs together, hoping to ease the building ache.

Ben got the message loud and clear. Dillyn was turned on enough that she might not shut down when he filled her. She was almost ready to trust him with her body completely

He tore his lips away from hers. "Can I touch you?"

"Yes." Her response came out on a gasp.

Gently, Ben pulled Dillyn down and onto the mattress. He lay down beside her, not sure if Dillyn was ready for him to settle between her thighs. "I didn't say where."

Dillyn squirmed. "I don't care."

"You sure?"

She was lost in the feeling of him—his touch, his kiss, his voice, his *everything*. "Yesss . . ."

Ben grinned as he quickly removed the last barrier of clothing separating their bodies. He slipped a hand between her thighs. "Mmm . . . You are wet, but not wet enough."

Ben dragged a single finger down the center of her sex and then back up.

Dillyn's back arched up into his hands. Her breathing became uneven. "Ben," she said his name in a breathy whisper. "I'm . . . I . . . ache."

"Good," Ben repeated the same motion over and over until he had Dillyn squirming uncontrollably. He was rewarded with the evidence of her arousal. Her cream covered his hands.

It was a miracle Ben hadn't already exploded from the sheer anticipation of being inside her, and that was before he inserted a digit into her opening. Slowly, he pulled his finger out only to reinsert it.

Dillyn lifted her hips off the mattress, searching for more, wanting and needing more.

Ben inserted a second digit.

Dillyn's head turned from side to side on the pillow as she bit down on her lower lip.

Ben watched Dillyn's face. Her eyes were closed, but she

178

looked like a woman ready to take the next step. He continued to make love to her with his fingers. He pulled them out only to thrust them back inside, alternating between slow and gentle, harder and faster.

Dillyn cried out when Ben found her g-spot.

She was ready. Ben moved in between her thighs and positioned himself just outside her opening. "Dillyn, look at me."

Her eyes had been closed but fluttered open.

"I want you to watch me. To look into my eyes when I enter you. I want you to know who it is inside you when we become one, and you become mine."

Dillyn nodded.

"Are you sure you're ready?" Ben asked one last time. If she said no, he'd be crushed but would respect her decision.

Dillyn lifted her legs, tenting her knees, and caressed the side of his face. "You said you would chase away the ghosts. I trust that you will, but more than anything, I want you to show me how it feels to make love."

Ben didn't take the amount of trust she gave him lightly.

Dillyn was nervous that she wouldn't be able to give Ben what he needed, but she wanted to try. She wanted to give him everything.

They held each other's gaze as Ben guided himself into the warmth of her body until he was fully seated.

Her heat surrounded him. His own eyes closed from pure pleasure. It had been so long. Dillyn was tight. *So tight.* She felt so damn good. Ben's natural instinct was to pound into her, but he had to reign those feelings in.

Ben knew Dillyn would feel amazing, but he couldn't imagine how good the reality was. Beads of sweat dotted his forehead as he fought for control. His eyes opened. He needed to see

Dillyn's face.

His voice was strained. "Are you okay?"

Dillyn's eyes glistened with unshed tears as a tear spilled over onto her cheek. "I'm better than okay. For the first time in my life, I'm making love."

Her smile was radiant.

Ben kissed away her tears as he began to move in and out of her. When her muscles clenched around him, he lost all restraint. Still, Ben did his best to make Dillyn feel beautiful and well-loved.

The power of their orgasm was nothing like either had ever experienced. Long after Dillyn had fallen asleep in his arms, Ben lay awake. He made a vow that he would love and protect her for the rest of his life. She may need some time to realize how she felt about him, but Ben knew. He'd always known.

Chapter 23

Ben faced away from Dillyn as she got out of her truck and walked up into his yard. She had no idea what he was doing, but he was shirtless and an incredible sight to behold. *Damn. He sure does wear those jeans well.* In this unguarded moment, Dillyn inhaled slowly and tilted her head slightly while admiring the view. *What has this man done to me?* The impossible. He'd awakened a monster. Over the past couple of weeks, all Dillyn wanted to do was be with him. She went from dreading being touched to wanting his hands all over all the time. Dillyn craved him. Every time they made love, Ben helped Dillyn learn more about the things that turned her on. Dillyn liked being on top. The expression on his face when she rode him hard made her feel powerful. The reverse cowgirl was pretty fun too. Dillyn caught herself in mid-thought. She didn't seem to have any control over them. She smiled inwardly. With a slight look of guilt on her face, Dylan glanced about as if she'd been caught checking him out. Luckily, everyone was still inside. She giggled like a schoolgirl. *Seriously, a body like his should be against the law.* "Stop it, Dillyn," she chided herself yet continued to study him.

The sun was hot and bearing down on Ben, and every single sinewy muscle glistened from sweat. Ben took his shovel and dug it into the ground. Each time the metal connected with the earth, his muscles tightened. Dillyn began to negotiate with herself. *Maybe I could talk him into a quickie.*

Steven had been dedicated to his fitness. He spent five days a week at the gym, but he never looked like Ben. Dillyn rolled her eyes. Why Steven popped into her head was a mystery.

181

Dillyn continued to stare as she gave Ben a slow but thorough once-over from the top of his head to the bottom of his booted feet. She didn't miss an inch. Dillyn whispered to herself, "He is absolutely perfect." There wasn't an ounce of fat on him. Without warning, Ben turned but was so engrossed in his task that he hadn't spotted her. His abs were so rock-hard they didn't even look real, but Dillyn knew better. She'd run her hands all over them. *That man is pure muscle. Look at his arms.* Yet, he could be so tender. She loved the way his strong arms held her. Dillyn nibbled on her lower lip, thinking about how it felt to have his body on top of hers. And how good it felt when Ben positioned himself between her thighs. The mere thought made her body throb. Dillyn pressed her lips together in a firm line to prevent a needy sigh from escaping. How she could still be so needy after their marathon love-making session the night before and early this morning was beyond her.

Selah bounded out the front doors. "Hey, Dillyn! Sorry, I'm running late."

At the sound of Dillyn's name, Ben glanced up.

"Hey! It's not a problem." Dillyn lied, "I just walked up."

Ben's ocean blue eyes connected with her rich chocolate ones. He used his forearm to wipe the sweat from his brow and started to walk over. Dillyn was glowing. He hoped he was the reason. The past couple of weeks with her had been fantastic.

Her eyes never left his as he made his way over. There was a hint of a smile at the edge of her lips as if she had a secret that was just for him. He wrapped one arm around her waist and pulled her body into his. "Hey, beautiful." Dillyn looked much too kissable. Ben couldn't resist. He lowered his head and covered her mouth with his.

Shamelessly, Dillyn kissed him back.

After a few minutes, Selah cleared her throat. "Hello? Sister standing here."

Ben and Dillyn broke a part. "Sorry," Dillyn said sheepishly.

"I'm not." Ben tried to kiss Dillyn again, but she moved out of his way.

Selah glanced between them. Ben was her brother, and it was gross to think of him in *that* way, but the sexual tension between him and Dillyn was hard to ignore. "Dillyn and I are going into town for a few things. We shouldn't be gone long."

"Sounds good to me."

Ben leaned in for another kiss, but Selah pulled Dillyn away. "Let's go before we have to postpone this little excursion."

Dillyn laughed. "I'll see you in a few hours."

Ben nodded. "Okay."

Selah whipped her head around to stare at him as if he were a two-headed monster. "Okay? No . . . when are you coming back? What are you going to get? Who is all going to be there?"

"Nope."

Someone could have knocked Selah over with a feather. "Nope?"

"Nope. You're with Dillyn." He glanced at her and smiled. "I'm sure you'll be fine."

Ben had caused Dillyn to have many wet dreams but watching the banter between brother and sister warmed her heart and reminded Dillyn that Ben was more than just the star of her sexual escapades. He was a thoughtful and caring man.

Dillyn's hands were dying to touch his heated skin. However, she kept them to herself by linking her fingers together and holding her hands behind her back.

"When y'all come back, maybe I can throw a few steaks

on the grill."

"Are you asking me to dinner?" The tone in Dillyn's voice changed. She turned her head and tried to speak low enough so that Selah couldn't hear. "Or are you asking me to dinner *dinner*?" She hoped he didn't miss the innuendo in her voice. Dillyn wasn't good at it yet, but she liked flirting with Ben. She wasn't even sure if she was doing it right. Flirting was more of a Cat and Palmer thing.

He leaned over, whispering into her ear, "I'm talkin' dinner *dinner* and dessert."

Dillyn backed away, grinning from ear to ear. Her voice still sounded sultry. "I do love a good thick steak and dessert, so that would be a yes."

Selah opened the door of the truck just in time to hear Dillyn's comeback. *Gross.* Selah hoisted herself up on the running board. "For the record, I have a date tonight. Don't worry about making enough for me. Now, can we *go*?"

Dillyn turned away from Ben and walked toward an impatient Selah. Dillyn's stomach was doing somersaults in anticipation of her evening. They would be alone since Lucas was out of town until tomorrow morning. "Sorry," she said meekly.

"Honestly, it's nice to see you and my brother flirting. Gross but nice."

"Flirting! We weren't flirting." The words rang hollow even to Dillyn.

Selah laughed. "Yeah, you were. You think I missed all that sexual innuendo? *Puhleeese.* I heard it loud and clear."

Selah's laughter faded as they drove away from the house and pulled out onto the road. "That's interesting."

"What?" Dillyn glanced over at her.

"I don't know. It feels like I see that silver car behind us

184

every time I turn around."

Dillyn looked up into her rearview mirror. "Is it anybody you know? Someone from Frank's?"

"Hmm . . . no. I don't recognize the car."

Dillyn stopped at a red light. When it turned green, she pulled off and kept straight while the silver car made a right turn.

Selah sighed. "Great. I'm just being a paranoid freak. I've been binging serial killer movies on Netflix for the past week. Maybe I should start watching *The Golden Girls*." She laughed. "That car was obviously not following us. It's just that Summer is small. We all know everybody. You see someone who is an out-of-towner and start to think all kinds of weird things."

Dillyn didn't think Selah was paranoid. She had noticed that same silver car around town too. She hoped it was innocent and not tied to Steven's empty threat. At least, Dillyn hoped it was an empty threat.

"So, are you going on a date with that one guy you met a little bit ago?"

Selah smiled mischievously. "Yes. Finally. It's been two long weeks of texts and phone calls. We FaceTimed the other day. We just click on so many levels, and my God is he's so cute. I can't wait to meet him in person."

"So, you *actually* saw him?"

"Yep. I know you're concerned, but I googled him. He's legit."

"That's good to know. What is his name?"

"Thomas Markum. We're going to meet at the Roadhouse for dinner."

Dillyn frowned. "I've never heard of that place. Is it close?"

"It's on the outskirts of town."

Warning bells started going off in Dillyn's head. Only she wasn't sure if her concern was due to Steven's threats more so than being realistic. Online dating was a thing. Many people did it safely. But there were also those *other* stories.

Selah could see the skepticism on Dillyn's face and wanted to reassure her. "I promise. I've done my research. Plus, if we met somewhere around here, it would get back to Ben and Lucas before our meal even came out from the kitchen. They would just so happen to show up and order steak."

"You're probably right." Dillyn still felt uneasy about it.

"If it'll make you feel better, let me call him, and you can talk with him."

"That's not a bad idea."

Selah punched in Thomas's number, and his face popped up on the screen almost immediately. "Hey, beautiful."

"Hey!" Selah rushed her words before Thomas said something embarrassing in front of Dillyn. "My friend would like to meet you. You got a sec?"

He shrugged. "Um . . . yeah. Of course." Selah turned her phone toward Dillyn.

"Hey. I hear you are taking Selah out to dinner tonight?"

"Yes, ma'am."

He looked around Selah's age and harmless enough, but Dillyn knew all too well looks could be deceiving. "I've got just one quick question?" Dillyn couldn't help herself. "What brought you to Summer?"

"Work. I'm doing some construction on the new bridge just across the way." Thomas flashed her an innocent smile. "I'm *single.* I'm twenty-four. I was born and raised in New Jersey as a devout Catholic. I'm a Scarlet Knight, and I have no political affiliations." He laughed. "Did that just about cover it?"

186

Dillyn laughed. "Children?"

"None but would like a few . . . way, way down the line."

Dillyn couldn't see anything wrong with him. "Okay, but just know that Selah is very, very special to a lot of people." Dillyn turned thoughtful eyes toward her. "So have a good time. But just remember, Selah also has *three* kick-ass brothers who will hunt you down and murder you if anything untoward happens."

Thomas' smile fell away, and Selah rolled her eyes. "Okay. That's good enough." Selah turned her phone back toward her. "I think you passed the test with Dillyn. I'll call you later after we finish running our errands."

After she disconnected, Dillyn couldn't help but ask, "Do you have the tracker on your phone turned on?"

"Tracker?" Selah laughed. "I don't think I'll need that. You just spoke to him. Thomas is a nice guy."

"I'm sure you're right. He seems like a nice guy, but I don't trust very easily. I keep mine on just in case."

"You do?"

"I sure do."

Selah seemed to take her words to heart. "I'm not even sure if I have one on my phone."

Dillyn smiled. "Everybody does. Can I see it?"

"Yeah, sure." Selah handed Dillyn her phone after they pulled into the strip mall's parking lot.

Dillyn's fingers moved lightning fast as she punched in numbers and brought up screens Selah had never seen.

Selah was in awe. "Wow, you must be good with computers and stuff. I have no idea what you just did."

"I just adjusted a few codes. I'm sure everything on your date will be fine, but it never hurts to be cautious." Dillyn wished she didn't get paranoid when meeting new people. "Just press this if you're ever in distress."

"What is that?"

Dillyn shrugged. "If you can't dial 9-1-1, you can still get emergency calls out if you hit that button. But if someone tries to take your phone, remove the SIM card. It'll send out an emergency signal to the police and stuff that can't be tracked or traced."

"Oh." Selah didn't understand what all of that meant.

"It's techie stuff, and know you can always call me."

"I'm starting to think you're worse than my brothers."

"Maybe. I've just . . ." Dillyn stopped short of telling her why she was so paranoid. "Be careful, okay?"

Selah could tell from Dillyn's expression that she'd experienced something traumatic. One day, Selah hoped she might be willing to share it with her. Selah's face softened. "I will. I promise, and if it puts you a little more at ease, I have mace."

The serious energy in the truck immediately changed. Dillyn laughed. "Mace is *always* a good idea. You can never go wrong with that."

Chapter 24

Dillyn didn't spend the night with Ben. It almost felt strange to sleep in bed alone since she hadn't done it over the past couple of weeks. Dillyn needed to get up early to prepare for several virtual meetings with her staff to catch up on a couple of important projects. She had been off-line and only available for emergencies since moving to Summer. Dillyn had left strict instructions not to contact her unless it was critical while she got settled into her new place.

Though she slept in her own bed, it didn't help. Dillyn was dragging. Ben hadn't brought her home till the wee hours of the morning. She currently had her bathroom steamed up like a sauna while standing underneath the hot water from the shower. It cascaded down her body and felt like heaven to her achy muscles. Between Ben and Whisper, Dillyn did not need a cardio workout. She smiled at the thought then stilled. Dillyn thought she'd heard her cell ring while she was in the shower. She shut off the water and stood completely still to listen. Everything was silent. At first, Dillyn didn't hear anything. She opened the glass door with tentative fingers and stepped out of the shower stall. Dillyn reached for a towel and wrapped it around her body. She waited to see if her phone would ring again.

Damn. There it was. Dillyn's eyes closed briefly at the sound after hoping she had imagined it the first time. She hadn't. The tone was different from her regular calls and messages.

Dillyn picked it up from off the sink. There was one message. She tapped in her passcode to unlock the screen. The text was simple. "Call me."

There wasn't a telephone number associated with the text,

but Dillyn knew exactly who it was. She released a pent-up breath. *Everything's been so peaceful. Please God, just a little longer.* Slowly, she lifted her head. Quickly, Dillyn went to her room and got dressed. She threw on a pair of joggers and ran-walked down the steps. The house was quiet save for Cat. She was in the kitchen making coffee. Cat was always up early and didn't miss a thing.

Cat called out to her from the kitchen. "Hey . . . where are you going this early? You've got to give Ben a rest!" Cat said cheekily.

Dillyn plastered on a fake smile. "I left something in my truck. I'll be back in a second." Swiftly, she turned on her heels and walked out of the house. The second Dillyn shut the door, she bounded down the steps and slowly jogged to her truck. Dillyn opened it, got inside, and locked the doors. She glanced around, taking in her surroundings to ensure she wasn't being watched as if it would matter. Dillyn wouldn't be able to see someone with a long-range lens. Getting out of her head, Dillyn placed the call to a number she had dialed so many times before.

The phone didn't finish the first ring before he answered. Dillyn didn't get a chance to speak before he started talking. "Steven's dead."

Dillyn's chest almost caved in. She felt like she'd been submerged in ice water. *Dead?* Her feelings for Steven were complicated, but she didn't want him dead. Dillyn was in complete shock. "Steven's dead?" The words came out hushed. Saying them aloud didn't make the news any more real. Thoughts began to rush inside her head as she struggled to speak. "I-I just saw him a couple of weeks ago!"

"I know."

"Of course you did." Dillyn had flashbacks of their last

conversation. "What happened?"

"We're still trying to figure it out."

"Do you know who would have done something like this?"

"Not yet. The police are on their way to his house."

Dillyn's brain could barely slow down long enough to form a coherent thought. However, one bubbled to the surface. "If the police are on their way to his house, how do you already know he's dead?"

"We have eyes."

In a moment of understanding, Dillyn sat up straight. "You were spying on us?"

There was a long pause before she received an answer. "Not until you left."

Dillyn raised her voice. She didn't believe that for a second. "Why?! Why would you be spying on us?"

There was no admission of guilt, but still, Dillyn received an answer. "We believe Steven may have compromised you."

Dillyn fell silent. He spoke in the present tense, not the past. "Compromised me? How in the world could he have done that?"

"We believe you might have stumbled upon more than just his affair."

Dillyn swallowed hard. "You know about that too? What am I asking? Of course you do. Look, I'm certain that I don't have anything so sensitive someone would want to kill him over. I mostly found pictures, emails, and several offshore banking accounts." Dillyn knew that Steven had been straddling the fence of the law but was skeptical about him being foolish enough to mess around with people who could bring about his death. "I can't believe Steven would have gotten involved in something that would have gotten him killed?" *How can you honestly say that after his warning?*

"What I know is that someone tried to access your account."

Her body went from cold to hot. The hairs on the back of Dillyn's neck stood straight up. Still, she tried to be the voice of reason. "Hackers are always trying to get into my accounts. I haven't had any recent breaches."

"This attempt was different. Much more sophisticated, and they didn't try to hack via your company. They went for your other access."

Dread spread throughout her body. Dillyn knew if Syntax was bringing that up, shit was serious. Dillyn closed her eyes and pinched the bridge of her nose. "Are my friends in danger?"

"We're not sure. That's why we're sending a couple of men over to your place. They'll be working undercover as extra hired hands. They've been assigned to protect you and your friends. But the clock is ticking. Find out what the people who killed Steven wanted, and we'll find out who's behind all of this. Your team is small, but you might want to double and triple check your security."

"My security is tighter than Fort Knox . . . you know that."

"True. But, knowingly or unknowingly, you triggered something and got into some pretty sophisticated systems. Make sure someone didn't plant a back door into yours."

Dillyn's security was so sophisticated even the best hackers in the world couldn't penetrate it. It was also programmed to change every three days. She was confident whatever someone may have wanted from her network . . . they didn't have. That meant not only was she in danger, so was everyone she cared

192

about. The silver car that she and Selah saw the day before popped into her mind. "I'll go through my metadata and get back to you with whatever I find." Dillyn disconnected the call.

She leaned back and rested her head on the headrest. Steven was an adulterer. He broke her heart into a million pieces. He was an asshole and had turned into someone she hadn't recognized, but he didn't deserve to be murdered. The worst part of it all was that Dillyn began to think his death might have been her fault.

Dillyn was completely frazzled after her phone call. The peace and security she had just ten short minutes ago were gone. She was jumpy and began to wonder if any of the people they'd hired in recent days were not who they appeared to be. *Would any of those people want to hurt my friends or me? And, if so, why?* Most of Steven's shady deals had to do with real estate. *What did I miss?* Dillyn would have to go back through her records with a fine-tooth comb. She needed to figure it out and fast because she couldn't allow anyone else to get hurt. Dillyn's business was legit, but no one knew about her role with CyberCom. Not a single soul. CyberCom was one of the eleven unified combatant commands of the United States Department of Defense. Contrary to what people might think about those roles, Dillyn couldn't fight, shoot straight, or run fast, but she was one of the best in cyber warfare and espionage. No one knew about that secret part of her life, which she'd been engaged in over the past twenty years.

A chill went down Dillyn's spine. *Steven knew.* Somehow, he must have found out, which is what probably got him killed. Her friends' and Ben's faces all flashed before her eyes. Dillyn was going to be sick.

Dillyn rushed to her room, locked, and closed the door.

193

She went straight to her walk-in closet. It had already been outfitted into a secure space. As Dillyn powered on her computers and hardware, she could only thank God Syn was sending over protection. Dillyn would have to come up with a cover story to explain their presence, but her main priority was to make sure everyone was safe. Dillyn grabbed her files marked "Steven," sat down in her chair, and got to work. The sooner she figured out what the hell was going on, the safer everyone around her would be.

Chapter 25

L ucas popped his head inside Ben's home office. "Hey. Morning."

Glancing up from his monitor, Ben sipped his coffee. "Morning."

"Dude. Have you seen Selah?"

Ben took a quick look at the time on his cell. "She's probably still in bed. That girl doesn't rise on a Sunday morning before ten."

"Nuh-uh." Lucas shook his head. "Her car was not outside when I got home this morning."

"What time did you get home?"

"I got back to town around four."

Ben frowned. "Are you sure? Did you check her room?"

"Of course, first thing." Lucas rolled his eyes. "Did she stay over at Dillyn's?"

"Dillyn was with me till around two. I know Selah had a date, but she wouldn't stay out all night." Ben picked up his phone and started scrolling through it. "She certainly wouldn't stay out all night and not tell us."

"She had a date? With whom?"

"Thomas Markum."

"Who the hell is that?" Lucas was irritated. "I ain't never heard of him."

"It's a guy she's been talking to for the past couple of weeks."

"Ain't no Markums in Summer. Who the hell is that?"

"He lives in the next town over and moved to the area a

few months ago. He's one of those out-of-towners who came here to work on the bridge."

"You let her go?"

"*Let her* is a pretty strong word." Ben dialed Selah's number. "As much as I want, Selah is grown, and I can't lock her up. Dillyn FaceTimed with him. She thought he was cool."

"Cool my ass. Basically, we don't know this fucker from Adam or his people, and Selah's not home. I'm gonna fuck him up when I see him. That's my sister he's screwing around with."

"Agreed." Ben's call to Selah went directly to voice mail. "Hey, call me when you get this message." Ben disconnected. "We don't exactly have nothing. I made Selah give me his home address and phone number." Ben had programmed Thomas's number into his phone too. He quickly dialed it. It also went to voice mail.

"If we know where he lives, what are we waiting on?"

"Not a damn thing. Let's roll."

*****

It was pouring rain when Ben and Lucas pulled up to their house. They were beside themselves with worry and had spent the better part of four hours trying to locate Selah before finally filing a police report.

"Fuck!" Ben yelled to no one in particular as he got out of his truck and slammed his car door. "Selah's not answering the *gaawdamned* phone, and the address Thomas gave us is bogus."

Lucas was equally worried and frustrated. "Those idiot cops didn't even want to report her as missing. You know they're sitting on their asses eating donuts."

They turned in the direction of blinding headlights pulling up behind Ben's truck. They couldn't see who it was because of the rain and lights. Both prayed it was Selah only to realize that it was Dillyn.

She hopped out of her truck along with Cat and Palmer. They'd raced over to the house as soon as Ben called looking for Selah.

"I think I might be able to help." Dillyn came prepared with her special bag.

Ben had no idea how Dillyn could help in this situation but was willing to cling on to any hope from any direction. He nodded.

As soon as they went into the house, Dillyn headed straight for the dining room and started setting up her equipment.

Everyone watched in awe as Dillyn went to work. Cat and Palmer knew Dillyn was a digital forensics investigator, but they didn't know what that was. And they had never actually seen her work. Lucas turned to Ben, and they both had the same looks on their faces.

Dillyn had her monitors set up in no time flat. Her hands began flying across her keyboard. Everyone's eyes were glued to the screen, but they had no idea what they were watching.

Finally, Ben asked, "Dillyn, what are you doing?"

Dillyn didn't miss a beat as she signed into her systems. "I programmed a tracker on Selah's phone. If she still has it on her, we can pinpoint almost her exact location."

"What's on that other monitor?"

"Thomas was stupid. They FaceTimed in the truck with me."

"What does that mean?" Ben asked. Confusion and worry clouded his features.

Dillyn explained as she worked. "Everything is out there. I just have to type in the right information to grab it."

"Make it make sense, Dillyn," Palmer said.

Dillyn's fingers froze for just a second. "Thomas called Selah's phone. I can pull a lot of information about him from that single phone call."

"What if he used a burner?" Lucas asked.

Dillyn went back to typing. "Doesn't matter. He's been calling her from that phone for the past couple of weeks. It might take a little longer to gather all the pieces, but I still should be able to put them together."

"What if they tossed the phone?"

"There would still be information I can gather."

If Selah still had her cell and it was on, Dillyn should have already picked up a signal. She wasn't but didn't say that part out loud. She was also worried that whatever was going on with Selah was connected to Steven.

Dillyn now had multiple screens running. "Okay. Let's see what we know so far. There are one-hundred and fourteen thousand Thomas Markum's. Let me narrow the search." Dillyn typed in more information. She spoke to herself. "Catholic. Iowa."

"Why'd you type in Iowa?" Ben asked. "He said he was from New Jersey."

"That's what he said, but he had a Midwestern accent, specifically northern dialect." A notification popped up on her screen. She clicked on it to enlarge it.

"What is that?" Ben and Lucas leaned in closer.

"I programmed a backdoor into Selah's phone. Even if I can't get a signal, I can get her last known whereabouts before it stopped tracking. I can also get any photos, emails, and whatever else they may have exchanged." Dillyn leaned in closer. "Like that." It was a selfie of *Thomas* leaning up against something that looked like a car.

The image was blurred.

"What kind of car is that?" Ben was frustrated. "Dammit. We can't really see it." He couldn't lose Selah. He'd already lost too many people. If he lost his baby sister, Ben would lose his mind.

"Not yet anyway." Dillyn's fingers were moving lightning fast. Seconds later, the blurred image came into focus. Dillyn was already running a trace on the plates.

"It's a rental."

"Got dammit!" Lucas cursed and turned around in a semi-circle.

"Just bear with me," Dillyn pleaded. "We'll find her." She continued to work her magic. "The car is rented to a Jarrod Smith." Dillyn feared that if Jarrod was an alias, this situation was not a run-of-the-mill deal. Another screen popped up. She clicked on it. "It's Selah's last known location." Dillyn dropped her head to her chest. "Shit."

"What?" Ben asked.

"It's from almost twelve hours ago." Dillyn took a deep breath and got back to it.

"Have you found her?" Everyone stopped to look at the person who'd just walked into the room.

Ben shook his head no. "Not yet."

"Fuck."

"Ladies, this is my brother, Wyatt."

There was no mistaking it. Dillyn thought it was super stranger how similar the Cash family looked. "Sorry to meet you this way," she said.

"Yeah. Agreed. I've called in some of my friends too. What do we know so far?"

"We believe his name is Jarrod Smith. If this alias is correct, he's twenty-four years old, five feet nine inches, dark hair, brown eyes, and driving a 2012 black Chevy Malibu, license plate N36259. It's a rental car from Budget Motors in Nashville, TN. The good news is he doesn't appear to have a criminal record."

All eyes turned to Dillyn. Everyone was shocked to realize how much information she had gathered in the past fifteen minutes. "I'm not sure who your people are, but I have my people getting facial recognition."

"Your people?" Wyatt asked.

"My staff over at Dot Matrix, a digital forensics firm."

His eyes narrowed. "I didn't know people in that field could just call up information like that."

Dillyn turned away from his intense scrutiny. "Depends on who you know. It's all out here." Dillyn's computer made a dinging nose. She whipped around and clicked on the new notification on her monitor. "Oh. My. God."

Chapter 26

"What?!" Ben was losing his mind. He ran a frustrated hand through his hair.

Dillyn turned to find everyone staring at her with anxious eyes. "I got her."

"How can you be sure?"

"I fixed her phone, so if the SIM card were ever removed, it would send an emergency signal and provide her last known location. I'm not sure if she removed it or—"

"It was destroyed." Wyatt finished her sentence.

"Where is she?" Ben asked.

"She's on Interstate 65 going south. Let me see something . . ." Dillyn was able to bring up satellite images. Her face turned white as a sheet.

"What?" Lucas asked.

"She's in a trailer" When Ben saw how pale Dillyn was, he thought he was going to be sick.

"What does that mean?" Palmer asked what Cat was thinking.

"She's being trafficked."

Dillyn glanced up at Ben with sad eyes. "I don't know what else to do." There was really nobody she could call for this. It would take them too long to get to Selah, and time was not on their side. "I can call the local police."

"Yes, do that. We'll take it from here." Ben looked at Wyatt.

"I'm going too," Lucas said.

Ben shook his head. "Sit this one out, little brother. We've got this."

"You might as well bury me right here and now if you think I'm sitting this one out." Lucas was determined.

"Lucas, you've never been in combat, we don't know who we're dealing with, and Ben, you haven't carried a weapon in almost ten years," Wyatt reminded them.

"I don't think it's anything you ever forget," Ben said.

Shock passed over Dillyn's face for a moment. She'd had no idea Ben had served.

"I'll follow y'all's lead," Lucas said.

It was settled. The Cash brothers were determined to bring their sister home safely.

Chapter 27

Selah was scared. She couldn't believe what was happening as she sat in the back of a semitrailer with about twenty other girls and women. Some looked to be as young as nine. *Dear God, what is going to happen to us?* Tears were streaming down her face. All of her brother's warnings came back to her memory.

Thomas and another guy were sitting in the back too but closer toward the door. They both had guns. He'd tricked her. As soon as Selah arrived at the Roadhouse restaurant, she was snatched from behind and put into a car before she could even go inside. She couldn't see anything because Thomas had placed his hands over her eyes and mouth. The men had taken her to a place like a warehouse where there were other women. She could even hear some of them being raped. She just knew it was only a matter-of-time before it was her turn. Thomas and another guy were going through purses and bags when they found her cell phone and mace. Thomas put it in a basket of other cellular devices. Though under the stress of the situation, Selah remembered what Dillyn had said. She had to get to her phone. If she could get to it and somehow retrieve her SIM card, then maybe she had a chance.

As Selah sat in the back of the semitrailer, she vacillated between rage and despair. At the moment, she wanted to scratch Thomas's eyeballs out. *How could I have been so stupid!* Selah had to figure something out. She wasn't going down without a fight.

She had no idea where they were going, but they had been

on the road for what felt like hours. The trailer started to slow until it finally stopped. Was she about to be put on a train? A plain? A boat and sold off like in the movie *Taken*?

Thomas stood. "If anyone makes a sound, we will gut you like a fish." He walked to the back and snatched Selah up. "I was told not to touch you by the bosses at the warehouse. But they ain't here, are they?"

Selah started to fight. She fought as hard as she could as Thomas led her toward the door. After that, everything else happened in a blur.

*****

The worst possible outcome in this situation was happening. It was as if the universe was trying to make Ben pay for shit his ancestors did.

Ben had to get out of his head and into action if they had even a prayer of saving Selah. Quickly, he and Wyatt went out to the stables. In a rarely used horse stall deep in the back was a door to a room. It was where Ben and Wyatt housed all of their weapons.

"So that's Dillyn?" Wyatt asked as they gathered several handguns, rifles, and ammunition.

Ben nodded.

"How much do you know about her?" Wyatt stuffed a backpack with several knives.

"I'm learning more and more every day," Ben said.

"You know she had a lot of heavy-duty equipment."

"I noticed." Ben wouldn't make eye contact with Wyatt. He knew where his brother was going with his inquiries.

"It's almost impossible to get satellite imagery as a civilian."

"I know." Ben heard the accusation in his brother's voice.

"I'm grateful."

"Me too," Ben agreed. Though Ben was relieved by Wyatt's answer, he didn't have the mental bandwidth to deal with all of his brother's questions regarding Dillyn. His only focus was to get Selah back safely.

"Based on Dillyn's tracking information, they've only got an hour head start on us. If we take a few shortcuts, we can catch them."

"That's provided they don't stop anywhere for an exchange."

Wyatt was aware of that but was trying to be hopeful. Instead, his jaw clenched in anger. "If they've hurt her in any way . . . I'm going to bury them and everyone connected to this outfit in ways they can't even imagine."

Ben zipped up his black bag filled with weapons. "I'll help and bring the shovels."

"What are we going to do about Lucas?" Ben lifted his eye to Wyatt's.

"He's a good shot." Ben reminded him.

"He hunts animals, not men. That's different." Wyatt shook his head. Lucas wasn't built for this situation.

"What would you do if you were in his shoes?" Ben asked.

Wyatt sighed. "I see your point."

"Exactly. Still, we'll keep him close. I'll take the front, we'll keep him in the middle, and you can bring up the rear. I don't think Lucas will need it, but just in case, he'll have protection from the front and the back."

Wyatt nodded in agreement. "We should take my truck. If that dude has been grooming Selah for the past couple of weeks, they probably have already checked you and Lucas out. That means they'll know what kind of vehicles you drive."

"They couldn't possibly have checked us out; otherwise, they would know better." The frown Wyatt gave him made Ben feel foolish. He'd always been vigilant, but since he'd been spending more time with Dillyn, Ben had lost focus on Selah. Wyatt was right. They probably did know. "Yeah. We can take your truck."

Lucas walked in on them. He'd missed their entire conversation. "Yo . . . Let's get moving. Dillyn sent a link to our phones. Once we click it, she'll be able to feed us information. She'll be our eyes and ears."

Everyone nodded in agreement. The brothers were hardened by anger and unified by a singular purpose.

Ben led the way. "Let's go get Selah."

*****

Selah struggled as Thomas gripped her wrists and dragged her along. "You bastard! Why would you do this?"

He didn't answer but kept walking away from the interstate where their trailer was parked on the shoulder and toward the dense trees. Thomas had one thing on his mind—to get a little taste of Selah before he had to hand her over. After all, he'd found her. She should have been his reward. His luck had turned around when the driver had to pull over due to tire pressure issues. Otherwise, they would have kept driving until they reached their destination, and *Thomas* would have been left wondering what it would have been like to have Selah.

Selah forced herself to stop panicking and think. She knew what he had planned but thought maybe she could use it to her advantage. Selah stopped struggling, knowing that she would need all her energy.

*****

206

Wyatt drove like a bat out of hell. "I can't believe the cops aren't there yet. That they haven't pulled them over."

Frustrated, Ben ran a hand down his face. "According to Dillyn, there is a delay in issuing a warrant because there is an inter-jurisdictional fight."

Lucas did his best to remain calm but was struggling. "So, are you trying to tell me that the city is fighting with the state on who can stop the damn truck? They're like twenty minutes from crossing the border!"

Wyatt nodded. "Then the case becomes Federal, and there will be even more red tape."

"How far away are we?" Ben asked Dillyn over the car speaker.

"You're close. They should be coming into your line of sight in about two minutes. The truck is stopped on the side of the road." Dillyn was doing her best to keep her own emotions at bay. This entire situation was reminiscent of her childhood. She could only hope and pray that they got to Selah in time.

"Slow down," Ben told Wyatt.

A corner of Wyatt's lips lifted. "You act like this is my first rodeo. I've got this." Wyatt asked Dillyn, "Are we sure that trailer doesn't have an escort?"

"Fairly certain. However, I'm not sure how many men you might come in contact with. I counted two in the cab and one that came out of the trailer. There is at least one more in the trailer since I don't see Thomas."

It seems like it might be a small team. I could've handled them by myself. Wyatt glanced back at Lucas in the rearview. The intel reinforced his feelings of leaving him at home with the ladies.

"Guys! How close are you?" The tone of Dillyn's voice

207

changed. It was elevated. "I have a visual on Selah. Thomas has taken her out of the trailer, and they're headed for the woods."

Wyatt passed the semi and pulled over onto the shoulder just a short distance away.

"We see 'em,'" Ben said. "We'll connect with you once we have Selah."

"Ben?" Dillyn tried to keep the worry out of her voice. "Please, be careful."

"We'll be home before you know it." Ben disconnected.

Wyatt took note of Ben and Dillyn's affection for one another. He wasn't sure about her. Ben was known for falling hard and fast. He just hoped his brother wouldn't get his heart ripped out of his chest this time. Wyatt pushed those thoughts away. Time wasn't on their side.

"Change of plans," Wyatt rushed his words. "Lucas, get out and raise the hood of the truck. It'll look like there's a problem with it. Keep an eye on them from there. If they get suspicious and give you any trouble . . . handle it. You've got good instincts. Do what you've got to do."

"Got it." Lucas pulled out his 9-millimeter Glock17. Lucas knew his way around long guns because he was an avid hunter. However, his only real experience with a Glock was at the gun range and survivalist training. He attended the school for two weeks every year. Lucas didn't know what they would be facing. Still, he knew his gun of choice held a seventeen-round magazine and nineteen holds fifteen rounds, meaning there wouldn't be any compromise on capacity. Basically, it was an *I wish muthafucka would* weapon.

When they all stepped out of the car, Ben spoke loud enough to be heard. "I've got to take a leak."

"Yeah, me too." Wyatt echoed.

208

Lucas nodded at the two and went around the front of the car, lifting the hood.

Quickly, Wyatt and Ben went into the trees and began to backtrack toward the trailer. In a matter of minutes, they could hear Selah screaming. She came into view just as she gave Thomas a right hook. He had her on the ground, trying to take advantage of her, but Selah was making it difficult.

Ben lifted the pistol that he'd outfitted with a scope. "I got him." The police didn't need to handle this. He would. "Go help Lucas."

Wyatt understood completely and had planned to do the exact same thing. Instead, he ran back toward his other brother. Just as Wyatt stepped into the clearing, he heard the shot. He knew Ben only needed one.

A commotion rose from near the semi. The two men in the cab, who had checked the tires, had drawn their guns and shouted to the other man in the trailer. They split up, taking different paths around the truck. It was clear the men had heard the shot too, which meant shit was about to get real fast.

"Go for the tires," Wyatt hollered over at Lucas.

Lucas quickly lowered the hood and followed instructions. Lifting his Glock, he fired four shots. Seconds later, the bastards returned fire.

Lucas dropped the guy who'd been working on the tire, and Wyatt took out two others coming up the side.

As soon as Wyatt gave the signal, they carefully made their way over to the trailer making sure the men they'd shot were dead. Once they confirmed, they continued to move slowly, unsure if they would encounter anyone else.

Wyatt and Lucas arrived at the back of the trailer without any problems. Lucas was on one side of the back end, and Wyatt was on the other. "On three." Wyatt had a hand on the latch to raise the door. He counted down then lifted.

They were fully prepared to blast anybody else who'd had a hand in abducting their sister. Instead, they only saw frightened women and girls. There were screams from the women closest to the doors. With all the gunfire, and now, those same guns drawn on them, they were understandably shaken.

Lucas was the first to put his gun away. He spoke to the women in reassuring tones. "It's okay. We won't hurt you." He put his hands up and looked to Wyatt, gesturing with his head that he should keep watch out of the women's view. Though he knew the gun had to trigger them, Lucas also knew one of them needed to remain ready and on guard.

As Lucas was helping a mass of women and girls down from the trailer, the State Police showed up. Wyatt put away his gun, shaking his head. *Of course. They get here after we've done all the dirty work.*

Wyatt turned to Lucas. "You good?" He knew Lucas had never killed a man before.

"Never better." Lucas turned away, but not before Wyatt noticed the hard glint in his eye.

Several squad cars and a sex trafficking unit pulled up close. The officers got out and rushed them with their weapons drawn. "Ben, Lucas, and Wyatt Cash?" Wyatt and Lucas both raised their empty hands.

"I'm Wyatt, and this is my brother, Lucas. There are three assailants down toward the front of this rig." Wyatt tipped his head toward the front of the semi.

The officer nodded, and his men went in search of them. "I'm Officer Joseph." The man lowered his weapon. "Dillyn Anderson already gave us the background regarding this situation and your images. Thank you for your service and for saving these girls. Are there any other people down?"

Wyatt lifted his chin toward the trees. "Maybe one more in the woods."

Just as several members on Officer Joseph's team were about to move out in that direction, they looked up to see Ben coming out from behind the trees. He walked down a slight slope and carried a motionless Selah. Her head lay cradled against his chest.

Lucas and Wyatt made eye contact. They could only pray they had arrived in time.

Chapter 28

It was well after midnight, and Dillyn and her friends were still waiting for word from Ben, Lucas, and Wyatt.

"Is there anything else you can tell us, Dillyn?" Palmer asked.

"No." She wished there was. "All I know is that the trailer hasn't moved in hours. I lost my satellite feed and have no idea what's going on."

"When you said you worked in IT, I thought that meant you helped people reset their password."

"I said I was a digital forensic investigator."

"But you were over here like that lady in the Bourne movies," Cat said in awe.

Her words hit too close to home for Dillyn. "No. It's typically nothing that exciting. Just boring stuff. I'm glad today I was able to help. Hopefully."

No sooner had Dillyn uttered the words did Ben walk through the door carrying Selah. They all breathed a sigh of relief and rushed over. Ben didn't stop. He stalked past the women, taking Selah straight to her room.

"Are you guys alright?" Palmer rushed to Lucas.

"We're fine. I'm just prayin' Selah will be."

Wyatt walked over to Dillyn with knowing eyes. "Thank you for your help. We would never have gotten our sister back without you." He glanced over at Cat, and his eyes lingered for a moment.

"I'm just glad I could. Is she okay?"

Wyatt knew what she was asking. "She will be." He turned to everyone in the room. "It's been a long evening. It's late. We have a ton of spare bedrooms. Pick one and get some rest. We can sort the rest of this in the morning."

Cat's eyes never left him as Wyatt walked out of the room.

Lucas was always so playful, so it was easy for Palmer to notice his eyes had a hardness about them they'd never had before. She could only assume it was because Lucas had to do some things he'd never had to do. Palmer shook her head. She believed there was going to be a lot of healing going around for a lot of people in the room. "I'm going to head up too."

Palmer's tone was low as she asked, "Would you like some company?"

Lucas stared at her for a moment before answering. "Yeah. I would." He grabbed her by the hand, and they walked out of the room together.

Cat and Dillyn were alone. So much had happened in the last twenty-four hours. Dillyn hadn't even told her friends about Steven. "Steven's dead." Her voice was just above a whisper.

"What?" Cat's eyes widened.

"I got a call earlier today telling me that he was gone. That he was murdered."

Cat didn't know what to say. She couldn't lie and say she was so sorry. Although she didn't want Steven dead, she also didn't care. So, in that respect, Cat wasn't sorry, but she knew she had to say something. "I'm sorry if you're hurt by his death."

Dillyn sighed as tears started to fall down her face. "I'm sorry about a lot. I am sorry that Steven is dead. I'm sorry that Selah just experienced such a horrendous situation." She dropped her head. "I'm just . . . sorry."

"Dillyn?"

She turned at the sound of her name. Ben stepped into the room. He looked exhausted. "Selah is asking for you. I can show

213

Cat to a guest room if you want to check on her."

Cat nodded. "Thanks. I'd appreciate that."

"Dillyn?"

"Yes?" Dillyn glanced up at Ben. The look he returned made her stomach bottom out.

"After you're done talking to Selah, then you and I need to have a heart-to-heart."

Dillyn nodded as she walked out of the room.

Chapter 29

Ben finally got the fire in his fireplace to blaze as he waited for Dillyn. Out of nowhere, an image of Lana appeared. If Ben believed in the paranormal, he'd be convinced Lana's ghost was standing right before him. But Ben knew it wasn't real. He was only haunted by his guilt and how, even now, he couldn't protect the people he loved. Still, he had to forgive Lana and himself. Ben couldn't move forward holding on to the past. *It's time.* Ben took a deep breath. "I hope you can forgive me because I have to forgive myself. Goodbye, Lana."

When Dillyn walked through the door, she could see by the set of Ben's shoulders the night had taken ten years off his life. Gently, she placed a hand on his shoulder. "Are you okay?"

Ben sighed. "Not really. How is Selah?"

"She's been through a lot, but the worst didn't happen. With time, I'm sure she will heal from this."

He nodded. "Dillyn, we need to talk."

She could have said, "We have. You know everything," but instead, Dillyn sighed. "I know."

"I don't want any more secrets between us. If I expect for you to tell me the whole truth, then I need to tell you the whole truth."

This was a pivotal moment. If she wanted a future with Ben, Dillyn would have to come completely clean. "Okay."

Ben continued to stare into the flickering flames.

Not only could Dillyn see the pain in his eyes, but she could also feel it. It was palpable.

Ben rolled his head around his shoulders and released a

loud sigh before he began to speak. "Her name was Lana Langston."

Dillyn already knew most of the story. After her first ride with Ben and Whisper, she'd come home and done her research. However, if Ben needed to tell her, she would listen.

"Lana was as smart as she was beautiful. I met her at a sustainable agricultural conference. I was on the panel, and she was in the audience. This might sound corny, but she literally snatched the breath right out of my body. I knew that I had to make it my business to meet her."

Dillyn listened intently.

"After the panel wrapped up, I made a beeline over to where she had been sitting. That was a challenge considering so many people wanted to ask me questions and me trying to get past the gaggle of reporters all wanting an interview, but I did it." A small smile appeared on his face before it faded away.

Dillyn didn't interrupt.

"We went for drinks. Lana was funny and shared my interest in sustainable agriculture. Something most folks don't even know exists."

Dillyn sure as hell didn't know what it was. She'd only heard of it while doing her Google search of him.

Ben continued. "After just one conversation, I knew she was the one." He paused for a moment, pressed to find the right words to continue.

Patiently, Dillyn waited.

"I fell hard and fast, not realizing we were as different as night and day. She was from Chicago, a city girl through and through, but I was determined to make a relationship work. I even convinced her to marry me after three months of dating."

"Wow." Dillyn didn't know that part. "She must have

loved you too."

It was something Ben often wondered about. It was also the heaviest part of his guilt. Ben hadn't really been *in* love with Lana. He loved her mind, her wit, and her humor, but he wasn't in love with her. More so than anything, Ben felt obligated. He lowered his head and pressed his chin to his chest. "Lana packed up her life and moved here to be with me. I learned pretty damn quickly that she was a fish out of water. Lana hated everything about the farm and living in Tennessee. On more than one occasion, she told me that she couldn't do forever on this ranch. Deep down, I knew it too. She was unhappy. I could see that light within her slowly start to dim. It wasn't just her passion that started to fade. It was her mind. I didn't understand depression and how it all worked back then, but I knew I had to figure something out. Not just for her but . . ." His voice trailed off. "She was pregnant."

Dillyn's heart ached. "Rylee?"

"Yes. Lana was barely six weeks."

Dillyn understood all too well how devastating losing a child could be on a woman and a marriage.

"I remember like it was yesterday. It was so cold and gray that morning when Lana decided to move back to Chicago."

"She left you?" Surprise was evident in Dillyn's voice. There were some things a person couldn't find on Google.

"For a little while. My life's work was and is on this farm. I spent a few months setting things up, so I could be with my family. I figured I could commute between there and the ranch. Relocating didn't seem to help us. Strangely enough, it put even more of a strain on our relationship."

"I'm so sorry," Dillyn said softly.

"Lana's depression kept getting worse. It was out of control, and I didn't know what to do. Mental healthcare in this country is a joke. Still, I tried everything I could think of. We went to counseling both together and individually. Nothing helped. I talked to every specialist available to us. My trips back here to the ranch became fewer because caring for Lana became an almost full-time job."

Dillyn's chest tightened. She felt the weight of his words.

"After our daughter was born, things seem to get better for a while. Lana was over the moon with happiness. She doted on Rylee."

Dillyn released a breath she hadn't realized she'd been holding until she remembered, and then despair spread throughout her entire being.

"Over the next couple of years, Lana would slip in and out of moderate depression, but she fought so hard. Finally, it got so bad I had to hire a full-time nanny and a part-time mental health expert because I was afraid Lana might hurt herself. Never in a million years did I think . . ." Ben's throat locked up.

Dillyn moved her hand to the center of his back and began to move it in a circular motion, massaging and trying to offer as much comfort as she could. She rested her chin on his shoulder and whispered into his ear, "You don't have to say anything else."

Ben knew he had to push forward. He had to finish the story. He cleared his throat a couple of times before continuing. "I hadn't been back to the ranch in over a year. There were some people I needed to meet with, so I flew back here for a weekend." Ben swallowed hard. "It was the weekend we met, and all I could think about was you. I could not get you off my mind. That guilt ate at me for a while."

Dillyn was shocked by that. They had only spent a few

hours together, but it made a profound impression on her life too.

"I knew something was wrong the second I returned home and walked through the door. It was so quiet. Eerily quiet. I called out to Lana and then to our nanny, Aimee, since they would have been the only ones home. Nobody answered. I rounded the corner, and I saw it. There was a large streak of blood on the floor. It led right to Aimee's body, pooled in blood. It was splattered everywhere. Blood was all over the furniture, the walls, and even the ceiling. She'd been stabbed several times, and her throat had been slashed. I freaked. I started searching for Lana and Rylee. I was screaming for them. I went from room to room searching. It was almost impossible. I kept sliding around. There was just so much blood. It was sticky and partly congealed, just pooling on the floor. I finally found Lana. She was lying in the center of our bed. Our sheets were white when I left. They were such a deep crimson, almost black under her. Lana had slit her wrists. I prayed like I'd never prayed before as I glanced over toward the door to our nursery. I lost hope when I saw a red handprint on it."

Dillyn's eyes were wet with not only her tears but Ben's as he had turned, and their foreheads were now touching.

"I walked into Rylee's room and found my two-year-old baby girl in her bed completely dismembered." Ben had never been able to say out loud to his family what he'd told Dillyn. "In a manic episode, Lana had killed them."

Dillyn pulled Ben into a tight embrace and held him close as he released the pain he'd been holding onto for the past couple of years. She whispered, "It wasn't your fault."

"If I had never left her . . ."

"It wasn't your fault, Ben." Dillyn lifted her head and cradled his within the palms of her hands. She held his gaze. "Lana was sick, and you did all that you could to help her. You are an amazing man, father, and husband. It's unrealistic to think you could be there twenty-four hours a day. You also didn't know how sick Lana truly was. There was nothing more you could have done. This wasn't your fault. It was just a tragedy I wish never happened."

"I'm not sure if I'll ever come to believe that, but I want to. I also want a life with you, but I can't be with someone who can't be honest with me. What is really going on? Why did you really move to Summer?"

Truth time. "Everything I told you about my life is true, but I left out some particularly vital facts. Things that I've never even told Cat and Palmer out of fear for their safety." Dillyn sighed. "I was able to help you find Selah tonight because . . ." Dillyn glanced down at her feet. "I work for an agency of the government that doesn't exist, and I used the tools that are available to me because of them. I have always been good at computers, cracking codes, and finding patterns. By the time I was sixteen, I had become a part of the anti-establishment network called Anonymous. At nineteen, a man you probably have never heard of, who goes by Syntax, recruited me. Think Morpheus from the Matrix movies. He brought me in to work for this non-existent government agency. I moved here because of the reasons I told you before. I've been searching for peace since I was nine, and I think I've found it, in this place, in myself, and in you."

"Did the attack on my sister happen because of you?" Ben asked pointedly.

"I don't know." Dillyn answered as honestly as she could. She didn't know how Ben would respond to that or what was about to happen between them. She had no idea if this were the moment that Ben told her she was too risky to be around or if he would give them a chance. "And that's not all. Steven was murdered yesterday, and I have no idea if it's at all related." She rushed her words. "But . . . I'm working hard to find out so that I can put all of this behind me. I . . ." Dillyn paused. "I like what we're building. For the first time in my life, I feel hopeful. I don't want to lose that or you."

Dillyn couldn't tell what Ben was thinking. He continued to stare into the fire. Finally, he turned and reached for her. "I want to build a life with you too, but no matter what, I always need you to be honest with me. Can you do that?"

Dillyn nodded vigorously.

"Good, because you mean a lot to me. I know it's only been a couple of weeks, but I think you've had me in the palm of your hand since the night you wouldn't even shake mine."

Dillyn was awash with relief. "I feel the same way. I've always felt a pull toward you even when I wasn't supposed to."

"I can now honestly say without any guilt that I feel the same."

Dillyn wanted to show Ben that she was committed to them in every way. She had never initiated sex before, and tonight would be a first. She was experiencing a lot of *firsts* when it came to him. With Ben, it wasn't so scary.

She reached out and gently cupped the side of his face. Ever so lightly, she placed her lips over his.

She spoke into their kiss. "I need this."

Ben understood what Dillyn was doing. "You don't have anything to prove." A lot had happened over the past twenty-four hours, and their emotions were all over the place. They were on the right track to a healthy relationship. Ben didn't want Dillyn confusing physical intimacy with emotional connection. He wanted her body *and* soul. When she was ready, he hoped to have

221

both.

"I might be a little clumsy." Dillyn walked Ben backward to the couch, and he lowered them down. Steadying herself by placing her palms on his shoulders, Dillyn got up on her knees. She lifted her leg and moved it over the side of his hip until she was in a straddling position. "But I need you." Her eyes bore into his. "I'm aching to be filled by you."

Ben was always hungry for her, and the look of pure desire in her eyes was almost his undoing. He didn't have the willpower or want to deny her.

Ben captured her hips in his hands as he kissed her. Wrapping her arms around his neck, Dillyn kissed him back with everything she had inside. He outlined the seam of her lips with his tongue and slipped it inside her mouth. Dillyn was throbbing and wet. It didn't take much with Ben. Slowly, she lowered her body onto the bulge in his jeans and rolled her hips.

He was hard.

The movement caused Ben to break the kiss so that he could take a breath, which lasted a second before he recaptured her mouth. Firmly, he gripped her hips and pressed her to his body. They were fully clothed, so it didn't give either of them the satisfaction they sought. They only felt needier.

Dillyn was anxious to feel him inside her and sped up her movements. She liked to ride. It was her favorite position. And every time she brought her body down, Ben lifted upward, pressing into her swollen core. It triggered a pleasure so intense that she bit her lower lip as her head fell backward. The feeling was delicious, and her body wanted more.

She began to roll her hips uncontrollably back and forth over him. It was as if her body had a mind of its own.

Their breathing filled the room as each worked harder to

222

get closer but not getting close enough.

Ben had been nervous that Dillyn might only be trying to make him feel better, but *she wanted him.* He could feel the evidence of it on his stomach through the thin layer of her yoga pants. Her pussy was moist and hot. Nothing was more intoxicating than knowing your woman wanted you.

Finally, Ben was tired of playing games. His hands traveled down to Dillyn's ass, and he got up from the sofa.

Dillyn's eyes connected with his as her legs automatically wrapped around him. "I think I'm going to burn up," she said in a breathless whisper.

Ben placed Dillyn on the bed and pulled those little black pants off in one single movement. I won't let you do that."

She was left wearing a little t-shirt. Dillyn lifted it from the bottom up and over her head as Ben removed his jeans and t-shirt.

"I still can't believe all of that fits inside of me." She rubbed her thighs together in anticipation.

Ben was fully aroused. His cocked jutted upward almost an inch or more above his navel. "I don't mind proving it to you over and over again."

Dillyn let her legs fall apart, exposing her slick folds. Her voice was husky. "Come here." She crooked her index finger and beckoned Ben to come to her.

Ben climbed onto the bed and between her welcoming thighs.

Dillyn couldn't stop squirming. His cock was pulsing, and it was positioned just underneath her ass.

"You're beautiful." Ben looked into desire-filled eyes that were half-closed. He'd made it a practice to always stare deeply into them before entering her. It coincided with a promise he'd

223

made to Dillyn—he would chase away the ghosts. It would take time, but it was a promise Ben planned to make good on. Knowing that he gave her pleasure unlike anyone else on the planet made him harder than anything.

Ben leaned down and kissed her again. Their tongues swirled hungrily around each other. With each passing moment, they became increasingly eager to become one.

Her nipples were pressed against his chest, causing an even more fiery reaction. They had already pebbled into tight little buds.

His hands roamed all over her body—touching, feeling, stroking—until Dillyn was almost begging for him.

Dillyn needed to touch him, and she did. Her hands were everywhere. Anywhere she could reach. At the same time, she rubbed her pussy lips up and down the length of his cock. Dillyn would get him close to entering her, but Ben kept denying her the satisfaction.

Finally, she captured the object of her desire in her hand. Her movements weren't soft or tender. It wasn't what either of them needed.

Ben lost all coherent thought at her touch, except one. "Look at me, Dillyn." He struggled to keep some measure of control as Dillyn pleasured him with her hand.

It was a miracle Ben's voice broke through her sexual haze. Dillyn's eyes fluttered open. She could tell by the look in his eyes that Ben didn't have any restraint left. *Thank God.*

Ben covered her hand with his and guided Dillyn toward her opening. She was dripping wet, and it was all over the sheets.

He needed to be buried balls deep inside of her.

Ben thrust forward, and Dillyn's body welcomed him.

"Mmm . . ." She moaned as her muscles clenched around his velvety thickness.

He captured the fleshy part of her ass in his hands and squeezed while holding her steady. Ben pulled almost all the way out only to surge forward even harder. He did it again and again and again.

Dillyn dug her nails into his back as she took pleasure from him. "I'm going to explode." She could already feel her body start to pulse.

Ben could feel it too. He wasn't ready and needed to slow things down. It took a superhuman effort, but he pulled himself out of the grip of her body.

Dillyn's eyes popped open. "What . . . what's wrong?"

He smiled. "Absolutely, nothing. Everything is right." Ben moved down her length until he was eye level with her breasts. Dying to taste her, Ben pulled the tight little bud into his mouth and sucked greedily.

Dillyn needed to do something with her hands. She entwined them in his hair as she continued to rotate her hips, searching for the satisfaction that only Ben could fill.

"Can I taste you?" he asked.

Form words? I can't. Instead, Dillyn just nodded.

Ben continued to move lower until he arrived at his destination. Initially, he placed feathery light kisses on her. Ben flattened his tongue. With one long stroke, he slowly licked Dillyn from the top of her pussy all the way down and all the way up—careful not to go inside her opening. "Damn. I knew you would taste good."

Her core clenched and throbbed, aching to be filled. "*Ahh . . . Ben. Umm . . . I . . .*" Several long, delicious licks later, Dillyn had a sheen of sweat covering her entire body.

Ben whispered into her silkiness. "I know, baby." Then he buried his tongue deep into her sex and fucked her with his tongue.

Dillyn exploded. "*Ahh . . . Ahh . . . Oooohhh . . . God!*"

Ben could feel her pulsing around him. He didn't stop but continued to swirl his tongue around.

Dillyn squeezed her eyes shut and screamed his name as the most intense orgasm she'd ever had rocked her body. She saw stars behind the darkness of her closed eyes. Ben didn't stop kissing and loving her until he sucked every last drop of her release.

Dillyn was breathing hard. She didn't know if she could catch her breath.

Nothing made a man feel more powerful than knowing they could satisfy their woman. He smiled knowingly. "My turn." Ben climbed up Dillyn's body as his mouth glistened from her release.

"I don't think I can feel my legs." Dillyn was still panting from her release.

He laughed. "I can promise you they're still there." Ben kissed her as he repositioned himself just outside of her entrance.

Dillyn tasted her cum on his lips. Something about it was so erotic that her body instantly started to heat up all over again.

Ben caged her head between his arms. "You ready?"

Dillyn nodded.

Everything up until that point had been about Dillyn, but Ben needed her in a raw, sensual way. He surged forward and almost immediately closed his eyes in pure ecstasy.

Dillyn's body tightened around him. Ben pulled out and slammed right back inside.

Neither of them could speak as they rode the wave of intense sexual satisfaction.

Her body wrapped around him so tightly that all Ben wanted to do was drill into her. He could live inside her body.

Dillyn lifted her knees so Ben could go even deeper. She accepted the hammering he gave as he pumped into her with everything he had.

Dillyn felt so damn good, and Ben didn't want it to end. Tonight, he needed Dillyn so much. Ben pounded and pounded into her. He gritted his teeth as he tried to hold on. "I'm gonna cum." He prayed that he could last until Dillyn found another release.

Words and thoughts were obsolete at this point. All Dillyn could do was feel. She started to tighten around him.

Sweat dripped off their bodies as they both built toward their release.

"Ben!" Dillyn screamed out his name. Her orgasm was intense and magical. Seconds later, Ben splashed his seed inside her body. It was the most powerful orgasm Ben had had in his life.

After several minutes, Dillyn finally found her voice. It was hoarse. "That was incredible."

Ben hated to pull out of her body, but he did. "Incredible is an understatement." He moved Dillyn into the crook of his arms, and Dillyn snuggled into his warmth.

Just as Dillyn was drifting off to sleep, she heard Ben sigh contentedly. It made her smile.

It didn't take long for them to fall off into a deep and peaceful sleep.

Chapter 30

Frustrated, Dillyn dropped her face into her hands. She'd been sitting in front of her monitors for hours staring at the screen. It had been a month since that harrowing night, and she was no closer to finding out if it was connected to Steven's murder or who was really behind Selah's abduction. And did either of the incidents have anything to do with the explosion at Frank's?

Dillyn had hit a dead end. She had gone through both Thomas's and Steven's files too many times to count but hadn't found anything that could help. Nothing she had discovered would rise to the level of someone taking Steven's life over it.

Dillyn got up and stretched. Her back was killing her. "I've been sitting for way too long." Her stomach growled too. She realized she hadn't eaten anything, and it was already past noon. Dillyn was just about to go downstairs to the kitchen to grab a quick snack when there was a knock on her bedroom door. "It's open."

Ben cracked open the door and came inside. He was carrying a brown paper bag. "You took a break yet?" She had been working like a maniac.

Dillyn rubbed her shoulders, hoping to relax those muscles. "I was just about to."

"Good." He'd been worried about her. Dillyn was burning it at both ends, trying to get to the bottom of Steven's murder and Selah's situation. "You look tired."

"Just what every woman wants to hear," Dillyn couldn't suppress a yawn. "Anyway, I can rest when I'm dea—" Dillyn caught herself. "There's too much at stake to take extended breaks."

"Your health is important too," he said with concern.

Dillyn walked over to him and wrapped her arms around his waist. She stood up on tiptoe and kissed him. "Thank you for your concern, but I promise I'm fine. How is Selah?"

"She's stronger than I ever imagined." His face held a thoughtful expression. "She's busy trying to take care of us and has a hard time letting us take care of her. That woman reminds me of someone else I know."

"Ben . . ." If Dillyn had a dollar for every time he'd thought she was overdoing it, Dillyn would be a billionaire. He had to understand how important her work was. She sighed out of frustration. "People I love might be in danger." She looked up into his eyes. "I wouldn't be able to survive it if anything were to happen to you."

"You don't think I feel the same?"

"Of course, I do, but even with your special skill set, you, Lucas, and Wyatt can't be with us twenty-four hours a day."

He smirked. "We can try. I like waking up and falling asleep next to you." Ben had also hired extra security and installed a state-of-the-art security system to look out over both their properties. Wyatt was also using his connections to gather as much information as possible. Ben wasn't leaving anything to chance.

"I won't lie. Waking up to you is almost as satisfying as our morning rides with Whisper."

"*Almost*? Am I really competing with a horse?" He chuckled.

"We both know that Whisper isn't just a horse. She's magical."

"True." Ben turned serious. "Hmm."

Her brows furrowed. "What? You don't believe me?"

"I know that Whisper's magical. She brought us together. That required a lot of magic. I was just curious." His tone was lighthearted, but his eyes were anything but. "Do you count me as one of the people you love?"

Dillyn was surprised at the question. "Don't you know?"

"You've never said it."

Dillyn's face softened. "Benjamin James Cash, I love the way you love me." She planted a butterfly kiss on his lips. "I love the way you allow me to be me," she said, kissing him lightly in between each declarative statement. "I love the way you support me." *Kiss.* "I love the way you love your family and those you care about." *Kiss.* "I love the way you've shown me what healthy love looks and feels like."

Ben held on to her every word . . . waiting.

"*I love you so much.* I love you with everything I am and everything I want to become."

The corners of his lips edged upward, revealing an incredible smile. Ben lowered his face close to hers and wrapped his arms around Dillyn's waist. "Now multiply that times infinity because that's how I feel about you." Ben leaned in and pressed his lips against hers.

The man knew how to make Dillyn weak in the knees. His kisses made her lose all track of space and time.

When they finally pulled apart, Dillyn was dizzy. *Like really dizzy.* She had to hold on to Ben for support. "Whoa."

Ben caught her. He swept Dillyn up into his arms and carried her over to the bed. "This is why you need to rest!"

"I'm fine." Dillyn dismissed his concern. "I just need to eat a little something."

"It's not just about you, Dillyn." Ben's concern sounded

angry to Dillyn's ears.

She was irritated too. "Who else would it be about then?" Were they about to have their first fight?

Ben handed her the brown paper bag.

"Is that a muffin or a donut?"

His voice was stern. "Open it."

Dillyn snatched the bag from Ben's hand, annoyance radiating off her waves. She opened it and stared at the contents for a long while before slowly raising her eyes to meet the intensity of Ben's gaze. "Ben, what am I going to do with a pregnancy test?"

"Take it."

Dillyn realized Ben was serious. She turned away to hide the pain. "I tried for years to get pregnant. It's not possible."

"Are you on the pill?"

She pressed her lips together, then whispered, "No."

"I never wear a condom. So, it's possible."

"It's possible but highly unlikely." Dillyn sighed. She took a moment, gathering her thoughts and swallowing back her tears. "I don't think I'll ever be able to give you children." Even though she was terrified of being a mother, it still broke her heart to utter those words.

Ben touched her face. "You are enough. If we decide to have kids, great. If we decide our family is complete with just the two of us, that's fine too, but Dillyn, you have all the symptoms." The thought that Dillyn could be pregnant hadn't entered Ben's mind until a couple of weeks ago when she had been overly tired and moody. Her breasts were super sensitive, and now she was having bouts of what seemed like morning sickness. It was possible she was just working too hard, but it was also possible Dillyn was pregnant.

Dillyn loved Ben's concern, but she knew better. "If it will put your mind at ease, I'll take it."

"It would."

Dillyn scooted off the bed and went to her bathroom.

Ben was a nervous wreck. He got up off her bed and started pacing. He'd tried to pretend as if he wasn't stressed out about the possibility of having another baby. He loved Dillyn, but they hadn't been dating that long. Did she even want kids? Ben wouldn't survive a repeat of his situation with Lana. *What the hell am I going to do if she is pregnant?*

Dillyn was only gone a few moments, but Ben couldn't read her expression when she came out of the bathroom.

"It'll take a few minutes before we can read it." Though Dillyn was certain she wasn't pregnant, the small chance that she might be scared her. She wasn't sure if Ben even wanted more children. It wasn't anything they ever talked about. However, she knew how much he doted on Rylee. *What if he does?* Dillyn wouldn't be able to bear disappointing him.

Dillyn used her hunger as an excuse to distract them both. "If I don't eat, I am going to fall out. I think I should grab something from the kitchen."

Ben had barely been able to breathe. He folded his arms across his chest doing his best not to appear frustrated. "Are you serious? You don't want to wait for the results?"

Dillyn shrugged and put her hands in the back pockets of her jeans, hoping to appear nonchalant when she was anything but. "Whatever it shows won't change in fifteen minutes."

Ben wanted to protest but thought better of it. Maybe it was best if they used the extra time to gather themselves—considering the results of that test could potentially change both of their lives.

*****

Dillyn had been locked in her room for hours before Ben arrived. When they finally came out, she had no idea what had been happening outside of her work. As they descended the stairs, Dillyn directed furtive glances toward the men Syntax sent to watch over them. It was a stark reminder of the danger she had put everyone in.

She sighed. *No more secrets.* Dillyn had made that promise to Ben and told him about their protectors. Unfortunately, Cat and Palmer were still in the dark. It was Dillyn's way of trying to protect them. The more they knew, the more in danger they were in.

As they made their way toward the kitchen, the loud and raucous laughter of her friends greeted her before she even walked into the room. A warmth spread through Dillyn's chest. Her heart felt full. *This* was her family. The one she always wished she had. A small smile tugged at the edge of her lips as they walked inside not only to see Cat and Palmer but Ben's siblings as well.

Palmer and Lucas were sitting at the table with their heads close together. It seemed they were unable to keep their hands off one another. It was obvious they were dating. Palmer said they weren't exclusive, but Ben had told her that Lucas wasn't seeing anyone else. Dillyn knew that Palmer wasn't either. So, while they might not be ready to admit it, they were a thing. Dillyn suspected something might have been going on since the night of the barbecue.

Dillyn's head tilted slightly as she observed Cat and Wyatt. They were a different story. Those two were definitely into each other same as Lucas and Palmer; however, Dillyn wasn't sure if they would ever actually acknowledge it. Instead, they played this weird game of cat and mouse. The most interesting part was the fact Cat hadn't slept with him. Given her history, *that* meant something.

Selah was sitting at the table too. She was reviewing some paperwork for their recently named business. In the end, they'd decided on *Uncorked Winery and Vineyard*. On the outside, Selah seemed as if everything was fine, but Dillyn's talks with her revealed there was still a lot more healing to do. In time and with the support of her family, she would recover. Dillyn was sure of it.

Lucas glanced up, grinning from ear to ear. He was the first to notice them. "Ben finally let you come up for air?" he said playfully to Dillyn.

Wyatt chimed in. "Y'all finally made it out of that room? We thought we were going to have to send in a search party."

They all laughed. Over the past few weeks, Wyatt had come to like *and* respect Dillyn.

"If I had my way, she'd never leave my side." Ben hugged her from behind. "But . . . she's starving. What's a man to do?"

"I don't know . . . feed me?" Dillyn joined in the banter and laughed too.

That seemed to be all it took to release the tension between Dillyn and Ben. Once the ice was broken, Dillyn turned into Ben's arms and mouthed the words, "I'm sorry."

He spoke for her ears only. "Me too."

Dillyn and Ben still had to deal with the *possible—but not really possible* in Dillyn's view—pregnancy. She hated that this topic was happening so soon in their relationship but felt no matter what, Ben would be there for her just as she would be there for him.

Pushing those thoughts away, Ben and Dillyn spent the rest of the afternoon enjoying each other and their newfound family. They ate. They laughed. They loved.

When the doorbell rang, Dillyn got up from Ben's lap. "I'll get it." Her cell phone also rang. It was that ring. *God, no.* She looked around to make sure she was alone before answering it and opening the door.

"Hey." She said.

"You can thank me later, but it's handled."

"What?" Dillyn was confused.

Syntax chuckled. "Congratulations and enjoy the time with your family. My guys will be out today."

"What are you talking about? Stop being cryptic. I hate when you're like this. What do you mean you *handled* it?"

"You think too hard and too much. Rest, relax, and enjoy this time." Syntax disconnected the call.

Dillyn stood in place dumbfounded. *What did he do?* Dillyn replaced her phone in her back pocket and went to the door. She opened it, but nobody was standing on the other side. Instead, there was an unmarked envelope on the ground.

Dillyn glanced about to see who could have left it, only to see the brake lights of that all too familiar silver car speeding away from their property. It was moving too fast to get a look at the license plates. Not that it mattered, Dillyn could work her magic and find the car easy enough.

Ben walked up behind her. "Who was at the door?"

"I don't know, but they left this." She bent low and picked it up. Dillyn stepped back inside of the house and closed the door. With trembling fingers, she opened the envelope. There was a note inside.

It's over.

S.

Ben looked over her shoulder as he read it. "Syntax?"

"Yes," she answered. "But exactly what is over? What was this even about?" Dillyn asked.

"Is it really over?" Ben asked skeptically. He hoped it would be for Dillyn, but there was no way Ben was going to let Selah's situation rest until he found the culprit.

She sighed. "Syntax is like the Wizard. He sees all, he knows all, and clearly, he knows more than he's willing to share. He's probably the reason I'm hitting a wall and have been coming up empty in my research."

Ben was relieved to hear that, in some ways, Syntax was trying to protect her. "If that's his way of keeping you safe, I'm all for it."

There was no way Dillyn was willing to let any of this go. There were too many unanswered questions. But for today, she had enough on her plate and would let it rest.

Epilogue

Dillyn was in no rush to go back to her room. She was in too good a headspace, and without a doubt, she knew the results of that pregnancy test would ruin it.

Ben, on the other hand, was anxious. He wanted to know if his suspicions were correct. Was he going to be a father again?

"I love it when we are all together like that. Everyone was in a great mood." Dillyn yawned. It was barely eight o'clock. Realization hit, and both looked in the direction of the place that housed the answer to a life-altering question.

Ben and Dillyn exchanged knowing glances. She released a breath. "I suppose I should go see, huh?"

"I'd like that." His tone was gentle but matter-of-fact. Ben did his best to keep the anxiousness out of it.

Dillyn nodded. She took another deep breath and walked into the bathroom. She stayed in there longer than Ben thought was necessary, but in actuality, it was only a few moments.

She came and stood in the doorway, holding the stick in her hand.

Ben couldn't tell by the look on her face what the test revealed. Was she pregnant? Was she happy? Was she disappointed? Her expression was a mixture of everything. Ben's heart was racing. "Well?" he prompted.

Dillyn walked over and handed Ben the stick. Closing his eyes, Ben swallowed hard before looking at it. He hadn't had a panic attack in a very long time. At the moment, though, he had to beat back the feeling of one coming on.

He opened his eyes and glanced down at the results. Briefly, his eyes shut as relief washed over him. "I'm going to be a father again, and you're going to be a mother."

Dillyn's mouth hung open. She couldn't believe it. She felt pale, like all her blood had abandoned her. *How is this possible?* Dillyn thought she'd feel devastated, but she felt—*joy*." She was both in disbelief and shock as she repeated his words. "I'm going to be a mother?" The mere thought was inconceivable. Dillyn was frightened but exhilarated too. It was the ultimate contradiction.

"Are you okay with having my child?" He held his breath, waiting for her answer.

Slowly, Dillyn lifted her eyes to meet his. "Yes," she said in a breathless whisper. "I'm better than okay. I'm actually kind of ecstatic!" Her eyes became glassy. "This isn't supposed to happen to me. The truth is, I was too afraid to hope. Too terrified to dream and too scared to even imagine the possibility. I really, really do want this baby and even more because you're the father."

Dillyn caught her breath and laughed. She still had fears about the kind of mother she would be, but she knew Ben would be with her every step of the way.

Ben's reaction wasn't anything he thought it would be. He gasped and joined Dillyn in laughter. His early reservations melted away. He was . . . *excited*. Life had given him another chance. No child could ever replace another, and Rylee would always be a part of him. He would forever miss her. Ben still had some fears, but he knew beyond a shadow of a doubt that he wanted to have this baby with Dillyn. Knowing that she was happy about it, too, caused his heart to swell. It was so damn full; he thought it would burst.

Ben reached for Dillyn, picked her up in his arms, and began spinning her around in circles.

She wrapped her arms around his neck and giggled like a

schoolgirl. "We're having a baby!"

Ben kissed her hard on the lips. "We're having a baby."

Dillyn wrapped her legs around his waist, and her eyes filled with desire. "I think we need to celebrate this miracle of life properly."

Ben had given her the miracle of life in more ways than one. He helped her find the joy in love when she had given up hope. And now, they were creating a life. For a woman who didn't believe in Prince Charming or fairytales, this was a pretty good happily ever after.

WHINE, WHISKEY, & LIPSTICK 2

I love the slow drip of a romance where the story is like an onion. If you pull back a layer, there is another and another. I thoroughly enjoyed writing about Ben and Dillyn but there is so much more to tell. Like, who is Syntax? Why was Steven killed? Is Dillyn truly safe (immediate answer is yes)? Do Lucas and Palmer, Wyatt and Cat get their own Happily Ever After?

If you enjoyed this story and would like to read more about these incredible characters please share your thoughts with your friends and leave a review!

FULL THROTTLE 2

**YOU WANTED BRIAN LOCKWOOD AND LILA JAMES'
STORY? YOU'RE GOING TO GET IT. FIND OUT WHAT
STARTED IT ALL - COMING 12/25/2022
PRE-ORDER NOW!**

CHAPTER 1

The club was packed with wall-to-wall people. The DJ had the place rockin' as the music blared through massive speakers placed strategically throughout the room. The base was pumping so hard it was bouncing off the walls. Anthony Luccesse could even feel the vibration beneath the soles of his feet as he and a group of friends sat at a corner table in the VIP.

Anthony lit a cigarette and took a long pull while looking less than enthused at the bevy of beautiful, half-naked women dancing and all vying for his attention. Franco Milani wasn't having the same problem. He enjoyed every ass that wiggled and jiggled in front of him. He leaned over toward his friend. "I don't know how you can sit there looking bored with all that good good staring you in your face." He laughed, then placed a hundred dollar bill into the g-string of one of the dancers.

Anthony blew out a breath releasing white smoke. "You have more than enough excitement for the both of us."

"Hell, yeah. And, if you ain't going to celebrate your twenty-seventh birthday, I certainly will." Franco pulled a busty

241

blonde down onto his lap. She was excited to be chosen and gave him an enthusiastic lap dance.

Anthony had been forced by a few of his friends into coming out. He wasn't exactly in the mood for celebrating. It had only been a few short months since his older brother was killed, and it hit him hard. Nick's death had thrown their businesses into complete chaos since he ran them. The natural order of succession should have been for Anthony's other brother, Gabe, to step up and take over. Gabe knew the business but didn't have a head for it. Gabe's talents lied in being the muscle. With the FEDs breathing down their necks, Gabe and his hot head would probably end up getting their assets frozen, or worse, sending them straight to prison.

Anthony took another pull on his cigarette. He couldn't shut off his brain. *What am I going to do about our money?* It was all he could think about. Their cleaner had been playing footsy with the FEDs, and Gabe had to drop him into the bottom of the ocean. It would have been cool if Gabe had found a new one first before leaving millions to be laundered.

Anthony sighed.

If their businesses were going to survive, he had to take the reins. His first order of business had to be finding a new cleaner. Someone with a company and reputation beyond reproach. That eliminated damn near ninety percent of all the businesses they dealt with, including the legitimate ones.

A commotion near the bar caught Anthony's attention. That's when he spotted a stumbling Brian Lockwood. Anthony hated the man. They couldn't have been more opposite. Brian was the fair-haired Prince of the Lockwood Empire who had been handed everything on a silver platter.

On the other hand, Anthony had come from a long line of criminals. His family had a reputation for being unscrupulous and unsavory characters. Anthony couldn't lie. The Luccesse family was one to be feared. After Nick's murder, they were mistakenly seen as being in a weakened position. That ended when he and Gabe massacred the people who killed Nick and everyone connected to them in a single day. Most days weren't as bloody.

Anthony watched in disgust as the club owners fell over themselves to roll out the red carpet for Brian. His jaw clenched with irritation. *Damn pretty boy wouldn't know anything about hard work.* Unfortunately, Anthony didn't get the same treatment when his group entered the VIP. It disgusted him that the Luccesse's massive fortune wasn't enough to be welcomed into the elite circles of society. Those people treated them with such disdain as if their money wasn't green or if most of them didn't have businesses with shady beginnings.

Anthony continued to silently brood as he watched Brian and his rowdy group walk over to their table. They were surrounded by many women, including a few celebrity models. Suddenly, Anthony sat up straight. It was like being punched in the gut. The answer to his problems was quite possibly just across the room as the beginnings of an idea popped into his head. The smile that had been so elusive began to slowly creep across Anthony's face. He crushed the end of his cigarette into the ashtray and stood. "I'll be right back."

Anthony strode over towards Brian's table. Immediately, Brian's security blocked his path. Anthony put up his hands as if to say *I come in peace*. "What? Can't say hello to an old friend?"

Brian looked around his men. He might be drunk, but he wasn't *that* drunk. "What do you want, Luccesse?"

"It's been six years since I last saw you. The way I figure it, that's enough time to lick your wounds and for us to call a truce."

"I don't think eternity is enough time for that." Brian said.

"C'mon. You can't still be mad over Lila?"

"Who?" Brian said casually. And, yes. He was still mad over Lila, but he for damn sure wasn't going to let Anthony know it.

"Exactly! Let me buy a round of drinks for you and your friends to celebrate our shared birthdays."

Despite Brian's brother's warnings about the Luccesse family, Brian and Anthony were once friends—in college—at least *he* had been a good friend. Unfortunately, Brian had realized too late that Anthony wasn't to be trusted.

However, tonight, Brian's ego got the best of him. He couldn't let Anthony think that his betrayal cut deep. He shrugged. "If you're spending your money, then I don't have to spend mine." Brian motioned for his security to allow Anthony entrance into his space.

Anthony yelled out over the music. "Bring my man a bottle of Asombroso Del Porto Extra Anejo and his friends too."

The waiter nodded.

Anthony sat down opposite Brian. "Seriously, this is my

peace offering."

"You think a few bottles of $4000 tequila is going to erase all the shit you did?"

"Look, I told you. Lila was a mistake. It never should have happened."

Brian cut him off. "I'm not talking about Lila."

"We both know you're definitely talking about Lila. We were young and stupid back then. We did stupid shit. After all this time, we've grown up, right?"

Brian would neither confirm nor deny Anthony's thoughts.

The waiter returned with their tequila and poured each of them a shot. Anthony raised his glass. "To old friends. Salute."

Anthony was a snake. One Brian probably shouldn't let within striking distance. Still, he lifted his glass. "Salute."

They tossed their glasses back. Anthony grinned. "Forgiven?"

"Let's just say it's my birthday, and I plan to enjoy it."

"Cool. Then, let's get it!" Anthony stood, pulling a curly-haired beauty up with him.

They partied hard over the next couple of hours, and Anthony continued to order more drinks. Brian continued to toss them back, not realizing that Anthony wasn't doing the same.

"Just like old times, huh?" Anthony asked as he sat back down at the table, taking a break from the dance floor.

Brian had to admit. It was like old times. At least before

he realized that Anthony was a no-good son-of-a-bitch. "The only difference is you're not trying to con me."

Anthony frowned. "You calling me a con?"

"I'm sure you've been called a lot worse."

Anthony's face grew tight, and he stood from his seat. "I came over to make amends, bought you drinks for your birthday, and this is how you repay my gesture? By insulting me? Calling me a con?!"

Brian stumbled to his feet. "Hell yeah! You're a con and a bum! Always have been, and no matter how much money you have, always will be!"

"Be careful, Brian. This ain't college where you were the man. I'm not going to take too many any insults from you, and words like that have been known to get men killed."

Brian slurred. "You think your threats scare me?"

"They should."

Brian narrowed his eyes. "Nothing about you scares me. Nothing!"

"Well, well, well . . . look at little Brian. Flexing?"

Brian stepped into Anthony's face. They were nose to nose. "If that's what you want to call it. I beat your ass in college, and even drunk, I have no problem repeating the lessons you clearly didn't learn."

Security for both men inched a bit closer just in case things got out of control.

Anthony really wasn't a fighter. He hired people for that shit. Still, he tried to hit Brian with a low blow. "I stole your woman." Anthony shrugged. "I didn't need to fight."

Brain lunged at Anthony, but his people held him back.

Anthony laughed. "You're seriously trying to write a check your ass can't cash. If you didn't know, you're in the deep end, Brian. You might want to call Liam to save you on this one."

Brian's voice dropped to a low menacing growl. "I can handle my own business. Unlike you, I don't hide behind my brother for shit!"

"Oh really? Well, if you really think you're a better man than me, prove it!"

"I don't have to prove a gaawdamn thing! But, just so we are clear, I'm a better man than you 365, 24/7, Monday thru Friday and twice on Sunday."

"We'll ask Lila about that." Anthony laughed. Playing Brian Lockwood was too easy. He had him exactly where he wanted him. This was going to be like taking candy from a baby.

THANK YOU

Thank you so much for reading WINE, WHISKEY, & LIPSTICK.

If you enjoyed Ben and Dillyn's story as much as I enjoyed writing them, please leave a review on **Goodreads** and the digital E-book platform of purchase.

Looking for more LaShawn Vasser Information? SIGN-UP to her Newsletter!

www.lashawnvasser.com

FACEBOOK (https://www.facebook.com/LVRomance/)

INSTAGRAM (https://www.instagram.com/lashawnvbooks/)

TWITTER (https://twitter.com/MsLaShawnVasser)

INSPIRATIONAL PLAYLIST
Available on Youtube and Tidal

Believe Me - Rej Archi

Bed on Fire - Teddy Swims

Lover's Prayer - Joe

Good Morning Gorgeous - Mary J Blige

Messy Love - Nao

All The Lovers - K Michelle

Why Should I Cry - Heather Headley

Best Thing - Inayah

I Bow Out - Whitney Houston

It's Been A Good Year - Tammi Savoy and Chris Casello

Black Girl Magic - Sierra McClain

Drank Too Much - Willie Jones

Drunk and I Miss You - Jimmie Allen and Mickey Guyton

What Hurts the Most - Keisha Renee

Hold On - Yola

Tennessee Whiskey - KeKe Wyatt

It Ain't Easy - Yola

Best Shot - Jimmy Allen

Soul In My Country - Mickey Guyton

My Masterpeace - Darius Rucker

Caught Up In Your Storm - Mickey Guyton

Take Me Home - Restless Road & Kane Brown

Fight With You - Ashlie Amber

Heavenly - Priscilla Renea

Another - Adam Doleac

Hold Us Together - H.E.R.

Soul Message - Rissi Palmer

67 - Reyner Roberts

Open - Ashlie Amber

Heaven - Kane Brown

Miles - Tiera ft. BRELAND

Found It In You - Tiera

Love On You - Rissi Palmer

I Hope You Dance - Keisha Renee

Blessed & Free - Kane Brown and H.E.R.

Same Space - Tiana Major9

Summer Rain - Leon Bridges

Say I Do - John Lundvik

I Promise - King South

249

OTHER BOOKS BY LASHAWN VASSER

HIS BABY HER GIFT (The Slow Burn Duology #2)

Harlem Thomas' world has crumbled into a million little pieces, and she's been left to deal with the aftermath–*alone*. Maybe not exactly alone. But she is single, pregnant, and wondering how she can fall in love with a completely off-limits and emotionally unavailable man.

Carter Owens has made a vow and plans to keep it. He will make sure that Harlem and her baby are well taken care of no matter how many times she pushes him away. *The problem*–he isn't supposed to fall for her. She's forbidden.

Find out what happens in the shocking conclusion to **Her Baby His Gift**, an enemies-to-lovers romance!

HER BABY HIS GIFT (The Slow Burn Duology #1)

Harlem Thomas has a plan for her life, and it is quickly falling off the rails. She's pregnant. The situation isn't ideal, and that's putting it mildly. Mommy, daddy and baby make three, right? Try four.

Could one call her predicament a love triangle when love isn't really involved? Harlem has no idea how she's fallen so far down the rabbit hole, but she has to climb up and out.

After the clouds of confusion lift, Harlem finds that she more than welcomes motherhood, but will she also find her soul mate?

FULL THROTTLE

Colby James can't seem to escape the world of stock-car racing, her father's first love. She wanted out and at the first opportunity, left it all behind. She needed to put as much distance as possible between that life and the pain it caused. But, after years of running, her father needs her. It was time to come home and well past time to lay old ghosts to rest.

Billionaire businessman Liam Lockwood does not like the unknown and usually has two or three plans for everything. He also hates being out of his element, which is where he found himself after being thrust into the chaotic world of stock-car racing.

Events place Liam and Colby on a surefire collision course. Find out what happens in this sexy, high-octane romance-*Full Throttle*.

SNOWBOUND

Novah Bankston's days are long, her nights are lonely, and her world is getting much too small. Still, her life isn't a complete dumpster fire. She has great friends. One in-particular makes her feel safe and protected, even if a bit sexually frustrated!

The thought of settling down has never appealed to Aiden Lawson. At least it hadn't until he met the smart, sexy, and utterly irresistible Novah Bankston. Every time she is around, crazy thoughts of forever pop into his head. It's too bad that she is *off-limits*.

No one could have predicted that a shared vacation among friends would turn into a fight for survival. The threat of death forces Aiden and Novah to confront their very real desire for one another. With temperatures dropping well below zero, and no shelter in sight, will the heat of their passion be enough to keep them alive?

A POWERFUL STORM - LOVING BRODY (The Storm Series 4)

I touched bliss for a little more than twenty-four hours before the chaos of my life turned it all to hell.

251

My head was spinning; to think I could have a future that in-cluded acceptance and love was ridiculous. Not when it was all-out war for control of my father's empire and what remained of my tarnished soul.

A coldness swept through me as I made plans for the final show-down. I'm preparing to do whatever it takes to keep those around me safe including *the unthinkable!*

I once told them it was my game, my rules. They obviously didn't believe me. I'll just have to show them.

A DANGEROUS STORM - LOVING GINA (The Storm Series 3)

There are two things I know for sure, the world is cold and men are bastards.

All of them.

A man I once idolized taught me that.

Another man I thought I loved reinforced it.

Then Brody Windham walked into my life, threatening to flip shit upside down. I was more than tempted until I remembered how impossible it was to mix The Family and love.

Love makes you stupid and vulnerable.

And The Family. . . Well, it's a whole other beast. One my father had led with an iron fist for over 30 years.

I have plans for my father and The Family.

I've played by their rules my entire life. That is all going to change. And, if all goes well, maybe I can have a little taste of Brody too.

That's right. It's My Game. My Rules. So, Let the Games Begin!

A PERFECT STORM - LOVING ALEXANDRO (The Storm Series Book 2)

A death and the potential loss of Manchetti Enterprises brought powerhouse attorney, Braylee Hinsdale together with Alexandro Manchetti. She managed the impossible - saved his business and his sanity. In turn, he was able to pierce through her tough armor and gently remove an intractable mask concealing deeply hidden wounds. While their attraction was immediate, each fought to protect their fragile hearts from hurt and harm; but instead found strength and love.

Just as Alexandro and Braylee seemed on the path to happily ever after, they found themselves in the middle of a storm. A powerful storm. A Perfect Storm. And, it had the name Gina Lee Xiou written all over it. Who was she? A lover from his past? What did she want? More importantly, could she blow up their lives with just a few words? And, would she dare? Find out in A Perfect Storm.

A BEAUTIFUL STORM - LOVING BRAYLEE (The Storm Series 1)

A Storm Is Coming is about a beautiful and tough as nails corporate attorney, Braylee Hinsdale, who must use every trick in the book to keep the handsome and powerful Alexandro Manchetti from losing everything. Alexandro is powerful, handsome, ridiculously sexy and has just suffered an unimaginable loss. He needs her skills as a ruthless attorney to win a case that he's being told is unwinnable. It is unlike anything Braylee has ever faced and will demand everything from her. Some have said they can sense when A Storm Is Coming, but neither was prepared for the storms ahead.

REMINGTON'S SKY

Sky Kirby is independent, arrogant, emotionally closed off, and owns it. She doesn't need anyone to fix or save her and makes no apologies—even when her choices may explain why love has been so elusive. Remington Kneeland is Sky's mirror image—only he is done with love. Cynical and bitter, he focuses on the one person that means the world to him—his daughter. When a terrible accident brings him and Sky together, fate steps in with a different idea. Find out what happens when an immovable object meets an unstoppable force—the results are soul-stirring, heart-pounding, and orgasmic.

The Right Side of My Pillow

Cricket Anderson and Cole Thornton were throwaways. The outside world didn't have room for them. Yet, from the tender age of nine, all they had was each other...until they didn't. Not only were promises broken but so was Cricket's heart. Focused and driven to create a life made of dreams, Cole Thornton succeeded only to be left feeling empty and alone. Ten years later, a chance encounter brings him together with the one person he's ever felt connected to – an angry, disconnected, and broken woman. They say time heals all wounds. But, can two damaged souls discover love and mend their hollowed hearts? Find out in The Right Side of My Pillow.

CREE

Cree Jacobs has ever only loved one man, and for years she's worked two jobs, sometimes three to support his dreams. Her entire world centered around Cameron Jacobs. What happens when his world no longer revolves around her? Distance has kept them apart for so long that they've become virtual strangers. Feeling lost and alone, Cree realized his goals were her goals. His dreams were her dreams until tragic events forced a path of self-discovery. Sometimes you have to stop, regroup, and find your center. Will that center lead back to love? The Stranger Next to Me

Tasha Stevens and Sabrina Links-Horne have been best friends since high school. Everyone always wondered how their friendship stood the test of time. Especially since they were polar opposites in every way, except for one thing. They were both in love with Tim Horne . . . Sabrina's husband. Although they've seen each other through the best and worst of times, one decision will change the course of their lives forever and leave them both wondering who is The Stranger Next to Me?

Out of Nowhere (Book 1)

He is the CEO of CkR International, Inc., a billion-dollar company. She is a struggling single mother working for his company in customer service. What happens during a chance meeting in his company's elevator will change their lives forever. Take the journey with Vicky and Jason as they fall in love. Will they overcome past hurts, society's demands, and family expectations?

NEW BEGINNINGS (Out of Nowhere Book 2)

Just when billionaire Jason Kincaid Rutherford was on the cusp of living happily ever after with the only woman who's ever lit a fire within him, tragedy strikes. Will it leave her so broken that her heart doesn't have room for him? Not if Jason can help it. Continue on with the journey of Jason and Vicky as they face their biggest challenge yet. LOVE, LIFE, and VOWS (Out of Nowhere Book 3) Jason and Vicky have fought hard for their relationship. They've overcome differences in culture, race, and social status. They've withstood an almost unimaginable tragedy and come out on the other side stronger than ever. Or, so they thought. Follow along as Jason and Vicky's love is pushed to the breaking point after life takes a devastating turn. Will they ever find their happily ever after?

Love, Life, & Vows (Out of Nowhere Book 3)

Jason and Vicky have fought hard for their relationship. They've overcome differences in culture, race, and social status. They've withstood an almost unimaginable tragedy and come out on the other side stronger than ever. Or, so they thought.

Follow along as Jason and Vicky's love is pushed to the breaking point after life takes a devastating turn. Will they ever find their happily ever after?

This is the final book to Out of Nowhere and New Beginnings.

PIECES OF ME (Book 1)

Their plane crashed in the South Pacific. It was a struggle to survive. Why after their rescue did life become more dangerous? Davis Chatham wasn't supposed to be on this flight, but a crisis with Chatham Industries demanded it. There was always a crisis—granted none like this, but his name was on the building, it was his problem to solve . . . right? Being an admitted workaholic was what destroyed his marriage—leaving him broken, bitter, and wishing he'd handled things differently. Life had not been kind to Nicole DonLeavy and the last year had been particularly brutal. She wanted a fresh start—a new beginning. When the opportunity of a lifetime presented itself, she jumped at the chance and all thanks to the man who made it possible—a man she'd never met—Davis Chatham. One fateful night changes the course of everything. Get to know Davis and Nicole as they fight to survive on and off an island paradise. Emotions collide, danger lurks, and ghosts of the past return. Prepare yourself; this is not your typical love story.

FRAGMENTS OF US (Book 2)

Who has the perfect love story? Certainly not Mr. and Mrs. Chatham . . .

It's been five years since Davis and Nicole said their I. Dos—five years, two children, and a mansion on the hill, let's not forget . . . their very own island. Perfect love story right? Wrong. Not when old habits die hard, and new ones are worse than the old.

This will be the ultimate fight for survival and takes them back to where it all started. In Fragments of Us, Davis and Nicole can only hope to put the broken pieces of their lives back together.